Rail pressed a stud on his wristwatch. The time didn't change. Arthwit Rail did. His skin dissolved, revealing three tiny pink eyes in a green face that looked like a miniature golf course speckled with water traps. Gripping the steering wheel were two long tentacles that subdivided into sets of smaller tentacles.

"Big deal," Miranda said. "An alien."

Kerwin stared at her. "You don't think it's weird that we're fleeing from homicidal, maybe not-human police, in a borrowed van driven by a creature from another planet?"

"I've been around." She shrugged. "Hey, I go to the movies. So he's an alien. So, like, nobody's perfect. I mean, you should see some of the dorks I've been out with."

A blaster bolt just missed the weaving van, melting the antenna aerial. Seeth pounded madly on the radio. "Dammit, that was a *great* song!" He stuck his head out the window and screamed, "You bastards ain't cops—you ain't even *meat!* Scum! Evil scourge of the universe!"

"How did *you* know?" Arthwit Rail murmured.

Other books by Alan Dean Foster

THE LAST STARFIGHTER
SLIPT

Alan Dean Foster
GLORY LANE

HAWK

ACE BOOKS, NEW YORK

This book is an Ace
original edition, and has never been
previously published.

GLORY LANE

An Ace Book/published by arrangement with
the author

PRINTING HISTORY
Ace edition/August 1987

ISBN: 0-441-51664-5

Ace Books are published by The Berkley Publishing Group,
200 Madison Avenue, New York, New York 10016.
The name "Ace" and the "A" logo are trademarks
belonging to Charter Communications, Inc.
PRINTED IN THE UNITED STATES OF AMERICA

10 9 8 7 6 5 4 3 2 1

Here's one for my sister Carol,
Who tried to imitate Lash Larue
And found a second life instead.
With love always.

There are certain queer times and occasions in this strange mixed affair we call life when a man takes his whole universe for a vast practical joke.

Herman Melville, *Moby Dick*, chapter XCIII

N I N

It was always slow in Albuquerque on Tuesday nights, but tonight was worse than usual. Man, it was *dead*, Seeth Ransom fumed. He couldn't even find a stray cat to kick around. So he was forced to fall back on the old standby of giving passing motorists the finger and smirking as they pretended not to notice, speeding up slightly as they hurried on past, their eyes fixed unswervingly to the road ahead. The pleasure this provided was decidedly muted, but it was better than nothing. At least the world was compelled to take notice of him.

Still, there was no denying the night was dull enough to bore a turtle.

He checked the watch he wore high up on his forearm so that his friends wouldn't know he had the slightest interest in what time it was. A little past nine. He considered returning to the apartment, just giving up on the night and crashing 'til tomorrow. Trouble was, the day would be more boring than the night. Besides which, the place was probably full to overflowing by now. The bed, couch, and kitchen table would be occupied. The Hole filled up fast. If you showed too late you had your choice of sleeping standing up or lying down on top of somebody else.

Seeth wasn't into that. He was pumped, full of adrenaline and suppressed energy and in no mood to close his eyes, even temporarily. Hyperactive, his high school counselors had called him. They'd called him other things as well. Seeth had responded in kind, with the result that he and his alma mater had parted company prior to his graduation. That Seethless ceremony had taken place a year ago. He told himself he wasn't missing anything. Street life was an education unto itself. Hanging out was an art. When you needed money you worked the odd job. When food or drink or the occasional recreational pharmaceutical was required, you shared with trusted friends.

The only real problem was the boredom—long stretches of nothing to do, nowhere to go. During such times he occasionally wondered if just maybe he might have screwed up his life.

No, no chance, he told himself firmly.

He thought about hitching out to Indian Petroglyph Park on the northwest side of town. It was a kick to scratch modern obscenities in the soft sandstone alongside the ancient drawings. The straights called it defacement and wailed and screamed. What the hell was the difference between what he did and what the Indians had done? Probably some of those little stick figures, crudely colored and inscribed, were just as obscene as the marks he and his friends made. A thousand years from now some other dumb archeologists would find Seeth Ransom's initials, and Piggie's, and Della's, and prize them for the tie they presented to the bad ol' twentieth century. The thought made him smile and smiling made him feel a little better.

By now the streets were pretty empty, the city's solid

citizens having retired to a soporific evening of contemplating the idiot box, voluntarily incurring the self-imposed death-state known as Prime Time without realizing it was a contradiction in terms. Couch potatoes hell, Seeth mused. The analogy was insulting to tubers.

Not much open now, either. All the malls and most of the markets were closed. All that stayed active through the Albuquerque night were 7-Elevens, K-Stores, and the occasional gas station.

He wandered over to the Shamrock station where Jean worked as a cashier and they chatted for a while. That was all they could do, since it was forbidden for her to unlock the office door for anyone after eight o'clock. That wouldn't have stopped Jean. She went her own way just like Seeth, but with all the people coming and going, the tourists trickling steadily off I-40, she didn't want to take the risk no matter how hard he pleaded. She needed the job. So he yelled at her and she yelled back, and with that acrimonious farewell ringing in his ears he had continued on his way.

There was always something doing around the University of New Mexico. Several pizza parlors and a club or two never closed. But he didn't have money to spare for pizza and he sure as hell wasn't interested in crashing any of the clubs. They played nothing but homogenized pap and their squeaky-clean patrons wore cotton shirts and shoes with laces. Nor did they offer the opportunity to pick up girls. Sorority sisters and pretty things deep into husband-searching tended to view him as something that had crawled up from beneath the sewers or invaded from another planet.

He knew the truth of it, of course. What they both despised and envied was his individuality, his readiness to express himself freely and openly when they were cramped and constrained by society. Screw 'em. He didn't need that kind of company.

He turned a corner. A police cruiser was coming down the boulevard toward him. It slowed. Though he kept his gaze on the street ahead he could sense the cops' eyes following him. He kept his hands outside his pockets where they could be seen. After a few minutes the patrol car accelerated slightly and left him in its wake.

The Albuquerque cops were what you could call half-cool. They let you know they were around and what your place was and that they could find you if they needed to, but as a rule they weren't into heavy-duty hassling. Albuquerque was just big enough, just cosmopolitan enough to barely tolerate Seeth and his friends, though the cops would come down on you hard and fast if you so much as parked ten minutes too long in a thirty-minute zone.

Where he really belonged was L.A. or New York. Not out here in the vast, stinking, conservative American heartland. Trouble was you couldn't pick up the bucks for relocation and cross-country airfare doing odd jobs at minimum wage. The good low-paying jobs were all taken by Hispanics. Not that Seeth blamed them. Most of them had wives and kids and dreams that would never be fulfilled. You could always try hitching, but he'd probably end up run down by some berserk redneck trucker. Bus fare was as bad as airfare. He was stuck.

He passed the big Diamond's department store and eyed the huge plate-glass windows longingly. The police cruiser might still be hanging around. It was a neat old building, rich with granite and concrete decoration. They'd probably replace it with a parking lot some time next year.

Checking himself out in the reflective window, he had to admit, as would anyone with an eye for fashion, that he looked his usual slick self. Black jacket dripping zippers, a few tastefully slung chromed chains, the black-and-white striped pants he'd had to get by mail order since you didn't find stuff like that on the rack at Sears, neatly set off by the lightning bolt earring dangling from his left earlobe. Above that was the Maltese cross ear bracelet, carefully shaved skin, and his three-inch Mohawk haircut. A little traditional, but a lot easier to maintain than those damn spikes.

Running fingers across the bald left side of his skull, he felt the beginnings of bristle. Time to shave again, he told himself. For all that, lookin' pretty good. A little black eye makeup and complementary lipstick would have really sharpened him up, but he didn't see the point in going all out just for a casual nocturnal stroll. The parallel red stripes he had painted on his neck and that ran from beneath his right ear to under his jacket collar were an original touch of his own. They were purely symbolic. He could have made them look a lot more like real blood, but then he would have had to deal with questions from the straights on the street.

He considered walking over to the university anyway. What stopped him was the possibility of encountering a couple of all-American frat types, jocks who'd enjoy nothing more than beating the crap out of a wayward punk. Though Seeth could take care of himself, he was only five-six and barely into three figures poundage-wise. There was the blade he concealed in his special pants-leg pocket, but if he actually had to stick somebody he'd be as bad off as if he just let himself get beaten up. The cops weren't likely to buy a claim of self-defense if his tormentor turned out to be, say, a star lineman on the football team.

His real destination was coming into view, but the

excitement it prompted quickly gave way to disappointment and then anger. He recognized one of those leaning up against the club doorway. Despite his arching, gravity-defying hairdo and artfully torn vest, Mangle still looked like a nerd. The kid was trying hard to fit in, but he didn't really have the spirit or the energy to make like a true anarchist. Mangle's real name was Michael Liverwort, or something like that.

The kid saw him and Seeth acknowledged the glance with a nod. There were a couple of girls hanging around and one other guy. The girls were both overweight, though the brunette would have been pretty if she'd dropped forty or fifty pounds. The sign over the door said

FISH HOOK

The door was covered with grafitti, much of it gross and obscene, some of it violent. Next to the handle someone had plastered a bumper sticker that screamed NUKE THE YUPPIES. He ignored the others and spoke to Mangle.

"What's the deal?"

"Closed," the younger boy told him mournfully.

"I can see that, pinhead. Why?"

The brunette spoke up. She sounded eager for another human contact. "Over there, on the front. Check it out. A real bummer."

Seeth studied the notice that had been stuck near the entrance. He'd always been a fast reader if not an enthusiastic one. The notice was from the Albuquerque Department of Health.

"Roaches." Mangle was trying to be helpful. "In the kitchen."

"So what's the big deal? So you get a roach in your burger."

The other girl made gagging noises while her friend giggled. Seeth couldn't stand giggling. They're playacting, he thought. They've no business here. Slumming. Mangle might be a pitiable case, but at least his heart was in the right place.

"So why didn't they just close the kitchen? Why shut down the whole club?"

Mangle spread long, skinny arms. "Hey, how should I know, man? When I got here they were chasing everybody out. I thought maybe there was a riot or something going on, but no such luck."

No such luck, Seeth mused. Not in Albuquerque. Nobody wanted to get thrown in jail in Albuquerque. Not with a bunch of wetbacks. The local straights found punks outrageous, but the poor Mexicans from across the border simply thought their appearance was hilarious. Better to get beat up than laughed at.

"It's no big deal," Mangle told him. "They'll be open again by the weekend. Nollie told me so. They just have to do some spraying in the kitchen."

"They ought to spray the whole building while they're at it. Get us some privacy." The girls giggled like mad. The brunette winked at him. Maybe he'd been too harsh on them too fast.

Then he caught a glimpse of their feet. Feet were dead giveaways for slummers. Both wore designer shoes. They were scuffed and muddy, but it was obvious they hadn't been picked up at Goodwill or the Salvation Army. His opinion of them fell back to zero.

Wasn't this the pits? Where the hell was he supposed to go now? Usually the Fish Hook opened at nine and stayed open until three or until the owners felt like closing up. It wasn't exactly Greenwich Village or Melrose. There was petrified gum lining the underside of every table, lumpy memorials to the days when the Hook had been a college club. But you could buy a fatburger cheap and this was where the local bands hung out. The real bands. You came for the camaraderie and the music anyway, not the food.

He looked around. The street was completely deserted, though the mindless traffic lights continued their winking regimen for nonexistent drivers. On-off, on and off, just like his parents and his teachers. Life by rote. He hated stop lights.

"So, hey, you wanna do something?" Mangle put a possessive arm around one of the girls. "Get laid?" The girl giggled. If she giggled one more time, Seeth knew, he was going to punch her out. He had to get away. He shook his head sharply, staring at the street.

"I don't know how you do it, man." There was admiration in Mangle's voice. "I've seen you walking at five in the morning and you look like you just got up."

"It's just energy," Seeth replied absently. "I've always had a lot of energy. Sleeping's the pits. You don't see anything, you don't experience anything. It's like death."

"Wow." The brunette stared at him out of wide eyes. "That's heavy!"

" 'Heavy'?" Seeth turned away in disgust and strode up the street.

Mangle called out hopefully, "Hey where you goin', Seeth?"

"To blow up a supermarket."

"Can we come?" shouted one of the girls.

He just shook his head and gritted his teeth. He *had* to get out of this town! New York, yeah, or even L.A. Los

8

Angeles was closer anyway. That's where he belonged. For the first time all night something made him feel good. You could bounce from club to club to club without seeing the same band twice. Find people who'd hire you without looking like they were going to throw up. Pay you some honest bucks so long as you did your job and wouldn't hassle you no matter *what* you looked like. Nobody coming down on you because of your hair. Even the cops wouldn't look twice at you. You could exist as an independent human being.

That was really why he'd gone punk and dropped out. It wasn't even for the music, though that was part of the whole scene. It was because after some painful introspection he'd discovered he really was antisocial. Sure, you could be antisocial in jeans and Nikes, but that marked you as a bum instead of a true rebel. Besides, he really liked the way he looked—and the way it outraged the straights.

All his life he'd been ignored, overlooked, teased. Nobody overlooked him now, nobody ignored him. Except his parents, but then they'd always ignored him. No loss there. He was himself, his own man, a distinct individual. That was what mattered. To stand out, to make a physical statement, to be able to linger on a street corner with your whole being screaming *I am not of the crowd, I am not of the herd*!

As he debated what to do next, he found himself angling toward the university. He'd just about decided to give up, to go back to the Hole and crash, hoping tomorrow would be better, when he found himself passing the Apache Bowlarama. It was dominated by a huge, ugly neon sign that depicted a stereotyped Indian bowling. Every few seconds the Indian would release a neon ball that would move five feet before knocking over a trio of neon cacti.

What the hell, he thought, smiling to himself. The parking lot was still pretty full and he was desperate. Some kind of league night. Be a shot to watch the reactions when he sauntered in. Wouldn't be as dangerous as the university. No linemen in here. Just ex-linemen carrying an extra twenty years and thirty pounds of beer flab. He could dance circles around them. Maybe he could get a few of them chasing him around the snack bar and, if he was lucky, the police would be called. They'd calm his would-be attackers and he could grin at them and watch their complexions darken.

"Why were you chasing that boy, Mr. Johnson?"

"Because—because, I mean, officer, just *look* at him!"

And Seeth would stand there running a hand through his mohawk and grinning while the cop patiently said, "I know, but that's not a crime, Mr. Johnson."

"Yeah, but," the fat guy would stutter, "it oughta be." Meanwhile, his buddies would be yelling at him because he'd be holding up the game and they'd get home late and their wives would yell at them.

Right, funtime. He crossed the street and made his way through the parking lot, which was full of pickups and ten-year-old sedans. Nobody challenged him either there or at the door.

The muzak almost drove him back outside. And they thought *his* kind of music was intolerable! He steeled himself and kept going.

There were a couple of leagues running simultaneously, one for men and another for women. The combined activity on the thirty-six lanes made a racket that sounded like the kamikazes at Iwo Jima.

He paused to consider the cacophony thoughtfully. When you thought about it, bowling was nothing more than

10

sublimated destruction. When he and his buddies smashed a car window or busted a few bottles in the park, they called it vandalism. Whereas here, in this temple of violence, hour after hour, day after day, the good citizens delighted in heaving fifteen pounds of hardened plastic at innocent, immobile targets. The fact that the pins didn't shatter in no way mitigated the delight the bowlers experienced at knocking down something that couldn't fight back.

Invent bowling pins that screamed and bled, he thought, and you'd make a fortune.

The steady din was easy to handle, but the music was actually painful. Merle Haggard was braying from the speakers now. Any minute Seeth expected to hear Johnny Cash or Hank Williams, Jr. or even the Judds. He'd seen a picture of the Judds once. Mama was pretty foxy. Give her some safety pins, warpaint and a decent hairdo and she could play the Hook.

He gravitated to the snack bar. The single attendant was close to his own age and pretty good looking. While he walked he jingled his chains and tried to make himself as conspicuous as possible. It didn't take much for heads to begin turning. When they thought he wasn't looking they made faces and whispered. He was enjoying himself immensely.

What was really riotous was that they thought *he* was funny-looking. This from middle-aged housewives in tight green pants and beehive hairdos. The first eighteen lanes were ladies league. From where he looked down on them it was like watching the debris from a wrecked eighteen-wheeler full of potatoes spilling across the road. He could sense if not actually hear the "Oh my dears" and "Would you look at thats."

The mutterings from the men, as he moved closer to their end of the building, were less amused and more dangerous. Even though there were dozens of them and only one of him he represented a threat—to order, stability, righteousness, God, and The American Way. The only ones who viewed him with anything close to tolerance were the dozen or so Navajos who formed two teams of their own. Most of them had the guts to wear their hair braided, in the traditional fashion. They were in no position to criticize another's coiffure.

Despite the growls and grumbles, no one started toward him. He took a seat at the snack bar counter. A second waitress had emerged from the bathroom subsequent to his arrival. Now they were debating which of them would be unlucky enough to have to serve him. He was glad when the younger one reluctantly approached. She spoke with obvious reluctance.

"Can I help you, sir?"

Sir. Riot, he thought. "Well now, that's a leading question, isn't it? I mean, it presupposes that I need help and that you could be of some assistance to me without even knowing what my problem is. Fascinating concept. You aren't by any chance telepathic, are you?"

Like a cow pausing with its cud, she halted her gum in mid-chew and gaped at him. "Huh?"

He sighed. "Got any Cherry Coke?"

"Cherry Coke?" She relaxed a little and managed a smile. "Oh, yeah." Her gums started working again as center control pushed GO. "What size?"

"Half a liter, but you're probably out of that." He smiled back at her. "Just make it medium."

"Medium, sure." She started to turn back toward the fountain, then hesitated, unsure whether to ask the question and, if so, how. Finally she just pushed ahead. "Uh, you got any money?"

"Money, money." Seeth's brow furrowed and he took on the appearance of a philosopher sunk deep in contemplation. "Let me see now: money." He dug into a pocket and began emptying the contents on the counter.

The pile included a handful of prophylactics, a very small but offensively engraved pocket knife that made her eyes widen, some pennies, a couple of quarters, a Mexican fifty-centavo piece, and some purplish-gray lint. He shoved the pennies and the quarters across the counter.

"That's not enough." She said it tentatively. At any moment he expected her to grab one of the butter knives and back up against the drink dispenser to defend herself. He was enjoying himself hugely.

"Not enough? Hey, hang on." He made a show of fumbling with his back pockets. "I know I've got my American Express platinum card back here somewhere. Wanna help me search?" That one went right by her.

"Here." He extracted a card and passed it to her. She took it carefully, as though it might contain some contagious disease, and read.

The Bearer of this Card is Neither a Convicted Felon nor a Libyan Terrorist, Nor does He Suffer From AIDS or Any Other Exotic Disease. He is Not Mute Nor is This a Solicitation for Money.

In Point of Fact This Card Has No Purpose Whatsoever Except to Occupy and Otherwise Waste Thirty Seconds of Another Overly Curious Person's Time. Successful, Isn't it?

She was slow, but she wasn't dense. And she did have a sense of humor, even if so far she'd taken pains to hide the fact. Now she grinned and handed the card back to him. As she did so she saw that he was holding a dollar out to her.

"Buy you one?"

"Sorry." She took the bill. "Not allowed to drink or eat in front of the customers."

"Sound policy. I mean, all those Cokes, you never know when you or that other waitress might go on a caffeine binge and tear the place apart, right?"

This time her smile wasn't forced. She moved a little nearer. "What's your name, anyway?"

"Wouldn't you be surprised if it *was* 'anyway'?"

She drew the Coke, twice pouring off foam to make sure that he got his money's worth, added a straw without being asked. He pushed the straw aside and took a long, cold swallow, spoke while crunching ice.

"I'm Seeth."

"That's a funny name."

"I'm a real funny guy." He leaned over the counter, trying to get close. "Want to see how funny?"

She ignored that, her gaze rising. "I like your hair."

"Thanks. Why not get one yourself?"

"Me?" She patted her carefully permed tresses. "Oh no, I couldn't."

"Why couldn't you?"

"Well for one thing, my parents would just *die*."

"Sorry. I've yet to see a documented case of hair causing a single parental fatality. Whose head is it growing out of? Your father's? Your mother's? Or yours?"

"Well, I. . . ."

"C'mon, I know there's a brain under there." Her smile

14

vanished. "Hey, lighten up. If I was trying to insult you I'd be more obvious about it. I'm just trying to make a point. If you like the way my hair looks and you want to do the same thing to your own, then who's to tell you you can't? It's not illegal—leastwise, not yet."

"You know, I think maybe I like. . . ." She shut up and backed off.

"Beat it, scum."

Seeth turned to see a taller, slightly older and considerably beefier man glaring down at him. He took his time inspecting the other.

"Beat it? Let's consider all the ramifications of that verb, shall we?" He swiveled on the stool and slugged down some cola. "There are several possibilities involved. First I'd like to know: if I don't beat it, are you going to make me beat it?"

"Yeah. What about it?"

Seeth turned to wink at the girl. She'd caught the joke instantly and was trying hard to stifle a laugh. The older man frowned at her, then back at Seeth.

"You trying to be funny?"

"What's with everybody tonight?" He spoke without looking at either of them. "The whole world thinks I'm trying to be funny. Here I'm wracking my brain striving to point out some of the inherent contradictions of our sociocultural matrix and everybody thinks I'm auditioning for late-night comedy. Somebody's missing a connection. As opposed to a link, which is standing here before me." He turned sharply back to the girl.

"Did you ever have the feeling that the world was an AC coffee pot and you were DC?"

A heavy hand landed on his shoulder. "I said, beat it. We don't want your kind in here."

"My kind?" Seeth tensed as he glanced diffidently at the big hand, but didn't otherwise react to the touch. "What kind might that be?"

"Bums. Jerks. Punks."

"Ah. Now there you have me, sir. I will admit to the third. As for the preceding pair I'm afraid you're way off base, but then I can see that you didn't quite complete your graduate degree in sociology so I suppose we need to make some allowances."

A couple of irritated shouts came from alley nineteen. The tall man yelled back in response. "I'll just be a minute!" He glared nastily at Seeth. "Come on now, beat it before I really get mad. You're holding up the game."

"Holding up? Hey, I wouldn't think of robbing you of your evening's intellectual stimulation." A sideways glance showed two of the man's partners starting up the stairs toward the snack bar. Seeth determined that, having made his point while gaining at least a semantic victory as well as impressing the girl, it might be time to move on.

He chug-a-luged the rest of his Coke, slipped off the counter stool and out from under the man's hand, pointedly hitching up his pants as he did so.

"Good riddance to bad rubbish," the man growled.

"Yeah, I can see that." Seeth talked over his shoulder as he strode away. "I can see that you're a true connoisseur of rubbish. Why, I've no doubt you'd be able to tell good rubbish from bad rubbish the instant you set eyes on it, which in your case is doubtless not an infrequent occurrence."

"Commie punk!" The man sneered at him, utilizing the strongest riposte at his command.

Seeth considered embellishing his verbal retreat with a few choice comments concerning the man's anatomy, but decided he wasn't close enough to the exit yet. While he did have masochistic friends, getting beaten up wasn't one of the finer pleasures of life as far as he was concerned.

He was halfway to the far exit, having crossed most of the building, when someone seated in the spectator seats caught his eye. The guy was a year older than himself, much taller, and neatly dressed in slacks and cotton shirt. His sandy blonde hair had been combed straight back, no-nonsense, except in front where it fell down and across. A light-blue jacket lay draped over the back of an empty seat nearby. A clipboard full of paper rested on one knee and its owner was scribbling furiously on the top page with a cheap ballpoint pen. Occasionally he would look up to observe the alleys, then return to his writing.

Seeth recognized him, wondered what he was doing here this time of night. Anytime of night, in fact. He was sure he wasn't keeping score for any of the groups below.

A glance over his shoulder showed that the snack bar mastodon had rejoined his companions, having done his bit tonight to make the world safe for democracy. As he headed down the stairs one of the other bowlers looked up, cupped his hands to his mouth and yelled.

"Hey kid, why don't you go back to the woods with the other animals?"

"No can do!" Seeth shouted back. "You and your buddies have shot 'em all!" This provoked laughter instead of anger from the first man and his friends.

What a bunch of cretins. They think mass extinction is funny. You could picture any one of 'em in uniform, laughing as they pushed the buttons that would launch nuclear missiles.

The brief, loud confrontation did serve to distract the scribbler from his work. He looked up long enough to spot

Seeth, then rapidly turned away and hunched low over his clipboard, trying to render himself invisible.

Seeth shook his head as he approached. "No good, man. I've already seen you. You has been identified."

"All right, so you've seen me." The man slowly straightened. "Now go away."

"Hey." Seeth raised his voice so that the nearest group of bowlers could hear. "I ask you, is that friendly?" A couple of them turned to frown in his direction.

"All right, all right," Kerwin said anxiously. "Sit down if you must, but shut up."

"Shut up? Me?" Seeth flopped down on the fiberglass seat opposite and put both feet over the seat in front of him, his legs blocking out the small sign that said PLEASE DO NOT REST YOUR FEET ON THE BACK OF THE CHAIR IN FRONT OF YOU.

"Who you hiding from out here? Mummy and daddy?" When the other man didn't respond, he picked his legs off the supporting seat back and leaned close, trying for a glimpse at the clipboard. "Lemme guess. You're doing a study on the physics of bowling, right?"

"Not exactly."

"You know," Seeth added casually as someone below made a strike to applause from his friends and groans from his opponents, "if you had glasses to go with that outfit you'd look so preppy ordinary that unwarned human beings would vomit at the sight of you."

"Yeah. And you just stepped off the cover of *GQ*, too."

"Actually I was supposed to be this month's centerfold in *Playgirl*, man, but I only filled up one page. They used me for a vodka ad instead. You know—silver Rolls, lady in a black satin dress, couple of wolfhounds sitting at my

18

feet looking like they're an hour overdue for a pee break but didn't dare move or they'd lose their residuals.''

"What are you on tonight, Seeth?" Kerwin said tiredly.

"Well," he replied with dubious gravity, "I did just down *all* of a medium Cherry Coke. What makes you think I am spending this particular evening indulging in designer pharmaceuticals?"

"Because you're in here. You wouldn't be in a place like this unless you were high."

"Is that a fact? It just so happens I thought flashing the yokels would be a neat way to pass an hour. They got the Fish Hook shut down. Health violation."

"Ought to condemn the dump."

"Ah, that's good old Kerwin. Always generous and understanding to a fault. At least I'm not stuck here scribbling garbage. What's your excuse?"

Kerwin fought an unsuccessful battle to conceal his clipboard. "Nothing. Just killing time."

"Oh sure. In here." Seeth raised both hands. "I believe you totally. I mean, just because I watched you writing like mad doesn't mean you're actually writing *about* anything, does it? Or could it be that we're both here to serve opposite sides of the same thing? I to be observed, you to do observing?"

"What makes you think I'm doing anything like that?" Kerwin sounded nervous.

"Because I'm not blind. Hey, come on," he said coaxingly, "what do you think I'm gonna do? Climb up on one of these rails and scream your secret to all these jokers? Promise I won't."

"You, promise? That's a laugh."

"Yeah? This must be my night for inducing humor in

others. Look, really, man, I won't tell. If you bore me more I might even leave.''

"If that's another promise, you're on." Seeth nodded and Kerwin slowly revealed his clipboard. "You had the right idea but the wrong subject. I'm here on assignment for my soph sociology class, not physics." He nodded toward the alleys.

The ninth frames were beginning to play themselves out. Quiet side bets were being paid off by good Baptists and Methodists. Final beers were being quaffed, chased by mints to kill the odor of alcohol. Husbands and wives said good-byes to friends and neighbors, cleaning up the residue of cheap cheeseburgers and greasy fries.

"I see. Stalking the wild lite beer drinkers? Baiting them in their natural habitat?''

"From what I saw when you came in, you seemed to be doing more of that than I ever could.''

Seeth glanced briefly back toward the snack bar. "Hell, you know me. I'm not like you." He used a finger to set the lightning bolt earring dancing.

"You're not like any living human being except those freaks you run around with.''

"Freaks? Check that out." He nodded toward a man with no hair and two hundred pounds of belly, liquid calories transformed as if by magic into useless flesh. "That's normal and my friends and I are freaks? Gimme a break.''

Kerwin just looked away. A hard man to provoke. Anyway, Seeth mused impatiently, it really was time to move on. He'd done about all he could in here. If he left before the last of them he could let the air out of a tire or two and stand off at a distance watching the owner get purple in the face.

At least Kerwin had half a brain. He'd actually talk to you instead of simply frothing at the mouth. As he was doing now.

"Did you know that bowling is the most popular sport in the United States? In some ways it's a perfect microcosm of a competitive society. There's a lot to be learned by observing the participants."

"Yeah, I can see that. Acres and acres of sub-intellect at work. I mean, the awesomeness of trying to calculate the relationship between beer consumed and concomitant trips to the john interpreted in the light of lost man-hours would tie up a departmental computer for several minutes at least."

Kerwin sounded slightly defensive. "It was something different, and anyway, this wasn't my choice. I wanted to do city hall, but by the time the subject list got down to me it was either this or go out to the reservation with a busload of other students."

"You just don't use your imagination. You could have studied your fellow students studying the natives. But I understand why you came here. I mean, if I was Navajo or Hopi and one more well-meaning white boy showed up to see how I put on my underwear, I'd probably unlatch the family shotgun and fill the jerk full of buckshot. Not that that would discourage the others. They'd probably just add it to their notes, right?"

Kerwin turned to shake his pen at the younger man. "That's your problem and you don't even see it. It's the attitude of your underculture. It's not the outrageous attire, the air of defiance; it's this reliance on violence both verbal and physical as a substitute for real self-expression."

"Like them, right?" He nodded toward the last of the bowlers. Most of the league games had concluded, but some were unable to tear themselves away from the alleys without rolling a few final practice frames. "You call it violence, I call it living. The Avoidance of Boredom Syndrome, if that's not a contradiction in terms. The difference between my friends and myself and those potato-heads down there is that we're tolerant. 'I don't like your lifestyle, I don't like your hair, I despise everything you stand for.' Man, I've been hearing that since I was old enough to understand words, but I'm still tolerant. It doesn't raise my blood pressure to see somebody dressed in cowboy boots, jeans and a flannel shirt decorated with remembrances of last week's meals.

"On the other hand, your 'normal' people get one look at me and they're ready to reach for their guns, except it takes 'em ten minutes to unlock the gun racks in the back windows of their pickups."

"You're stereotyping." Kerwin said it with a smile. "You're stereotyping them the way they stereotype you."

"They're the real stereotypes. No, monotypes. Not an individual in the bunch."

"No? See that couple getting ready to leave, alley twelve? His ball is red, hers is light green. A minor example, but it's still individualism."

"Ah yes, a vibrant aesthetic difference. How could I have overlooked it? 'His ball is red and hers is light green.' Why, they're as different as Turner and Goya."

"Actually, I don't find Turner and Goya all that different. One was interested in the expressions on human faces and the other in expressions of the sea. Both used light to reflect an inner feeling."

"Speaking of inner feelings," Seeth said, feeling pretty good with himself, "how about another Coke?"

22

Kerwin looked dubious. "Sure you haven't got something better to do?"

"Well, they say death is a real high, but I'm not into suicide tonight."

"All right. I couldn't make you leave anyway."

"Sure you could. Just say 'leave, Seeth.' "

"All right. Leave, Seeth."

"No way. Not when I'm having such a good time. How about those Cokes?"

"How about them?" Kerwin sounded resigned.

Seeth dug in a pocket. "If you don't mind, man, I'm a little short."

Shaking his head, Kerwin fumbled out a couple of crumpled bills. "And this time bring me back the change."

"Hey, I may be an anarchist but I'm no thief."

"Then don't be a forgetful anarchist either, okay? I need the gas money."

"Relax. I'm your original returnoid." He spun and headed for the snack bar, leaving Kerwin to jot down a few final notes.

Poor old Kerwin, Seeth mused as he took the steps two at a time. He was almost human. And the boy could talk. Definitely some brain up there hiding in the solid bone. It just wasn't connected to eyes and ears. As he approached the snack bar he glanced around, but his original tormentor had long since departed. Sadly, so had the two waitresses. The assistant manager was cleaning up.

"Hey, where's the good-looking one?"

The guy eyed him distastefully. "Nancy's gone home."

"Nancy? You mean her name's really Nancy? I thought that was a dead moniker, like Ethel. Two Cokes, please." He pushed the two bills across the countertop. "I mean, can you imagine a pair of proud parents in their early

23

twenties standing in an observation room looking into a hospital nursery at this little wrinkled pink thing and saying, 'Let's call her Ethel'?''

''I wouldn't know. I'm not married myself.'' The night manager turned his back on Seeth as he drew the drinks.

No, and if you were you wouldn't tell me, Seeth thought bitterly, because you're afraid I might sneak up on your house in the middle of the night and torch the place.

''She work here every night?''

''Off and on.''

Yeah, I didn't think you'd tell me that, either, nerdo. He smiled as he swept up his change. There was almost a buck. He debated whether or not to keep it and decided to split it down the middle. Not that he really needed the forty cents but it was a matter of principle. He wouldn't want Kerwin to get the right idea.

His friend didn't comment as he pocketed the three coins. He didn't come here often enough to know the price of a Coke or anything else.

Seeth hung around a little longer, but the joy of bugging the older student waned as Kerwin fielded his comments calmly and politely. What the hell, you couldn't get him upset. Self-control. Seeth always tried rattling him and only rarely succeeded. He could ''accidentally'' have tipped his drink all over Kerwin's neat, meticulously arranged notes, but that might've prompted something stronger than just angry words even from someone as even-tempered as the sociology student.

Anyway, the fun was in upsetting him emotionally, not physically.

He bade farewell with a last comment concerning his parents that added just a hint of color to Kerwin's face. It was still early. Maybe he could find Midge and Dreko and

24

the three of them could take Dreko's car and go cruising down the Interstate and moon some tourists. If not, well, there was always the Hole and a good morning's sleep. With any luck he wouldn't wake up again until the sun was going down tomorrow night.

Nothing wrong with living like a troglodyte, he told himself. He didn't get a tan, but he wouldn't get skin cancer, either. Besides, pale skin looked better against the blacks and purples he favored. Made it easier to gross someone out with the occasional, minor self-inflicted wound, too. Red showed up much better against white skin than beige.

He was almost out the door when he noticed the bowler working lane thirty-six, the last one, the one next to the painted concrete-block wall. Nothing special about him. Just another guy. Not much bigger than Seeth himself. Brown Levis, long-sleeved shirt. That was a little odd. It was plenty warm in the Bowlarama even this late at night, but lots of people were easily chilled.

The man had a seven-ten spare to pick up. The toughest shot in the game, or at least it was insofar as Seeth knew anything about the game. He didn't exactly follow the professional averages, though one time he and some friends had spent three hours watching a national bowling match—only to find it numbed their brains as thoroughly as any drugs.

He wasn't really watching the man at all and he just sort of caught the throw out of the corner of his eye. What made him halt was not the fact that the guy picked up the spare, but the way he did it.

He tossed the ball down the right side of the lane and it rolled straight and true for the ten pin, knocking it nob over tail. The ball then vanished from sight, back in the pickup area. At which point Seeth stopped as sharply as if he'd walked into a wall of inch-thick safety glass. The ball popped back *out* from the grasp of the automatic return, hovered above the wood like a mongoose taking a bead on a cobra, turned ninety degrees to its right and clobbered the seven pin.

All *right*.

⚡ II ⚡

His first thought was that something weird had happened with the automatic return to throw the ball back out onto the alley. He was still dealing with the realm of the possible. But if the ball had been kicked or bounced back out it should have come rolling back up the lane. It most definitely should not have bounced back out, halted, then pivoted and rolled decisively to its right. You could do that in a Saturday morning cartoon, but you couldn't do it with a fifteen-pound bowling ball.

Seeth just slowly turned around and stood motionless, watching, holding the last of his cola in one fist. The man bowled again but the miracle shot wasn't repeated. Everything else he threw looked normal. He was running up a good score but not an exceptional one.

Just when he was starting to wonder if he was beginning to hallucinate a little early tonight, Seeth saw the guy throw a strike. Not a normal strike, where the ball hits to the left or right of the head pin or even straight on the head pin itself, but one where the ball went down the right side of the alley, halted almost three feet from the pin, jumped sideways into the center of the pins and commenced to transcribe an outward flowing spiral until the last pin had been flattened. Whereupon the ball then leisurely spun over to the rightside gutter and slid out of sight back among the auto-pickup.

An inside-out strike. An utterly impossible sight. He fully expected the ball to levitate on its way back to its owner. But the guy just waited calmly like everybody else, sipping at his Bud while he waited for the automatic return to shoot the orb back to him. Which it did.

So, okay. One defiance of nature's laws was a coincidence. Two of a completely different nature suggested something else. Not that it mattered to Seeth, he wasn't the would-be scientist here. Let Kerwin make something out of it.

The older man looked up in surprise. "I thought you were leaving."

"Makes two of us."

"So what brought you back? The pleasure of my company?"

"Yeah, sure, I just can't pull myself away from the insights of Beaver Cleaver's clone." He turned and gestured subtly. "See that guy over there on the end?"

Kerwin turned to look. Most of the alleys in between were empty now and he could see the man clearly. "What about him?"

"Might be an interesting footnote for your paper."

"Why?" He squinted. "I didn't see anything unusual about him."

"Maybe not him, but he's got some interesting shots."

"Sorry. I'm into watching people who aren't bowling. This just happens to be a bowling alley."

"And this guy just happens to be contra-Newton. I don't mean fig. I saw him throw the ball, have it stop dead

28

and then accelerate perpendicular to the lane. Maybe you can make that work on paper but not with a bowling ball.''

''That's real amusing.'' Kerwin made it sound like a curse as he turned back to his clipboard, checking. ''I'll be done here in a minute and you can stay 'til they turn out the lights.''

''Look, man, I'm serious. Just watch the guy, will you? I saw him do it twice. The second time was even weirder than the first. Maybe he's some kind of electronics expert or something and he's trying out some kind of new remote control on the ball—though I didn't see him push any buttons or give any verbal orders or anything. Maybe he's gonna go pro and cheat. Or maybe he's just developed a couple of shots that contravene all the known laws of thermodynamics.''

Kerwin frowned at him. ''What do you know about thermodynamics?''

''Remind me to tell you about the date I had last week, but for right now let's just watch this guy, huh? Isn't that what you're into, observing?''

''All right. But only because it's the first time I can remember you asking me for anything besides money.''

So they watched while the man threw shot after shot, leisurely and calmly doing all the things bowlers normally do. None of them were miracle shots.

''Right, so I'm going over the edge,'' said Seeth, wondering if he really was. ''But I saw him do those shots, I really did!''

Kerwin didn't look over at him. ''I don't know about what you saw or didn't see, but you were right about one thing. He's unusual.''

Now it was Seeth's turn to be confused. He didn't like being confused. ''What are you talking about, man? He

29

hasn't thrown anything but regular stuff since I told you about him. I've been watching too."

"You're correct. All of his shots have been normal. However, something else is not."

Seeth stared at the bowler, watching as he tossed a simple two-pin spare pickup. "Like what? He's not doing anything."

"Watch him. Watch his hands right when he gets ready to release the ball."

Quietly Seeth did exactly as ordered, trying to find something unusual in the man's release. A hidden switch or something. The guy took his three steps and flung the ball, watched as it rolled down the lane to knock down half the pins. Then he turned to take another methodical sip of beer while waiting for the automatic to return the ball.

A contemplative Seeth muttered softly. "Far out. The guy's got six fingers on his right hand."

Kerwin responded with a slow shake of his head. "No. Seven."

"Cute. I wonder how he does it? What about his left hand?"

"That's even funnier," said Kerwin. "It's normal. Seven fingers on the right hand, five on the left. I wonder if he's got seven toes."

"Yeah. Maybe he's messed up somewhere else, too."

Kerwin made a face. "You're sick."

"Maybe, but there's nothing I can do about it because I'm fifty years short of qualifying for Medicare and they'll be broke by the time I qualify anyway. I never saw a guy with seven fingers before. I knew a gal once who had a cat had seven toes on a front paw and six on a back."

"People aren't cats. Sometimes they're born with two

heads or no fingers, but you don't get extra ones. They're not just ossified offshoots, either. I can see them working. They're functional."

"So what happened to this guy? I mean, is he a by-product of the H-bomb or something, like Mothra? Or did he hit up Chippendale's emporium for a couple of extra digits?"

"I don't know."

"You're not the only one. The dude could have thirty fingers on one hand. That wouldn't explain how he managed the two shots I saw."

"I'm beginning to think you saw what you say you saw. Wish I'd seen them."

"I wish you had, too. So what do we do about it?"

Kerwin shrugged. "I dunno. It's not a crime to have seven fingers on one hand." The Bowlarama was all but deserted now. The night crew was cleaning up the first eighteen lanes. He checked his watch. "We've got to be out of here in fifteen minutes. They're getting ready to close."

"What about plastic man over there?"

"Don't ask me."

"So ask him."

"Ask him what? He's probably sensitive about the deformity. The guy can have as many fingers as he wants. It's nobody else's business."

"Some scientist. Where's your sense of curiosity? Think Hillary would've climbed Everest if it had been five thousand feet lower? What's he going to do if you ask him about it—punch you out?"

"So you ask him, you're so curious."

Seeth straightened. "Hey, you're the male Margaret Mead, not me, Jack. I'll hold your Coke."

"I'm through with my Coke. I'm through with tonight, too." Kerwin started to rise, then suddenly sat back down and bent over his notes. "Take a look at these," he said under his breath.

"What, are you whacko?" Seeth sounded as if his friend's sanity was no longer in question. "I'm not interested in your stupid notes."

Kerwin reached up to grab the smaller man's jacket and pull him close. "Just pretend," he whispered tightly.

Seeth lowered his voice appropriately, his eyes darting around like a cat sure there were mice about. "A new game, right? So what's it called?"

"It's called don't attract attention to yourself."

"Are you kidding? That's my whole reason for being." He stepped back and shrugged off Kerwin's hand, thrusting both hands into the air. "See, I love attracting attention! I . . . ," he caught sight of the thing that had caused Kerwin to turn back to his notes with single-minded intentness.

The pair who'd entered via the back door might have been off-duty football players. Not for the university. Maybe for the Dallas Cowboys. Offensive linemen, and not for the power company. Both wore identical, trim brown suits. Their faces looked soft, almost puffy, but their shoulders were wide enough to skateboard on.

What had caught Kerwin's attention, however, was not their size but their expressions. The way their eyes moved, the set of their jaws. Put eyes and mouths and attitudes together and they spelled C-O-P. Seeth abruptly developed an intense interest in Kerwin's notes.

"Shit," he muttered, "I'm holding."

"Holding? You *are* crazy." Kerwin glanced anxiously

at the two men as they came down the steps leading to the lanes. "Holding what?"

"What do you think, man." Seeth's face was shoved up close to Kerwin's. "U.S. Mail?" He looked around wildly. "I've got to get to the john." He started to move, then hesitated. There was fear in his expression. "I can't. They're liable to stop me." He started fumbling in his pockets. "Here, you take the stuff."

"What, are you nuts?" Kerwin pushed him away. "I'm not having anything to do with anything you've got in your pockets, whether it's smokable, drinkable, or breathable!"

"Calm down, man! It's all right, it's all right. See?"

The two new arrivals were ignoring everyone else in the Bowlarama, including the two quietly arguing young men nearby. They were heading for lane thirty-six. The bowler with the extra grip didn't see them coming. He was standing by the return waiting for his ball and concentrating on the seven pin still standing subsequent to his last throw.

One of the cops put a paw on the man's shoulder and spun him around. The bowler's eyes got real wide, wide enough for Kerwin and Seeth to see his reaction clearly. They stared at each other, bowler and much bigger man. Then the bowler cautiously reached down to recover the ball. The other cop blocked any retreat.

The bowler looked exactly like someone on a TV show hunting for a place to hide. Since this was real life, no mysterious pathways suddenly appeared in the middle of the floor or the concrete wall. The cops each took an arm and started hustling him up the steps, just sort of urging him along, though Kerwin hadn't the slightest doubt they could carry him if it proved necessary.

"Hey, that ain't right," Seeth said suddenly.

"That isn't right." Kerwin wasn't so preoccupied he couldn't correct his companion.

"I mean, they didn't talk to him or nothing. They just grabbed him."

"Maybe he's been arrested before and they all know each other." He turned back to his notes. "In any case, it's none of our business."

"Typical yuppie. Mouth off about truth and justice, but when it comes down to it what you really want is not to have to get involved."

"You don't either. Sit down."

"No way, man. This stinks." His eyes glittered in the light from the batteries of overhead fluorescents. "Besides, this is the first interesting thing I've seen all night."

"Stay out of it, Seeth."

The younger man had already slipped out of reach. "How can I stay out of it? I've spent the whole night trying to get into it."

Kerwin glanced nervously around the alley. Only half a dozen die-hards remained. The nearest was ten lanes away. So far, none of them had taken any notice of the largely silent drama that was playing itself out on lane thirty-six.

The two cops were so big they would have overlooked Seeth if he hadn't stepped directly in their path. The extra-digited bowler looked at him too, both arms wrapped tightly around his bowling ball. It glowed slightly, Seeth noted. Obviously a custom job.

"Hi guys. What's on the program for tonight? Too late to hand out jaywalking tickets?"

The cops exchanged a glance, then simultaneously stared down at the pint-sized human blocking their path. Their silence convinced Seeth his first impressions were correct. Something was definitely unkosher here.

Instead of saying, "Get out of the way, punk," they tried to sidestep around him.

"You guys don't talk much, do you?" Seeth easily darted sideways to confront them a second time. "C'mon, I've got all night. What's going on here?" He eyed the bowler. "Hey, Jack, what's the story, huh? What're they leaning on you for?"

The bowler was either too preoccupied or too terrified to reply. His captors hustled him sideways between two rows of seats, heading for the next aisle over. Seeth stayed where he was, letting them think he wasn't going to interfere again, before clearing seats and rows to block them yet a third time. He'd already determined he could run circles around them if he needed to.

"You oinkers got a warrant for this guy's arrest? I mean, you can't put anything over on anybody here. We know what the score is. We all watch the tube."

For the second time the men eyed each other. Then the one on Seeth's right finally spoke.

"Go—away." It was a deep voice and it came rumbling up from somewhere far below, like bubbles in oil seeping to the surface. While hardly an elaborate response, it appeared to require a considerable effort on hulk number two's part to produce it.

"Away? Okay, where would you like me to go away to?" He glanced sharply at the bowler, who'd remained silent. "Look, man, if you're having problems here, I know a good lawyer. Bailed me out a couple of times. He's got a twenty-four hour phone, he's fast, and he doesn't ask a lot of awkward questions. Want me to give him a call for you?"

"I—I . . . ," the bowler stuttered. He was more than

frightened: he was terrified. More than anyone who'd simply been placed under arrest had any reason to be.

"Look, it's pretty obvious you guys are in violation of New Mexico municipal code statutes twenty-four and twenty-five, paragraphs six through ten. So unless you can show me a warrant or a badge or a letter from your mommies right now I think you'd better let this guy go."

Over on alley thirty-two, Kerwin was staring dumbfounded at his diminutive acquaintance. His jaw dropped as Seeth unclipped a long chrome chain and began swinging it casually from his right fist. Attached to the chain were a handful of keys, a battered Mercedes symbol, two handles scavenged from a pair of junked toilets and an ancient beer can opener. The chain was a good two feet long.

Seeth spoke as he twirled the chain in slow, lazy circles. "No badges? No warrants? Then let him go." He grinned over at Kerwin. "Hey, check this out, man! Showdown at the OK Corral."

Kerwin turned away and tried to bury himself in his seat.

"Go away," the first cop said again, "or you will get—hurt."

"What's this?" Seeth's eyes went wide with mock fear. "Threats of physical violence from a member of the department of public safety? Here in a public place, in front of witnesses? Oh my, oh horror, whatever shall we do? You're going to beat up on poor innocent little me? What if I told you I like it?"

The second cop extended a hand that looked big enough to pinch off Seeth's head as if it were a pimple. "Go—*now*."

Seeth skipped back out of reach and the mischief drained

from his expression. "Hey, what the hell's going on here? You guys aren't cops, are you? You don't *have* any badges to show." He looked at the bowler. "What's the deal, Jack? What's this all about?"

"I. . . ." The man tried to speak anew, then slumped as if he was going to faint. The first cop reached down and grabbed him by the neck, lifting him straight up until his feet were barely skimming the floor. Seeth's expression tightened.

"Right, bozo. That's enough. Leave him alone."

The other cop grabbed for him again. Serious now. Seeth ducked to one side and swung the twirling chain. It made a whistling sound as it screamed through the air to strike his massive opponent on the left side of his face. Kerwin moaned.

Seeth expected the man to flinch, or at least blink reflexively. He did neither. A chunk of flesh and skin went flying, but that wasn't surprising. What was surprising was that there was no blood. Not a drop. Even more surprising was that, instead of bloody flesh, the inch-square gash revealed something that looked like greenish-black sheet metal. But it wasn't metal, because as Seeth stared at it, it twitched.

"Oh wow." He took a step backward. "Trippy."

The expression on the cop's face, if cop he was, changed as he let go of his prisoner and lunged at Seeth. The younger man ran backward up the stairs faster than the man could move forward. Reclipping his chain as he darted around the edge of the rack, Seeth grabbed the first bowling ball he could reach and heaved it with both hands at his lumbering pursuer. The ball made a distinct *thunk* as it bounced off the man's forehead and fell to the floor. It didn't appear to affect him in the least. It certainly didn't slow him down.

Nor did his expression change. Seeth was starting to wonder if it could. The man kept coming and Seeth kept throwing bowling balls. Despite the first glimmerings of panic, he was thoroughly enjoying the excitement. His blood was racing, the adrenaline flowing for the first time in over a week.

Bowling balls slammed into the man's mouth, his chest, his knees. For all the good they did, Seeth might as well have dumped them on the floor. By this time, Kerwin had managed to shove his notes into his small briefcase. He was trying to dodge around Seeth and his determined pursuer to reach the upper concourse. Having finally noticed what was going on, the night manager was yelling frantically at the combatants while the remaining six bowlers had stopped to stare stupidly at the unequal fight.

Meanwhile, the other cop clung loosely to his prisoner while watching his companion track the nimble Seeth. He failed to notice that the bowler had switched from holding the ball with both hands to one. Now the man brought the ball up and around in a sweeping arc to smash it against his captor's nose. Hard.

Unlike Seeth's wild efforts, this produced some results. His captor let go of him, clutched wildly at the damaged spot and staggered backward until he reached the first step. He promptly went over backward while the bowler sprinted for the exit.

"All *right!*" Seeth yelled delightedly at the top of his lungs. He was jumping back and forth, taunting his pursuer. The man's chest appeared slightly indented where he'd caught a good dozen bowling balls, but it didn't slow him down. He lunged again.

Laughing, Seeth sprang to his right, cleared two seats, and climbed on top of the four-foot high bowling ball rack. He gestured past the cop.

"C'mon, man! What are you waiting for? Let's get out of here!"

Kerwin was almost to the concourse. Now he gaped at Seeth. "Me? But I don't. . . ."

The battered cop hesitated, then turned and started toward Kerwin.

"Hey, look." Kerwin backed away fearfully. "I don't know this guy. I'm just standing here. I don't know what's going on, I don't want to know what's going on. I—oh hell."

The cop lunged at him and Kerwin barely managed to dodge those huge hands. An arm like iron just brushed his side as he stumbled clear. It still had enough force to spin him around. His briefcase went flying, slammed into the ball rack and sprung, sending his notes and pens and blank paper flying all over the floor. Automatically he bent to pick them up.

There was a hand on his shoulder. "Come on, man!" Seeth started dragging him toward the exit. The cop the bowler had slugged was climbing back to his feet. Any normal individual would have suffered massive contusions, a fractured skull and severe haematoma from the blow he'd taken, but repeated head-bashing just seemed to put these guys slightly off stride.

"My notes." The cop was coming for him again, staggering from side to side. His companion was slowly mounting the far stairs. "Dammit!" Leaving notes, briefcase, and everything else behind, he turned with Seeth as the two of them bolted for the door.

"Save your head, use your legs." Seeth was covering their retreat, twirling his chain like a gladiator's mace.

"What've you got me into?" No athlete, Kerwin was already panting as they plunged out into the cool night air. "What am I going to do if they take me down to a station for questioning? We don't even know what that guy they were holding is guilty of."

"Hey, I'm not sure he's guilty of anything. I don't think these guys came from no station. Twilight Zone, maybe. I cut one of 'em and you know what he's wearing under his skin?"

"More skin?"

"I wish. It was all green and black and shiny. I know a chick uses makeup that color, but on the outside. It moved, man. It moved like real flesh. But it wasn't. It was something else. Listen to me, Jack. Tweedledum and Tweedledee back there, they ain't meat." He was jumping up and down like a berserk pogo stick, trying to see over the tops of parked cars. There was an all-night Denny's next to the Bowlarama and the mutual lot was pretty full.

"There he is." He pointed, then started running. Kerwin had no choice but to follow, since his brain was still numbed by the events of the past ten minutes.

Sure enough, they found the bowler huddled behind a low-rider Riviera. As he saw them approach, he rose and turned as if to run. He was still holding onto the ball, Kerwin noticed. Maybe it was an expensive custom job.

"Hey, hang on, man! We're the guys who helped you, remember? We just want to know what's going on."

The man took a couple of steps, then stopped, cradling the ball protectively in both arms. Some of the fear left him.

"Yes, right, sure; I remember now."

Funny sort of voice, Kerwin thought. Smooth, but with the emphasis on all the wrong syllables, and spit out fast, like a DJ on amphetamines.

"I should thank you. I do thank you. Thank you both. I don't know how they found me." He hunkered back down behind the Riviera, peering nervously over the long trunk. "I was careful, so careful, but you know, they'll find you no matter where you ever go. Just when you think maybe you've finally lost them, just when you think you've put yourself in an away-place so obscure nobody's ever heard of it, they find you. Damn them. They never give up. Never give up 'til they get you."

"Yeah, I've known cops like that." Seeth stared at the double glass doors that formed the Bowlarama's exit. "The thing now is to get you away from here."

"Look, you don't have to thank me," Kerwin told the man. "I had nothing to do with this. It's all a mistake. I was just taking some notes, getting ready for a class, minding my own business. My being here now's a mistake." He checked his watch. "I've got two exams tomorrow, both of them weeklies, and while I'd like to know what's going on here I really can't hang around."

"We need a car," Seeth muttered. "We've gotta get out of here." He glanced over at Kerwin. "I don't suppose . . . ?"

The taller man shook his head. "I took the bus from the dorm."

"Yeah, you would. How you plan on getting back?"

"There's a bus every hour."

"We can't hang around waiting on it." He looked at the bowler. "I don't suppose you've got a car."

The man shook his head. "I have no personal transporation in this area. I have. . . ."

41

Kerwin ducked and pointed. "Here they come!"

As they emerged, the two men blotted out almost all the light pouring from the bowling alley. Thus silhouetted from behind, their inhuman aspect was enhanced. They'd straightened their clothing and looked none the worse for wear, including the one who'd taken a bowling ball flush on the nose.

"Hey, the guy on the left, the one I cut?" Seeth was staring. "He doesn't look hurt. What happened to the gash?"

"Band-Aid," Kerwin suggested.

"Yeah, or a quick welding job. Come on." Bent over, he started making his way toward the restaurant. The bowler seemed to hesitate, then followed. So did Kerwin, until realization struck home.

"Hey, wait a minute. I don't have anything to worry about. I didn't do anything." He straightened despite the bowler's insistent tugs on his arm. "Lay off." He turned to look back toward the Bowlarama. "They can't do anything to me. I'm going into Denny's and I'm going to call my friend Jerry and have him come out and pick me up. I don't know what you two are going to do and right now I don't—"

The air was filled with the sharp tang of ozone and burnt caramel. Something that looked like a wayward lightning bolt crackled close to the left side of his face. A moment later the first odors were replaced by the stink of singed hair. His own.

Turning, he stared blankly toward the bowling alley. The cops had seen him and were lumbering toward him. Each carried a gun. At least, they looked like guns. Toy guns. Narrow, thin chrome tubes with sleeves at the back large enough to accommodate a pair of hands. As he gaped, one of them fired again. Fortunately, the weapons were difficult to aim when running. The bolt or whatever it was passed through three car windows and the bed of a pickup truck on its way to Kerwin's face. This time it missed slightly to the right.

Next time it might not miss.

He stared not at the onrushing pair but at the molten steel that was running in rivulets down the side of the pickup truck, at the slag glass that was dripping from windows.

"How'd they do that? They can't do that."

"Yeah, you tell 'em." Seeth reached up, grabbed Kerwin's belt and jerked him back down. "Come on, Miss Muffet. Move your tuffet or it's going to get shot off. This way." He turned and started moving. Kerwin and the bowler followed, keeping low as Seeth led them through the maze of parked vehicles.

"Who are those guys, anyway? Bullets, okay, but what's with the light show?"

"It's all right." The bowler whispered as rapidly as he talked. "They don't want to harm me, they don't. It'll go bad for them if they harm me."

"Won't do me any good either. Bring 'em back alive, huh?" Seeth voiced his crude Jimmy Cagney imitation. "The dirty rats."

"You two, however, I'm afraid they will not hesitate to kill. If they can, they will melt your heads."

"Hey, no big deal. I got my head melted years ago. Kerwin, now, he'd be a loss. He's original issue, a real antique."

"Just shut up and keep moving." Kerwin stuck his head up for a quick look, ducked back down. "They're still coming, but back toward the buildings. I think we're losing them."

"They will not ever give up," said the bowler. "They will keep following until they have us."

"This duck-walking sucks." Seeth raised his head slightly. "We need wheels."

As he hunted for possible transportation, Kerwin took the opportunity to question the man they'd rescued. "Look, what's going on here? Who are you? What's this all about?"

"They want to take me and to kill you. Isn't that obvious, man?"

Seeth spoke without looking over at them, still inspecting cars. "Be gentle with him, Jack. He's a little slow." He chuckled to himself. "Kong and Dong are talking. Can't figure out where the mice got to. Hey, where'd they get those guns? Those are slick."

"They carry standard police weapons."

"Then they are cops." Kerwin was more puzzled than ever. "Seeth said, he said he hit one of them and when the skin came off there was something else underneath. They wouldn't be some kind of robots, would they?"

"Oh heavens no, man, no. Robots I could deal with. No matter how well designed and determined a machine, if one is fast enough and clever enough and skilled enough—and I am—you can usually convolute their logic circuits and leave them standing arguing with themselves. Robots I could handle. But these are Oomemians."

⚡ III ⚡

"Say what?"

"Oomemians. Lots of Oomemians go into police work. They're big and strong and dedicated and not too bright."

Seeth nodded agreeably. "Sounds just like the cops here in Albuquerque."

"My name, by the way, is Arthwit Rail. I am sorry I didn't introduce myself earlier but the circumstances were not sanguine."

"No kidding," said Seeth.

"I'm Kerwin. This is," he hesitated, knowing what his friend's real first name was and knowing how he'd react if it was mentioned. This wasn't the time to provoke internal dissension. "His name's Seeth."

"Oomemian cops, huh?" Seeth continued to study the ranked automobiles. "They like Nicaraguans or something?" His expression lit up. "Hey, you wouldn't be a dope smuggler, would you?"

Rail looked confused. "Why would anyone wish to smuggle stupidity when there is so much of it readily available?"

"He means drugs," Kerwin muttered. "You must be a foreigner to miss that one."

"Yes, true, I am from not around here."

"Like the cops?" Seeth glanced over at the man they'd rescued. "This is really getting interesting. You an illegal alien or something?"

"Something like that, yes, true."

Kerwin had to admire the single-mindedness with which the man clung to the bowling ball. In times of crisis familiar objects could be soothing to the psyche. Or so his profs claimed.

"Not that I'm real big on anthropology," Seeth was saying, "but I kind of thought Central Americans were like kind of brown, not black and green."

"That's Oomemians for you." The more time passed without their discovery, the more Rail's confidence appeared to be returning. "Nobody thinks they're good-looking. Their pigmentation's about as nasty as their dispositions."

"I can go with that. You sure you're not carrying drugs?"

"Absolutely not. I do not indulge in artificial stimulants nor do I approve of their use by others."

"Skip it." Seeth didn't try to hide his disappointment. Suddenly he grinned. "Hey, I got it! You're smuggling bowling balls, right?" He glanced toward Kerwin. "See, there's this multimillion dollar market in illegal bowling balls. The great thing is you don't have to pack 'em in. You just stand on the Mexican side and roll 'em across."

"Funny." Kerwin didn't smile. "For someone with a destroyed brain you're a real wit."

"At least I've still got a brain and not a lump of saltwater taffy any retardo can stretch and pull at his will."

"That so? Lemme tell you that—"

"Gentlemen, please," said Rail anxiously. "Save the philosophy of cognition for when we have assured our mutual continued existence."

"Potato brain," Seeth muttered under his breath.

"Anarchistic twit," Kerwin hissed by way of reply.

Seeth looked back over the Riviera's hood. "I think they're leaving, heading off the other way. Gonna check out Denny's, maybe."

"They won't give up," Rail reminded them warningly. "Oomemians never give up."

"You said that. Check that out." Seeth pointed at a customized Dodge van parked three lanes away. The front door stood slightly ajar.

"Wonder if they left the keys inside?" Kerwin strained for a better look while Seeth stared at him.

"What's this? Can it be? The boy wonderbread thinking of stealing a vehicle that belongs not to him but another?"

"Borrowing," Kerwin corrected him. "This is a matter of life and death."

"Excuses. Maybe there's hope for you yet. We don't need keys."

As they moved toward the van, Kerwin considered asking Rail about his obsession with the bowling ball. Expensive it might be, but it was getting a little ridiculous to keep hauling it around when they might have to make a run for it.

Seeth opened the door noiselessly and slid inside. Rail and Kerwin followed. The front was dominated by a pair of oversized captain's chairs. Seeth didn't have to demonstrate his antisocial skills because the van's owner had thoughtfully left the keys in the ignition. It was slightly crowded up front with the three of them, not to mention the bowling ball. Music blared from the radio.

"Please, let me drive." Rail's request was unexpected.

Seeth eyed him briefly, then shrugged. He was listening to the rock pouring out of the custom speakers and feeling good. "Sure man, why not?" He moved aside and let the man slip behind the wheel.

Rail appeared to hesitate over the automatic shift. Maybe he was used to a stick, Kerwin mused. He turned the key and slowly eased forward. The loud music helped to muffle the sound of the engine turning over. They began easing out of the parking lot.

A blast of white-hot energy scorched the left side of the van.

"Hit it, hit it!" Kerwin yelled over the heavy-metal riffs of KDKW. Rail responded by slamming his foot down on the accelerator, leaving rubber behind as the van peeled out of the lot and roared eastward.

"All *right*!" Seeth was bouncing up and down in time to the music, jabbing Kerwin in the ribs with an elbow. He leaned out of the passenger window and looked back the way they'd come as another bolt of energy, weaker with distance, seared the pavement behind them.

"Eat hot lead, Oomemian scum!" He cocked his thumb and forefinger and began shouting as he shot imaginary slugs. "Bang—bang!" Kerwin had to grab him by the seat of his pants to keep him from tumbling out as Rail sent the van careening wildly around a corner.

Their driver looked a little steadier now. He glanced uncertainly at Kerwin.

"What weapon is your friend firing?"

"Whaaa?" Crammed in between the enigmatic Rail on one side and Seeth-the-mental-case on the other, Kerwin

48

began to feel like a Tenniel illustration from *Alice in Wonderland*. "He's not shooting anything."

"Oh." Rail sounded disappointed.

"Look, this whole business is insane. What are we running from, anyway?"

"It is not insane," said Rail evenly. "It is inconvenient, which is not quite the same thing."

He'd finally put the bowling ball down. It was rolling around, bumping up against the door and center console and the seat posts. It didn't seem to affect his driving. A third energy bolt was barely audible as it sizzled by overhead.

"Wonder if *they've* got a car?" Seeth had finally come back inside. His Mohawk was frazzled and he wore a look of exhilaration.

"I am sure they must." Rail turned another corner. He seemed to know where he was going. "They would not be as ill prepared as I and their resources are greater. Once more I extend my gratitude to you for saving me from a fate worse than death."

"Heyyy." Seeth looked nonchalant. "What are casual acquaintances for?" He turned the radio up and the music blasted through the van. "Much better. What do you think?"

"Catchy. Maybe they'll play some *X* or Dead Kennedys or Siouxsie and the Banshees or Crumple."

Seeth's eyebrows rose slightly. "I'll be damned. A classics lover." He reached in front of Kerwin with an open palm. "Put 'er there, compadre."

Rail stared at the palm. "Put what where?"

"Forget it. You drive and I'll cover us." He leaned back out the open window, flinging pinging sounds into the New Mexico night.

Kerwin strained to see past him, trying to get a look at the outside rear view mirror. "Are they following?"

"Can't tell."

This late, the roads were almost deserted. Cops would be changing shifts, late-night giving way to graveyard. With luck, most of them would still be swapping stories in the doughnut shops down on Central, which was fortunate, considering Rail was exceeding the speed limit by double figures. Those police already on station were probably busy trying to bust underage drinkers near the campus. The presence of a pair of speeding vehicles, with the occupants of one of them firing a weapon of unknown potential at the other, should escape the constabulary's notice entirely.

"Crap, here they come!" Seeth ducked back inside as another blast of flame just missed the weaving van. Kerwin stared as the upper half of the van's antenna melted and ran like quicksilver. Reception suffered.

Seeth was bouncing up and down in the seat, pounding madly on the radio's controls. "Dammit, that was Blowfish! I haven't heard that song in years." He leaned back out, screaming at the road. "Come on, you bastards, I'll wrap you around a telephone pole! Blast you, evil scourge of the universe!"

Rail clung tightly to the wheel and murmured something that sounded like "How did he know?" but as Kerwin was about to question him he veered hard to port, almost rolling the van. The two wheels on the right side actually rose from the pavement before slamming back down. The radials held.

"Hey, take it easy! You total us and your Oomemians won't have to shoot us."

Rail spared him a glance. "I assure you I am perfectly

quite aware of the relationship between gravity, mass, and velocity. I will keep us absolute straight upright.''

''So enough twenty questions already. Why are they chasing you and why are they shooting at us? Why are . . . ?''

This time the interruption arose not from their pursuers but from the rear of the van. Kerwin and Seeth stared. Rail seemed to have no trouble keeping his eyes on the road.

The guy who was sitting up in the back of the van was big, though not nearly as big as the pursuing Oomemians. He was trying to extricate himself from a bevy of entangling blankets. The girl who sat up alongside him was exceedingly pretty. No, not exceedingly pretty, Kerwin corrected himself. Ravishing. Gorgeous. Overpoweringly radiant. And a few equally descriptive if less formal adjectives applied also. He applied them.

''Well helloooo.'' Seeth leaned over the back of the captain's chair and leered.

''What's going on? Who are you people?'' The guy looked slightly dazed, as though he was emerging from deep sleep. Or something else. Except for the rumpled blankets, he and his female companion were stark pale naked.

''I told you,'' she said, sounding bored. ''I told you I heard the van start up. Couldn't you feel it moving?''

''Uh, no, not under the circumstances.''

''Man, what I wouldn't give to be under the circumstances!'' Seeth was trying hard not to pant. The girl ignored him, indifferent to his stare, his comments, and her partial nudity.

''Creep,'' she finally murmured.

''Can't,'' Seeth told her. ''I'm not on my knees. But gimme a minute and I'll give it a try.''

The big guy glared at him. ''Bug off, jerk.''

"Bugoff?" Seeth adopted a look of false concentration. "Sorry, the name's Ransom. Seeth Ransom. Don't know any Bugoffs. Hey, great haircut. I don't think I've ever seen anybody who's had their hair cut with a chainsaw before."

The guy started to lunge at Seeth, remembered suddenly he wore nothing beneath the blankets. He started hunting around in the dark at the rear of the van. "Where the hell are my clothes? Miranda, have you seen my underwear?"

"I've seen your underwear, sweet thing," simpered Seeth, "and frankly, I'm not impressed."

The guy looked needles at him. "As soon as I find some clothes I'm gonna come up there and kill you, you little creep. You think you can steal my van with me in it and get away with it? I'm gonna pound you!"

"We're not stealing your van." Kerwin tried to placate him. "We're just borrowing it for a minute. See, there are some people chasing us—at least, I think they're people—and they're trying to kill our friend here."

"Chase? Kill? What are you mumbling about?" Another energy bolt crackled past and the van's owner looked wildly at the roof. "What the hell was that?" He turned and Kerwin heard him banging around as he walked on his knees to the rear of the vehicle. He stared out the back window and Kerwin saw he wasn't much older than himself. Rail sent them screeching up a side street.

"Jesus!" The guy turned to his girl. "Somebody's shooting at us!"

Seeth made a show of checking a nonexistent watch. "Twenty-two seconds for basic message to travel from tympanum to central cortex. Another ten for preliminary interpretation. Not bad, for an orangutan."

The girl leaned back against one wall, composed and

relaxed. "So they're shooting at us. What can we do about it?"

"Not a lot," Seeth told her. "Not without underwear. Now, if you'll give me a general idea of where yours might be located, I'll be happy to. . . ."

"Thanks, I'll find it myself."

"Did anyone ever tell you you're the most beautiful organism ever to walk the Earth?"

"Lots of guys." She started searching through the blankets for unmentionables.

She had better luck than her boyfriend. Soon she was trying to arrange her hair.

"Wanna borrow my comb?" Seeth dug in a pocket and produced a piece of black plastic six inches long. A few tines still showed forlornly among the gaps. She eyed it distastefully.

"Thanks. Let's keep the oil in the engine, okay?"

"Hey, anytime," he replied, blithey ignoring the sarcasm. He repocketed the comb. "So your name's Miranda, huh? Wanna know why everybody calls me Seeth?"

"Not especially."

"Glad you asked. It's because I'm mad all the time. Seething. Get it?"

"Do I have a choice?"

"Seeth Manitoba Ransom, but that sounds too much like a seaport in Massachusetts, so everybody just calls me Seeth."

"I'm Kerwin. Our friend here is Arthwit Rail."

"Pleased to make your friendship acquaintance, madam." Rail didn't take his eyes off the road, for which Kerwin was persistently grateful.

"Hey, like, I'm no madam, you know? Just Miranda."

"Miranda." Seeth stared solemnly at the roof. "A name

that should be applied to one of the major constellations so that all the heavens might glory in its sound.''

She stared at him a moment before looking over at Kerwin. ''Is he for real?''

''I'm afraid he is.''

''I'm gonna kill him!'' This from the back of the van.

''That's Brock.'' She gestured in his direction with a casual thumb.

''Brock?'' Seeth turned to Kerwin. ''And you thought Arthwit was a funny name.'' He turned back to her. ''Nobody's really named Brock. Are they, Brock? You find your Fruit Of The Loom yet, fruit?''

An inarticulate cry sounded from the back of the van as Miranda's boyfriend lunged forward—to stumble over something in the darkness and whack his head pretty good against the small bar sink that was sunk into the service counter on the left side of the van. The girl just shook her head.

''How do I end up with these clowns? I think, you know, like, I'm just unlucky.''

''Not to worry, sweetness,'' Seeth reassured her. ''You now have me here to protect you.''

''Swell. Protect me from you, will you?''

Rail was muttering to himself, squinting into the darkness. ''Up this way; no, no, it must be over here.'' He yanked hard on the wheel, sent the van bouncing and rattling up a steep dirt road that led back into the foothills of the Sangre de Cristo mountains. The persistent glare of twin headlights abruptly faded from behind them.

''Hey, I think maybe you lost them!'' Kerwin shouted.

''Only temporarily, if at all. They are relentless trackers. They will find us again soon enough.''

''Not soon enough for me. Look, would you *please* tell

us what this is all about? It's bad enough you've ruined my project. . . ."

"Ah, a scholar!" Rail seemed pleased. "Interesting."

"Him, a scholar?" Seeth laughed unpleasantly. "That's a joke. He's a professional student. All he does is take every course they'll let him into in the hope it'll lead to something when he graduates."

"I am a Renaissance man," Kerwin said with dignity.

"Yeah, sure," Seeth sneered. "Borgia, not Medici."

"At least I can lay claim to being human."

A puzzled Rail glanced from one young man to the other. "I should say you both qualify as human."

"Not him." Kerwin nodded at the smaller occupant of the passenger's chair. "He's a sub-species. Freaks."

"That's funny, coming from a zombie with play-dough for a moral conscience."

The van slid wildly as Rail took another corner. "Hey, take it easy up there, damn you!" Brock bawled. "You know how much the flares on this mother cost? You know how hard it is to get good fiberglass bodywork?"

"Not really," Seeth said conversationally, "but I'd say they did a pretty good job on your head."

"You little prick! As soon as I get my pants on I'm going to beat the crap out of you!"

"Oh Bret, don't be so crude," Miranda admonished him tiredly.

"Crude? What the hell do you mean, crude? And my name's *Brock*."

She looked up at Kerwin out of mesmerizingly huge blue eyes. "Have you seen my blouse?"

Kerwin swallowed, staring. "Uh, no, but if I do, you'll be the first to know."

"Get your elbow out of my face, man," Seeth snapped at him.

"Sorry." He sat back, looked over at Rail. "You have any idea where you're going? Some of these roads, when they get up into the national forest, they just run up to the edges of cliffs and stuff."

Rail sounded more relaxed than at any time since they'd made his acquaintance. "No need to worry concern yourself needlessly. We are now traveling the correct course."

Kerwin stared out into the night. The headlights illuminated nothing but dirt road and trees. "The correct course for what?"

"For losing cops, spitwad," snapped Seeth. "Leave him alone. He knows what he's doing. Don't you, Rail?"

"Assuredly absolute."

I am going to wake up, Kerwin told himself silently. Any minute now I am going to wake up. I am not an extra in a Spielberg or Lucas movie and any second now I will wake up.

"I've never been shot at before in my life."

"Liar," said Seeth.

"Will you kindly SHUT UP." Kerwin turned back to Rail. "I'm not enjoying this, you know."

"I understand, and I apologize for inadvertently having involved you in my problems. What can I do to make you understand?" The look in his eyes was considerably less maniacal since they'd shaken their pursuers.

"You could start by telling us how you happen to have seven fingers on one hand."

Rail looked down at the hand in question. "Seven? I thought it was six."

"Sorry. I definitely counted seven."

"But I don't have seven fingers." He held up the

controversial right hand and Kerwin was stunned to see five perfectly normal-looking digits. There was no sign of the additional pair.

"Now, that's a neat trick," said Seeth softly.

"Oh dear, now you've got *me* confused. I suppose I owe you a full explanation. Considering how things have gone and how many edicts I've broken already, I don't suppose it will hurt to break one more."

"Yeah, come on, bowling fiend, come clean," said Seeth.

"That is precisely just what I intend to do."

Rail put is hand over what looked like an ordinary wristwatch and ran fingers along both sides. The watch didn't change. Rail did. His epidermis seemed to flow, like a copper plate undergoing an acid bath preparatory to being used to make etchings. His skin dissolved into nothingness and yet his clothes remained intact.

Thus revealed, Arthwit Rail looked over at them out of three small eyes set in a green ellipsoidal skull. The pink pupils were so tiny they looked like specks floating in pools of white water. Narrower than a human head, the skull was set on the end of a long wiry neck and was completely covered in a dark olive-green fuzz, which had been shaved to form intricate whorls and curlicues similar to Maori tattoos. His face looked like a miniature golf course speckled with water traps.

Gripping the steering wheel were two long tentacles that subdivided into double sets of smaller tentacles that subdivided still a third time. As Kerwin stared goggle-eyed at these limbs, the smallest tentacles shrank and disappeared— only to reappear at regular intervals, like sea anemones at a bridge party.

The only thing that hadn't changed besides his attire was Rail's voice.

"You see, the confusion arises from the fact that I can have as many digits as I want. Extending and withdrawing them is a nervous reaction among the Prufillia, much as your terrestrial felines extend and retract their claws according to their moods. When I'm especially uneasy it becomes particularly difficult for me to control my patterns, hence the additional digits you noticed back in your recreation center. Sometimes even the camouflage field can't cover everything. You were most very observant."

"Good study habits," said Seeth.

"Big deal." Miranda was slipping her right arm into the sleeve of her blouse. "An alien."

Kerwin chose his next words carefully. "You don't find it somewhat unusual to be fleeing from a couple of homicidal, maybe not-human police in a borrowed van that's being driven up into the mountains by someone not of this world?"

"Look, Keith, I mean, I've been around, you know?"

"Kerwin," he corrected her absently. It was apparent that Miranda didn't have much of a memory for names.

"Yeah, well, whatever. Like, if you think *he's* funny looking you should see some of the losers I've been out with. I mean, sometimes I think half the men at school are majoring in post-doctorate dorkism." She glanced toward the rear of the van. "Present company excepted of course, Brick."

"Brock, it's Brock, dammit! Where the hell's my belt?"

"That's more like it," said Seeth. "Belts I can get into."

"That's good. That's real good. Because as soon as I find mine I'm going to—ow!"

The van slammed through another pothole. The forestry road wasn't exactly the Interstate and the unfortunate owner of the van was thrown sideways into a wall.

Kerwin was still staring in wonder at Miranda. "Amazing. Simply amazing. No surprise, no shock, no fear."

"Why should there be? Hey, I go to the movies. So he's an alien. So, like, none of us is perfect. What are you, prejudiced or something?" She eyed their driver thoughtfully. "So maybe he's not a real good *looking* alien. . . ."

"How would you know?" Rail sounded a bit miffed.

"Yeah, right. Hey, nothing personal like, you know? It's been a weird night for me."

Seeth was inspecting Rail's true appearance. "Actually, man, I think that haircut's far out. Who mows your fuzz?"

"I primp myself, thank you. When I have the time and when I'm not operating under the restraints of a camouflage field."

"That the little bugger that makes you look human?" Seeth nodded toward the unwatch.

"An expensive piece of equipment, but for one in my circumstances well worth it. Particularly when one's on the run from the authorities." He reached down and caressed the watch anew. "As you will see, in a moment I will have reformed my human aspect."

The moment passed, the light seemed to ripple, and sure enough, there in the driver's chair sat a bright blue porcupine.

"No sale," Kerwin told him apologetically. "Maybe you'd better try again."

"What?" The porcupine frowned and quills touched the watch. The porcupine vanished, to be replaced by something like a cross between a vampire bat and a swordfish. "Drat. I think the modulator's jammed."

Kerwin tried to be sympathetic. "Computers at school are always going down, too."

"This is wild." Seeth put his hands behind his head and

leaned back. "Do another one. When this is over I'm gonna try and book you on the Dick Clark show. He *loves* acts he doesn't understand."

"What's he talking about?" Rail looked confused. "I thought I understood your language quite well. I took a crash course before setting down here, you know."

"Don't mind him. First of all, our language is in a constant state of flux. Second of all, so's his brain. He usually doesn't know what he's saying, either. Remember, I told you he's a member of a subspecies. They usually converse in monosyllables. Anything more complex tends to confuse them."

Seeth threw him a finger. "Just for that, man, you don't get any peanuts when the zoo closes."

"That's about enough of this!" Having sufficiently attired himself, Brock loomed in the light pouring through the back windows. "I want everybody out. You hear me? Out! Everybody out of my van except Miranda. Right now, or I start kicking ass!" He started forward.

The high-backed captain's chair had concealed Rail from his view. Now the driver turned to look back at him. He'd managed to unjam the camouflage generator to the point where he once again looked like himself: tri-eyed and green.

Brock-boy got a look at him and his eyes got real big. He started making odd, blubbering noises.

Miranda shook her head and sighed. "Settle down, Brian. It's only an alien."

Brock retreated several steps, mumbling. "You mean a real alien? Like, from up there?" He gestured skyward with a finger.

"It is all right, Mr. Bloke," said Rail. "I will not harm you." Clinging to the wheel with his left tentacles, he reached back with his right to reassure the van's owner with a friendly caress. As no joints were involved, he didn't have to turn his body from the road ahead. To Miranda's boyfriend it looked like a dozen writhing green snakes were reaching for his chest.

Screaming, he staggered to the back of the van and slammed into the rear doors. The impact sprung the latch and he tumbled out onto the dirt road. Because of the bumps and ruts, they weren't going much more than twenty miles an hour. He was still screaming as Miranda sighed again and crawled back to resecure the doors.

"Like, what a drip. I mean, he was built, a real hunk, but I guess muscles aren't everything, you know?"

"Muscles aren't anything," Seeth assured her.

"Yeah. There's always brains." Kerwin jerked a thumb in the smaller man's direction. "Like there's always sewage."

"And where would the world be today without sewage? Up to its earlobes in undigested waste, man." His expression brightened. "Hey, that's not a bad name for a group. Undigested Sewage. I ought to get some of the guys together. We been thinking about forming a band. Maybe we could. . . ."

Miranda interrupted him. It wasn't so much that she interrupted, it was as though no other vocalizations of consequence disturbed the ether in her immediate vicinity, as if there was some kind of mysterious cloud of radiation that automatically shut out all forms of communication other than her own.

"Can you guys get me back to Eighty-Third and Thunderbird? I mean, my parents are going to be pissed if I'm not home pretty soon. They think I went roller skating. Would you *believe?* I mean, roller skating! Now that Bjorn has freaked out he's liable to do something really stupid like call them up. So if you could just turn around, like right now, okay?''

Seeth was staring into a side mirror. ''Better gun it, Rail. I think I see headlights again. Way back.''

''It could be someone else,'' said Kerwin hopefully.

''Not on this freeway, man. Just rabbits and skunks.''

''I told you the Oomemians were persistent.'' Rail accelerated as much as he dared. The transmission was starting to complain.

''They missed you when you made that last big turn. How'd they get on you again?''

''I fear they are attuned to my *sumash*.''

''Right, yeah. Why the hell didn't I think of that? You AM or FM sumash?''

Miranda slumped back against one paneled wall and crossed her arms, pouting. She managed to look wonderful despite her rumpled hair and clothing, one of those unique young women who could drive the Baja 500 and emerge at the end with makeup perfectly intact. She moved in a different dimension than he did, Kerwin knew, which was why he'd never encountered her on campus. Circumstances had put them in close proximity.

''Look, as soon as we get to wherever Mr. Rail's going and lose the people who are chasing him, we'll take you straight home. I promise.''

''Big deal. I'm gonna be grounded for *weeks* after this.''

Far back on the dirt road, Brock was trying to button his shirt. A car bore down on him and he moved out into its lights, waving frantically.

''Hey, hold up there, stop!''

The car slowed. Gratefully, he ran toward it. No telling

when another vehicle would come along on this isolated forestry road, and it was a long hike back to town.

"Listen," he said excitedly as he neared the open window on the driver's side, "those guys up ahead, they stole my van, and they've got something driving it that looks like—" He stopped in mid-sentence as a creature with the face of a cancerous toad peered up at him.

Away from humans, the Oomemians no longer needed to waste the power necessary to maintain their own camouflage fields, with the result that Miranda's exceedingly unfortunate date became the first person on planet Earth to see an Oomemian as it truly was. In addition to being persistent, they were also exceptionally ugly; maybe not ugly enough to win a galaxy-wide ugly contest, but gruesome enough to at least qualify for the semi-finals.

As Brock staggered away making interesting gurgling noises, the two aliens consulted and then roared off up the road, tires squealing, dirt flying into the air behind their late-model sedan. Having struck out twice on the road, Brock turned and made a mad dash for the nearest woods. At this point he would have been extremely grateful for the sight of something as normal-looking as a bear.

N IV N

Once Rail got started it was hard to turn him off. As he talked, the green fuzz that covered his head rippled like an unripened wheat field in the wind. Kerwin suspected that each ripple conveyed a whole range of feeling, though to him it looked only like blowing grass.

"Part of the problem is that we Prufillians are a very gentle race. We don't like it when someone else tries to set themselves up as lords of the universe. Besides, the Oomemians have no sense of humor. If there's anything a Prufillian can't stand it's a race with no sense of humor." He smiled. His teeth were thin and short.

"That's one reason why I have enjoyed my stay on your world so much. Your kind has a wonderful sense of humor— when you're not giving vent to your homicidal urges." He glanced into the rearview mirror. "They think they're so smart, they do. Cleverer by half than anyone else, especially a lowly Prufillian. They don't have me yet. We'll show them a thing or three."

Seeth continued to leer at Miranda. "Want me to show you a thing or three, creamkiss?"

She was working with her hair. "No thanks. One boring

date a night's enough. Why don't you just leave? Go on, get out.''

"And where would you like me to get out to, honeylips?"

She made a face. "Don't tempt me."

"Why are they after you?" Kerwin asked their driver as the van turned down a narrow track leading through the trees. Something went *spang* beneath the van. Miranda's ex-boyfriend wasn't going to get his machine back in like-new condition.

"Oh, a little of this and a little of that."

Kerwin couldn't tell if Rail was being deliberately evasive, was just concentrating on the road ahead, or was actually telling the truth.

"I'm what you'd call a freelance espial."

"A what?" He turned back to Seeth, who continued to stare over the back of the captain's chair at Miranda. "You know what an espial is?"

"Sounds like an abbreviation, man. Hey, you're the college boy. Isn't that one of your pet words? Some people have dogs and cats, you have words."

"Not this one."

"A word you do not know, in your own language." Rail shook his head and Kerwin assumed it meant the same thing on Prufillia it did on Earth—unless you were from Bulgaria. "That's something else I love about you humans. Your linguistic diversity. Of course, it has mucked you up no end but I'm sure you'll straighten it out soon. Who would have thought that any one race could create so many words that mean so little? Could construct elaborate sentences that contradict themselves and yet appear to actually mean something? When you join the galactic community you will make wonderful diplomats."

"Galactic community?" Kerwin swallowed. "You

mean there are others out there besides you and the Oomemians?''

"Certainly. Intelligent life is as common as dirt. There are hundreds of sentient races, maybe thousands. I don't know the actual number at last count, but there's an entire administrative department whose job it is to keep track. Occasionally an intelligent race will be bypassed or overlooked by the Development and Integration people. Then they tend to extinct themselves. Terrible waste. Hard to get credit if you extinct yourselves. Bureaucrats.'' He shook his head again.

"You'd think advanced computers would be able to keep track of everything, but sometimes they just make it more confusing for us poor organics. Though when you're trying to keep track of an entire galaxy, you don't have much choice but to make use of them. You give machines artificial intelligence, next thing you know they want to use the same bathroom. If it was up to me—but nobody asks my advice. Nobody wants to listen to a lowly espial.''

"That still doesn't tell us why the Oomemians are after you.''

Rail smiled wanly. "It's all a misunderstanding, of course.''

"Oh. Good. Then you haven't actually done anything bad.''

"Naw,'' Seeth sneered. "He's innocent as a newborn juniper. Come on, man! Who's kidding who here? He's guilty as sin. It's written all over his face. Or maybe I should say mowed. He's guilty, I'm guilty, we're all guilty.''

"Not me,'' said Miranda with perfect self-assurance. "I'm not guilty of anything.''

"No? How about being too beautiful?''

"Nobody can be too beautiful." She said it without attempting to argue his compliment.

Rail dimmed the van's headlights. "I suppose from the Oomemians' point of view it's not a misunderstanding. But I assure you that to the rest of the civilized galaxy I am as innocent as the driven frooflak."

"So what do they call this misunderstanding?" Kerwin pressed him.

The green fringe on his head moved south. "Not much. Kidnapping."

"Kidnapping?" Kerwin drew back. "Hey, I don't know how they evaluate crimes where you come from, but here on Earth kidnapping's not just a 'misunderstanding'."

"Relax, my friend. It is what the Oomemians call it, but I am not guilty. Just accused."

Kerwin breathed a little easier. "Okay then."

"That's why they've sent those two trackers after me, because they know they haven't a chance of proving their case to any court. It would be much better for them to avoid the publicity an open trial could produce. In an open proceeding they would have to admit to some things they would prefer to keep secret. In other than an Oomemian court their accusations wouldn't hold a sorbil."

Kerwin mulled this over as he took another look in the sideview mirror. Only rarely could he glimpse a glow that might come from pursuing headlights. Rail hadn't been kidding when he'd told them the Oomemians were persistent.

"If you're not guilty, we're going to help you all we can. I don't like the idea of somebody else picking on an innocent traveler no matter where he's from."

"So you didn't kidnap anybody?" Miranda had finished with her hair and was slipping on her shoes.

"Of course not." Rail smiled broadly. "I liberated something. You can't really call it someone."

Kerwin's expression fell. "Hold on. You mean, you really did kidnap somebody?"

"I said liberate. Admittedly, it would be up to a court to draw the requisite distinctions. Wonderfully duplicitous, your language."

"So who or what did you liberate?" Seeth asked him.

"Izmir the Astarach."

"*Got* to get a group together. Can't waste all these names. You got whoever this Izmir is stashed out in the woods somewhere?"

"I refer to it as a he because it makes for simpler semantics. No, he's right here. He has accompanied us all along."

Kerwin's eyes searched the van. "You mean you've kidnapped somebody invisible?"

"Hardly. Come on, Izmir, reveal yourself. We're not playing that game anymore." With his right foot he nudged the bowling ball that lay close to his leg. It rolled forward slightly and bounced off the engine housing. For the first time all night Seeth and Kerwin wore similar expressions. Kerwin stared hard at their driver.

"Let me make sure I've got this straight. These Oomemians have tracked you across no telling how many light years and are trying to kill all of us because you've kidnapped a bowling ball?"

"Don't be absurd." Rail did not appear particularly upset. Maybe, Kerwin thought, he was used to the question. He nudged the ball again. "That's enough, Izmir. Game's over, finished."

"Blitheract," said the bowling ball quite clearly.

Kerwin gaped at it. He was sure it was the ball that had

69

spoken and not Rail, not unless he was some kind of interstellar Edgar Bergen. Reaching down hesitantly he touched the shiny, almost iridescent curved surface.

"Glumelmerk!" the ball snapped.

Kerwin yanked his hand back. The surface of the ball rippled and flowed, extending a thin black pseudopod that encircled his right wrist. It was as gentle and strong as a baby elephant's trunk.

"Leave him alone." Rail added something in an entirely different language. It sounded like radio static.

Obediently, the tendril freed Kerwin's wrist. He clutched it with his other hand. It tingled from the brief contact. As the three humans looked on, the bowling ball levitated soundlessly and settled down on the drink-holder tray that covered the engine console. As soon as it made contact it silently commenced to explode, surfaces shifting, running down the front of the console, rising toward the ceiling. Tiny explosions were visible within this flexible matrix, small bursts of intense energy.

As the malleable surface continued to flow, the color changed from black to a deep navy blue. The tiny explosions changed from pure white to red, blue, and tangerine, began to run together in glowing strips. The result was something that looked like a giant, animated candy cane. A single large blue eye appeared atop the cylindrical shape. A pair of short arms, each ending in four fingers, extended from the main body to push off from the console. It floated in the space between the chairs, its base rippling like a skirt blowing in the wind, and gazed intently at Miranda.

A few minutes passed before she spoke. "Hey, give it a rest, will ya? First Bowen, then this joker," she jabbed a finger in Seeth's direction, "and now you—and I don't even know what you are."

"Ffirzzen hobewl menawick."

Words from several languages or one unknown one, Kerwin thought.

"See, he thinks you're pretty too," Seeth told her. "You oughta be flattered, woman."

She sighed indifferently. "I don't need the flattery." Ignoring the exotic alien thing floating less than a foot away, she lifted her arm and eyed the candy-colored Swatch on her wrist. "Jesus, my mother's gonna kill me."

Seeth leaned toward Izmir. "That's not bad, but can you do a real red?"

The blue eye turned toward him by migrating through the fluidlike body. The Astarach promptly turned a bright candy-apple red, the kind of red usually seen on show cars at fancy auto expositions.

"Pretty good. How about matching her watchband?" Izmir became a bright, hot pink. "Wild! How's that for matching accessories? Every girl needs an alien to go with her handbag. You ever been in a band, man?"

Kerwin eyed the smaller man pityingly. "Seeth, this is an alien lifeform. It doesn't know what you're talking about."

Clearly, the entire cosmos was conspiring to prove that he was the biggest idiot alive, because Izmir the Astarach's flanks shifted and flowed to form half a dozen unrecognizable shapes. Their purpose was clear enough, however, as the imitated instruments proceeded to fill the van with a discordant but not entirely unpleasant music. Even Seeth was rendered momentarily speechless. But only momentarily.

"When we lose these Oomemians or whatever they are, Arthwit old buddy, I want you to help me get this guy on MTV. I mean, if we can get Stevie Wonder or Dave

Stewart to produce for this whatsis, we're all gonna be rich!"

"I fear there will be no time for that, much as the prospect of such an adventure intrigues me." Rail was searching the woods now, obviously hunting for something.

Kerwin kept a wary eye on Izmir, who had abandoned his band self in exchange for a shape like a hot fudge sundae, complete with dark brown and white fluids coursing down his flanks. He looked soft, almost rubbery, a feeling enhanced by his obvious flexibility. In actuality the Astarach's softly glowing body had the consistency of steel, but Kerwin didn't know that because no way was he going to touch it again.

"Why is he so important to the Oomemians? I mean, he's pretty and clever, but that doesn't make him valuable. Does it?"

"Ain't it obvious, man?" said Seeth. "I mean, he's an *artist*. Maybe the greatest artist these Oomemians have ever developed. Or greatest work of art. Yeah, that's it, he's got to be a work of art. A continually changing piece of art. He can't be an artist because he doesn't look anything like these Oomemians, unless they can do these shape changes too."

"No, unfortunately for them, the Oomemians, like the rest of us, inhabit the shapes they are born to." Rail slowed a little more, not wanting to miss something in the dark. "I do not know exactly what Izmir is, but an Oomemian he is not. As to why they consider him so valuable, I really have no idea."

"You mean, you kidnapped him without knowing why he's important?" said Kerwin.

"It was enough to know that he *is* important. Very important. What is stranger still is that, from what I heard and learned, the Oomemians don't know what he is either. But they guarded him heavily and were studying him intently close, so I figured that if he was that valuable to them he ought also to be valuable to Prufillia. Besides, if nothing else, by borrowing him I could at least deny him to the Oomemians.'' Without altering his tone in the slightest he added casually, "It's all because of the war, of course.''

The short hairs went up on the back of Kerwin's neck. "War? What war?'' Suddenly the wild terrain and the night-shrouded forest, which under ordinary circumstances he would have found threatening and lonely, began to look exceedingly inviting.

"Why, *the* war, naturally. Ah, here we are. I was starting to get concerned.''

"Uh, I don't want to sound obtuse,'' Kerwin told him, trying to remain halfway calm, "but there's no road here.''

This observation did nothing to dissuade Rail. Seeth let out a shout as the alien sent the van over an embankment and into the bushes below. Miranda was tossed all over the back of the van by the terrific bouncing and jouncing, complaining nonstop. Something about her hair, Kerwin thought as he found himself thrown to the floor between the two front seats. Seeth grabbed the high back of the chair and hung on.

Kerwin couldn't imagine how Rail kept the van upright as it crashed down the steep slope. He couldn't see, either, because he was tangled up in flying blankets, cushions, pillows and other loose paraphernalia. Miranda was thrown into his field of vision momentarily—a bouncing, tumbling compendium of perfect eyes and lips, wrinkled yellow pants and multicolored blouse, dangling earrings like strips of paint hanging from her ears, and other interesting accoutrements. Then she was gone again. His life didn't flash before his eyes, but the complete contents of the van did.

Eventually they came to a halt, not so much because Rail had reached his destination as because of the presence of a very large pine tree directly in their path. Large pine trees being decidedly unreasonable in matters of right-of-way, it behooved Rail to alter his course in an attempt to go around it. In this he only partly succeeded.

The right side of the van got crumpled. The windshield shattered and diamondlike glass fragments flew everywhere. Miraculously, no one was cut, though you couldn't tell it by listening to Seeth. Kerwin fought to sit up.

"What's wrong? Leg, arm?"

"I should be so lucky." Seeth leaned toward him, his face contorted, one arm extended. "Look at this, man! That's friggin' glove leather. Four hundred bucks this jacket cost. Four hundred bucks!" He glared at Rail, who was trying to extricate himself from behind the wheel. "I'm gonna take it out of your green hide, man."

"I am sorry about the damage to your attire."

"Sorry? *Sorry?* Didn't you hear me? Read my lips, turkey: four hundred bucks!"

"Wait a minute." Kerwin was looking around anxiously. "Where's Izmir?"

A gurgle came from behind the driver's chair and a shifting shape emerged. The blue eye stared blankly back at him.

"Here, Izmir." Rail molded an invisible sphere with his tentacles. The Astarach promptly assumed the form of a ball again, not a bowling ball this time, but one that resembled a gigantic marble. However, he retained the blue eye and arms. If anything, this was more disconcerting than his previous forms.

"He responds pretty well to you for a kidnap victim," Kerwin observed.

"He would do the same for certain Oomemians. Or for you, if you wish to try."

"Thanks, I'll pass and admire him from a distance, if you don't mind." He indicated their silent surroundings. "What's the big idea? I thought you knew how to drive."

"I do know how to drive." Rail was trying to open his door. Locking himself in place with his tentacles, he began trying to kick it open. "This is exactly where I wanted to come."

"Oh, fine, yeah. What do we do now? Play hide-and-seek in the woods with the Oomemians?"

"I fear am afraid we have no time for games. Having come so near, our pursuers will not rest until they have closed upon us all. We cannot remain in this vicinity any longer." The door popped open.

"That makes sense." He followed Rail outside, glad to be standing up again. "Hey, wait a second. What do you mean *we* can't? I've got to get back to school, my dorm."

"What's the matter, man," Kerwin taunted, "no guts? Where's your sense of adventure?"

"My guts are right where I want 'em, between my thighs and navel." Both young men turned in response to a loud sigh.

"My parents are absolutely going to *die*. I'll be grounded *forever*."

"Don't sweat it," Seeth told her. "I'll come over and keep you company. We can put *Leave it to Beaver* reruns on and ignore them while we—"

"You're getting tiresome, you know that?" She was sitting in the driver's seat, staring disgustedly at the broken speedometer. "This is great, just great. It isn't bad enough

I have to make do with a dumb jock like Brock, I have to go bashing through the woods with a freak, a nerd, an alien, and a bowling ball that's broken loose from a Levi's commercial. I mean, it's not like I don't take care of myself. What did I do wrong today? Did I get up wrong? Did I eat the wrong breakfast?''

"I resent being called a nerd," said Kerwin with dignity.

"You think I'm a freak, sister?" Seeth gestured toward her legs. "Get a load of those pants!"

Miranda glanced down at herself and plucked at the bright yellow material. "What's wrong with my pants?"

"Nothing's wrong with 'em, that's what's wrong. They're straight off the rack. Untouched. Virgin polyester. No individuality. There's nothing there that screams *you*."

"It all screams me," she argued.

He shook his head sadly. "Vinyl body, vacuum brain."

"Well at least I look like a human being," she replied huffily.

"Excuse me." Rail had moved several yards away and now turned to look back at them. Izmir was cradled under one tentacle, his two arms extended to lock around Rail's long neck. In that guise he looked something like a one-eyed monkey hunting for his tin cup. "We cannot stay here. We must hurry."

"What do you mean, hurry?" Kerwin started around the van. "I'm going to hike back up to the main road and flag down the first car I see. I've got a mid-term in Biology coming up."

"If the Oomemians encounter you they will melt your brain head."

"Cool," said Seeth. "He'll never miss it."

Kerwin paused, his eyes shifting from the punker to Miranda as she delicately exited the van. "Are you guys gonna wait here and play patty-cake, or are you going to make a run for it with me?''

"Run?" Seeth turned a slow circle. "Run where, man?"

"Look, we don't have anything tying us to him." Kerwin nodded at Rail. "If we do run into these Oomemians or whatever they are I'm sure they'll listen to reason."

"Sure they will. Like they did in the lot outside the Bowlarama. Me, I think these Oomemians are your standard massacre first, ask questions later types. Why should they listen to you when it's easier to remove your head? Probably simplifies their paperwork. Typical cops." He walked over to stand next to Rail, stared hard at him.

"In any case, Jack, I'm not letting you out of my sight until somebody pays for this jacket."

"I'm sure I can arrange recompense once we are safe."

"That's better." He looked back at Miranda. "Coming, sweetlegs?"

"I might as well." She indicated her watch. "You know what time it is? I'm already gonna get killed. I don't want to get shot, too."

Kerwin tried to keep it simple for her. "Look. This guy is an alien. We don't really know anything about him except that he's green, and that might be another disguise, too. He's a self-confessed kidnapper." He found himself studying her hair. There was a great deal of it and it was a mixture of blonde and black. Blonde with streaks of black. Or was it black with streaks of blonde? And what difference did it make?

"All right, go with him. I'm getting back to the real world." He turned to start up the hill.

"OH MY GOD!"

Seeth dropped into a fighting crouch. Kerwin whirled, wildly looking around in the darkness while Rail tensed.

"What? What is it!" Kerwin yelled. Then he saw she was bent over, staring at the dark ground.

"I've lost an *earring*, dammit! That was one of my favorite earrings. I've had it for almost a *year*."

Kerwin slumped. He would have said something, except for the lights that suddenly appeared high up on the hillside.

"Oomemians," whispered Rail. "Time to go. Come or stay as you please." He headed off into the woods.

"Damn." Kerwin hesitated, then moved to follow. He and Seeth had to take Miranda by the arms and hustle her along or she would have stayed to get her skull melted over an earring.

"I'll buy you a new one. Two, even," Seeth told her sweetly. "If the gruesome twosome chasing us shoot off your ears, you won't have to worry about it."

She shook herself free. "All right. I know when I'm being made fun of."

"Somehow I knew you possessed great reserves of perception," Seeth said.

"You think I'm being silly about it, don't you?" In the moonlight she looked like a goddess, Kerwin thought. Except for the remaining earring. "That's because neither of you knows what's really important in life."

Rail seemed to know exactly where he was headed, despite the absence of sunlight. They stumbled through the trees in his wake. Kerwin spent plenty of time watching the ground. He didn't want to find out how the Oomemians would treat a sprained ankle.

"So tell us," Seeth implored her, "what is really important in life?"

She looked defiantly at both of them. "Clothes. Clothes are the most important thing. I mean, if you don't have decent clothes you're just *nobody*."

Kerwin nodded absently. "I'm sure Einstein felt the same way."

"Go on, make fun of me. One of these days you'll see."

Twenty minutes later a wheezing Kerwin called a halt. "Hey, are we walking to Texas, or what?"

"Not much farther," Rail assured him. "In fact, we have arrived." He put Izmir aside and began pulling at a mound of brush and branches, his multiple tentacles making quick work of the pile. Something like a dull platinum frisbee appeared from beneath the dead leaves. It didn't reflect the moonlight so much as it seemed to absorb it.

Kerwin bent to help with the clearing. "Doesn't look big enough to hide all of us."

"Most of it is buried. I wasn't able to dig in completely. There's a lot great deal of metamorphic rock in this region and I was in somewhat of a hurry rush. The Oomemians were right behind me, relatively speaking."

"How long have you been hiding here like this? How long have they been chasing you?"

"Oh, they've been chasing me for quite a while, quite a while. But they haven't caught me, not yet. This is the closest they've come, but thanks to your intervention they have missed me again." He grinned. "I am sure they are most positively furious."

When the last of the brush had been shoved aside, the platinum dome turned out to be about the size of a buried Greyhound bus. If most of it still remained below ground it would be of considerable size, Kerwin mused. He had a pretty good idea what "it" was, though he still found himself doubting his own sanity.

Rail touched the device on his wrist and a door appeared in the metallic surface. The large, inviting oval opening seemed to melt through the solid wall. Light poured out of the gap, illuminating their faces and revealing a corkscrewing ramp leading inward and down.

The alien glanced back into the trees. "They can't be far behind us. We must hurry." He started toward the opening and vanished within. Seeth was right behind him, looked back at his friend.

"Hey, you heard the greenie. We gotta hurry or the head-melters'll catch us. What are you waiting on?"

"It just occurred to me what this thing is. It's not just a hideaway, Seeth."

"Naw, gotta be a ship. What did you think he was heading for, a tree house? Come *on*, man."

"It's just that I think we're going," he tilted back his head and stared up at the stars, "you know."

"Maybe even New York. Move your butt."

"But what about my exams?" He found his feet moving one at a time toward the entrance to the buried spacecraft. Miranda strode unconcernedly past him.

"Might as well kill the whole evening." She paused outside the opening and bent to shout inside. "I've just got one question!"

Rail's voice drifted out to her. "I will answer reply if I can."

"Where we're going . . . is there shopping?"

"Most definitely for certain."

"Okay then." She smiled sweetly back at Kerwin. "I wouldn't go anyplace I couldn't shop." Whereupon she tiptoed elegantly down the ramp. Seeth blew Kerwin a kiss and followed.

Then Kerwin did too. It wasn't like he had any choice.

The door flowed shut behind him. Rail led his guests deeper into the bowels of the ship, which was indeed far larger than the tiny portion visible from above would have led anyone to believe.

"I would prefer to find another uninhabited world," he murmured as they descended.

"Uninhabited? But Earth isn't uninhabited," Kerwin pointed out.

"Sorry, but according to official galographics that's how it's classified. Not your fault."

"Now wait a minute." Miranda halted and crossed her arms again. "You said we were going to be able to go shopping."

"Some of the best and most unique items obtainable are to be found on worlds classified as uninhabited."

This mollified her slightly. "Well—okay. But remember, you promised."

Rail eventually led them into a large, domed chamber, which Kerwin felt must be located somewhere near the middle of the ship. A broad, sweeping window dominated the far wall. Presently it displayed layers of earth and rock, plus one family of gophers who were about to be rudely awakened. Their host oozed into a lounge-style chair, and Kerwin wondered aloud as he took note of several similar seats nearby if he and his friends should do likewise.

"Only if you'd feel more comfortable. The field will keep everything steady and stable. You will experience only a slight sense of movement as we depart. Unless the Oomemians start shooting, in which event I may be compelled to take evasive action. But I think we will surprise them."

Miranda promptly settled herself on one of the inviting lounges. It was much too big for her, but shaped close enough to the human form to be comfortable. She began fumbling in her purse, which was slightly smaller than your average steamer trunk.

"I am going to sit right here and do my nails. With all that bouncing around you just wouldn't believe how banged up they got."

Kerwin was inspecting the enclosing walls. They were lined with inch-wide metallic strips that resembled mylar but obviously ran much deeper.

"Fascinating," he murmured.

"Bull," said Seeth. "You don't even know what you're looking at. You haven't got enough point-of-reference to figure out where the toilet is."

"It's highly advanced technology." Kerwin assumed a superior air. "That much is obvious."

"Actually, this wreck's on the old side." Rail ran his tentacle tips over a knot of intersecting mylar strips on the console in front of him. "It was the best I could do on short notice. I was in a hurry and had to borrow whatever was available."

"You mean you borrowed this ship, too? The way you 'borrowed' Izmir?" Kerwin nodded in the direction of the ex-bowling ball. It had adopted a pole shape, plonked itself down on the console next to Rail, and balanced itself on both arms while staring intently at nothing out of that single, unblinking blue eye. A bright purple-and-pink striped pattern flowed across it in endless streams.

"The pressure of circumstances compelled me to." The ship lurched sharply, nearly knocking Kerwin off his feet.

"Hey, watch it!" Miranda had to juggle her nail polish.

"Apologies sorry." Rail bent low over his control strips.

"I thought you said we wouldn't feel any movement." Kerwin looked around for something to hang onto, but the chamber walls were smooth as the inside of a billiard ball. He started cautiously toward one of the chairs.

"Did I? Excuse me. I am doing the best I can. If we get off a little odd, the field should compensate. Anyway, the ceiling is soft."

"Soft ceiling?" Kerwin hastily slid onto the lounge chair, hunted frantically for straps or belts. "Anything to hold you down here?"

Rail didn't look back. "Touch the strip on your left, halfway down."

Kerwin found the metallic surface in question and followed instructions. Something like an invisible hand grasped him gently around the upper chest and legs. It was light as a feather and, he had no doubt, far more secure than leather. A touch lower down on the strap released the hold instantly.

"Nice and neat, anyway," he muttered.

"Oh, the ship takes care of that, insofar as it's able," Rail told him. "I'm a terrible housekeeper. There are places even the automatic cleaning devices refuse to go. Absolutely filthy. Chambers and rooms that haven't been cleaned out in years. Besides being ugly, the Oomemians are slobs. There are things left behind by previous users of this vessel whose origin and purpose I do not care to contemplate. Some of it moves, I think. I wouldn't go wandering about the ship once we're on our way."

"Don't worry." Kerwin reactivated the restraints. "I may not get out of this chair again until we make landfall."

Seeth was the only one still walking about, even though the vessel was now shuddering and jerking in response to Rail's instructions. "You know what, man? You've really blown it."

"Blown it?" Kerwin looked over towards him. "What are you talking about?"

"You were in that stupid bowling alley to take notes for a class paper, right?"

"That's right. So what does . . . ?" His voice trailed off as he realized what Seeth was driving at.

Of course! In ruining one project, fate had presented him with another, far greater opportunity. Positively unique. Why study the social habits of middle-class American bowlers when he could take notes on the lifestyle of not one, but two alien races—Prufillian and Oomemian. Three, if you counted Izmir as alive. The report he could make!

"Notes," he began muttering, "got to start taking notes." He released his restraints and sat up, ignoring the shivering beneath him. "Hey, Arthwit, have you got a pad and pencil around here somewhere? I've got to do some writing."

"Sorry again." Rail was concentrating on his strip instrumentation. The ship was fully alive now. You could feel it in your feet, in your whole body. Power. "We Prufillians did away with such recording methods eons ago, when it was discovered that trees can feel pain. Writing on paper became rather like writing on dried skin. Now we only use the stuff for ceremonial purposes, and then only when the tree perishes of natural causes."

"Gee." Miranda looked up from her intricate nail work. "How do you pass notes in class?"

"Telepathically is the best way, unless you're stuck with a sensitive instructor. Then it can be embarrassing sure." He touched a blue strip.

The ship rose a foot. Beyond the sweeping window, the gophers looked agitated. One was trying to bite through the transparency.

"Only a very few are capable of true telepathy, though. We try instead to convey much feeling through expression.

84

As you do, only without the gross and unpleasant facial distortions.''

"Good thing you never got to his club." Kerwin nodded toward Seeth. "You would've seen some really gross distortions."

"Your dancing is better, I suppose? Foxtrot and two-step?"

"At least it was designed for human bodies. Break dancing works for chimps and gibbons, not people."

"I thought Rome was for gibbons. You're just jealous because you can't coordinate arm and leg movements without tripping over your own feet."

Kerwin felt the ship twitch and restored his restraints, closing his eyes tightly. I don't believe it, he thought. We're getting ready to flee the planet to escape alien cops in the company of an interstellar kidnapper and I'm sitting here arguing with a jerk like Seeth about break dancing.

"I am familiar with the recreational activity to which you refer," said Rail unexpectedly. "What I was able to observe of it via one of your video transmissions was intriguing, though I think it would work better with a couple of additional pairs of limbs."

"There you go," said Seeth, vindicated. "Soon as we get back from this I'm gonna run down to the nearest leg store and pick up a few extra pairs. Maybe I'll catch 'em on sale."

"I do not recall seeing such available on your world," said Rail thoughtfully. "However, your internal structure is simple enough so that a properly designed set of neuronic prostheses could be attached. Ah, there we are."

A throaty rumble sounded somewhere far below. The ship rose three yards. The gophers gave up and fled down a tunnel that led toward unseen regions. Kerwin thought they looked disgusted.

"This isn't the first world you fled to after borrowing Izmir, is it?"

"No. It's most peculiar, but as you've noticed he doesn't act like he's at all upset by his change of locale. I'm not sure he is conscious in the sense we think of it. He may not know what is happening to him, though he is aware of what is happening around him. He appears quite comfortable in the company of whomever he happens to be with.

"He and I have been hopscotching from one world to another in this little-visited part of the galaxy. Out here toward the edge, civilization is more spread out and it's easier to throw the Oomemians off your trail. It's taking a lot longer than if I'd simply set a straight course for Prufillia, but I'd never have made it that way. There'll be all sorts of monitoring stations and relays between Oomemia and home. Sometimes the surest way is not the most direct way."

Izmir pushed away from the console and drifted across the room, bouncing once off the ceiling and executing several aerial somersaults with the same ease as he altered shape and color, before finally settling down in an empty chair. With his hands he began to pick at his now triangular body.

"What I don't understand," Kerwin murmured, "is why the Oomemians or anyone else would think a levitating imbecile is valuable."

"No one understands," said Rail. "I've measured and tested and probed until I've gone pink in the face, and I know less than when I began. He's not putting out any radiation I can detect, though my instruments are not the most sensitive. I thought to try and analyze his substance, but every time I attempted a tiny biopsy I met with failure. Metal blades, lasers, nothing worked. Any solid instrument simply broke or snapped against his body, while radiant energy like that produced by a laser is absorbed. Nothing damages him. Not only is he a shape-changer, he appears to be quite invulnerable.

"As to what he mumbles from time to time, according to the ship's translator it's nothing but drivel, quite meaningless. There is no recognizable pattern to it, nothing like language, not even code."

"How come we're not moving any faster, and how long has this war you mentioned before been going on?"

"We're still underground because this is an old ship and it takes a long time to warm up, besides which I'm scanning for Oomemian weapons.

"As to your first query, it's not really a war. Then again, it is. The Prufillians and the Oomemians have never gotten on well, but neither have we tried to annihilate each other. Genocide is impolite. You might characterize our long-term relationship as one of infrequent conflict interrupted by periods of uneasy peace. You see, Prufillia and Oomemia are located so far apart that for one to mount a major offensive against the other would be not only exceedingly difficult but inordinately expensive. So the war consists mostly of calling each other dirty names and broadcasting endless threats. Only occasionally out in open space or on other worlds does actual combat sometimes take place. The respective populations seem satisfied with this state of affairs and the rest of the civilized galaxy tolerates it, so long as no innocent bystanders are incinerated. Every so often peace breaks out, but it rarely lasts for long. The Oomemians are intemperate.

"Both sides spend a great deal trying to think up ways to deal the other a finishing blow, but, because of the costs involved, grandiose battle fleets and so forth never get beyond the propaganda stage. Financing an interstellar war over any distance at all is simply impractical. People would quit paying their taxes. Even totalitarian governments can't sustain them."

"Then there aren't any empires?"

"Empires? Goodness gracious no, young human Kerwin. What good is an interstellar empire? Prohibitively expensive to keep even a single obstreperous world in line. The administration costs alone—no, it's purely a romantic notion. Not practical at all. If you're interested in settling on another world or opening a business there or doing some minerals exploitation, it's a lot simpler and cheaper just to secure the necessary permits and pay the requisite fees than to try and take over. There's pretty much free movement between worlds. Everybody seems to think their planet is the best, so why try to take over another that's not as nice?" He sighed a long, drawn-out whistle.

"There's no place like Prufillia. Most of the other races feel likewise as concerns their own home worlds. I mean, someplace like Varnial is okay for a vacation, but you wouldn't want to live there.

"Despite distance and difficulties, there remain ways of harrying the enemy. Sending someone like myself to make trouble problems is not quite the same as funding a warship. I obtained backers for my vessel and managed to slip behind Oomemian screens. This sort of minor irritation is performed constantly by both sides, but once in a while someone manages to accomplish something substantial. Such was my hope, for my people, for my planet—and for the enormous bonus that would greet me upon my return.

"Hence my interest in Izmir, once I found out about him. You cannot believe the secrecy with which the Oomemians surrounded him, but I found out about the Izmir project despite all their safeguards, and managed to spirit him away from underneath their very mometils." He glanced over to where Izmir was turning lazy somersaults.

"To tell you the honest complete whole truth, I am beginning to wonder why I bothered. I had no idea the Oomemians would so relentlessly seek the return of something so patently useless. Oh, he may respond to you, and he babbles incomprehensibly, but not in response to any questions. You don't know if he's understanding you, and in any event there's no way to understand any possible answers.

"About all that's distinctive about him is his ability to shape-change. No other true shape-changers are known, though there are always rumors. He certainly can be colorful when he wants to be. He also seems to be able to change his density at will. I worry constantly that he will one day wander through the wall of the ship when I am in the same room. He's quite capable of doing that, you know. Most remarkable of all, when he alters density it does not appear to hinder his ability to levitate."

"On the face of it," Kerwin commented, at the same time praying fervently that Izmir wouldn't choose to walk through any walls when they were out in space, "I'd have to say that my people would be interested in studying a shape-changing, density-altering, invulnerable creature too. Especially if he's the only one of his kind."

"Oh, he's the only one, all right," said Rail. "The only Astarach in existence. If he wasn't, I don't think the Oomemians would be so anxious to get him back."

"Maybe they think he holds the secret to personal levitation."

"I don't know. Perhaps. What matters is that I have denied him to them. It matters not why he is important, only that he is important to Oomemia."

"That's nasty, really nasty," said Seeth.

"Thank you."

"Kerwin here, he can change the density of his brain, from near vacuum to total vacuum."

"Give it a rest, guys." Miranda had finished her nails and was already looking bored. "Wish I had my radio."

The ship continued to rumble, gathering strength. "I apologize," said Rail, "for having forgotten the customs of local late-period adolescence. I've had other many things on my mind, as you have seen." He ran a tentacle tip along a control strip.

Static filled the room, followed by a ripple of unfocused music before the heavy-metal thunder of KMUT-FM out of Los Angeles assailed their ears.

"All *right!*" Miranda put her purse aside, slid off the lounge and began to move to the music.

"Hey, it works." Seeth came over to join her.

"Couldn't you find something a little mellower?" Kerwin asked their pilot. "Or at least lower the volume?"

"Oh no—you can't noway fool me," said Rail proudly. "I've studied this phenomenon closely. The volume is correct proper for this type of music." He looked back at Seeth. "Is it not?"

Seeth gave him a thumbs up sign.

"Fascinating, your rituals. See how effectively they communicate without the use of words or telepathy."

Kerwin watched Seeth dancing with Miranda and found to his surprise that he was madly jealous. Maybe it had something to do with Miranda's exceptional beauty. Or maybe it was the fact that she was about to become the only human female for light years around.

"Your hair!" Seeth shouted over the wail.

"What about it?"

"You've got to do something with it. It's too—too *safe*."

"No thanks. I'm not into punk styles." Somehow she managed to convey an air of boredom even while putting her body through some extraordinary gyrations. Was it an attitude, Kerwin wondered, or was there simply nothing up there between the ears?

He turned away, knowing full well that if he tried to join in he'd end up by falling flat on his face, or worse. Instead, he hesitantly unlatched himself and walked over to watch Rail conclude his liftoff preparations. The console was a total loss, a blank white curving surface lined with crisscrossing metallic strips, Scotch Tape gone punk.

"If nothing else, you could always use Izmir for a bowling ball."

"Perhaps. That was his idea, you see. He does what he wants and he can convey intention by simply doing it. We ended up in that recreation center quite by accident chance. I was wandering about the area—I don't sleep much, and it is difficult in some of your smaller metropolitan areas to find things to do at night. Apparently he found the motion of the balls the other bowlers were throwing of interest.

"He indicated he wished to do likewise simply by eliminating his eye and arms and providing a number of finger holes for my digits. I confess to finding it of interest myself. The need to calculate the proper sine curves stimulates the brain."

"That's not why most people bowl."

"Really? Another revelation surprise. I did not actually throw Izmir, of course. I merely went through the motions and he did the rest. After a while I believe he grew bored with the limitations and chose to try some dimensional variations, which is what first attracted your friend's attention, I believe. That made me uneasy, though I can usually talk my way out of any awkward confrontation with primitives.

"I don't know if Izmir considered the activity recreation. I don't know that he would comprehend the term. I don't know if he comprehends anything much. I'm still not sure if he's a living creature or a machine or what. You might wish to return to your chair or otherwise stabilize yourself, Kerwin. We are leaving now."

Not far away, Miranda's ex-boyfriend had finally stopped running, his panic having given way to exhaustion. Besides which, his bladder was making physical demands that paid no attention to emotional considerations.

As a result, he was just in the middle of relieving himself when Rail's starship began to emerge from the ground almost directly beneath his feet. In spite of the fact that he was completely winded, he still managed a respectable sprint in the opposite direction.

If for the rest of his life Brock was convinced that the universe was out to get him, well, who could blame him?

N V N

Kerwin was too overwhelmed by the sight that suddenly appeared beyond the sweeping port to worry about keeping his balance. He stood close by Rail's shoulder and stared.

Below lay the moonlit green foam of the national forest, and beyond, the gray shadows of the Sangre de Cristo mountains. Rail had the ship rotating slowly to insure that his instrumentation wouldn't miss any communications that might be disturbing the firmament in their vicinity. Oomemian conversation, for example.

"Looks clear clean so far."

"What about our people?" Kerwin asked him. "Aren't you worried about being picked up on local radar? Albuquerque's a major FAA center, and there's an important missile-testing facility in the southern part of the state."

Three eyes turned to him. "Such simple detection methods are easily confused. I am concerned only about the Oomemians, whose devices can penetrate any cloaking field."

Seeth had moved to the far end of the window and was staring eagerly at the rapidly receding ground. "Wild."

Miranda looked up from her chair. "I don't suppose at

this point it would do me any good to ask you to drop me off by my house. I mean, it doesn't have to be right by the driveway."

"Apologies regrets." Rail ran two tentacletips down a gleaming silvery strip. "We cannot linger in this vicinity."

She sighed. "Somehow I knew that's what you were going to say. I'll bet there's no FM where we're going, either."

"You may be in for some surprises, young female woman. There is a great deal more variety in the universe than you or your people have ever dreamt of. One can find entertainments to suit just nearly about any taste."

"No kiddin'? Really?"

"Straight," he told her.

She swung her legs around and sat on the edge of the lounge, fumbling through her commodious purse. "Maybe this won't be such a bad trip after all. As for my parents, I guess I can bullshit them about where I've been. I've done it before. Hey, you want some gum?" She extended an open pack of Juicy Fruit toward their pilot.

"No thank you not. I am familiar with the dreadful composition you refer to as 'gum.' Being an advanced race, our teeth are somewhat more delicate than yours. Attempting to masticate the substance you hold in your hand would result in severe orthodontal damage."

"Suit yourself." She unwrapped a stick, shoved it in her mouth, and returned the rest to her purse. "I had a cousin like that. Had to have all false teeth put in when she turned twenty. Weird." She began chewing noisily, then somewhat reluctantly removed the pack again and gestured at Seeth. "You want some?"

"Me? Good gracious no! Being a member of a more

primitive race I'm afraid I just can't handle anything that strong."

"Wise ass." She turned to Kerwin. "You?"

"No thanks." He didn't turn from the curving port.

"Oh, well. See if I offer you two anything again."

The ship accelerated, climbing out of atmosphere. Their velocity must have been phenomenal, but Kerwin had no sense of moving at high speed. The only indication that they were moving at all came from the slight vibration in the deck.

They were at least a dozen miles up now. Off to the north you could see the lights of Albuquerque, and beyond, the smaller pockets of illumination that marked the locations of Taos and Santa Fe. The surface sparkled with small towns that glowed like jewels against the quiet, dark Earth.

"How fast can your ship go?"

"You don't want to know. I mean, it's not the newest model but it moves good fast."

Miranda had slid off her lounge. "Where's the ladies' room on this thing?"

"The hygienic facilities lie through the hall we entered by, first door on your right," Rail told her. "I'm afraid you may find the design somewhat obscure, but if you will simply carry out the necessary functions, the equipment will compensate. It has been built to accommodate the needs of different species and will respond appropriately."

"Yeah, well, okay. It better." She started toward the doorway. "I mean, it's not like I have a choice, you know. A girl's gotta go when a girl's gotta go."

"So go already," said Seeth. "What do you want from us, a testimonial?"

"You—you're just so, so *crude*!"

He grinned disarmingly. "That's my middle name, snugglebuns." After she'd left, he looked up at Kerwin. "Know what I think? I think her IQ and your shoe size are about the same."

"Maybe so, but she's got great. . . ."

As he tried to finish the sentence, the ship rose. Not slowly this time. It didn't so much accelerate as lurch away from North America.

"I thought it'd be prettier than this." Seeth eyed the gleaming curvature of the globe and the gleaming, masked sun. "Looks just like a movie."

"Life's a movie."

"Wow! I mean, that's really *profound*, man. Can I use that?"

"Morgleweez gluh norpsis," said Izmir from his position near the ceiling.

"If you'd read an occasional book," Kerwin began, but again he didn't get the chance to finish. This seemed to be his day for not finishing sentences.

Everything Rail had told them about intertialess fields and not experiencing a feeling of motion was abruptly given the lie as his fingers raced over the strip controls and the ship rolled sharply to the left. The Earth spun like a pinwheel before vanishing entirely. Ahead now lay only a wildly contorting starfield, and once or twice an intense light that wiped out the view completely.

Kerwin carefully picked himself off the floor and stumbled over to an empty lounge, relaxing only when the restraining fields had locked him in place.

"What's the matter? What's going on?"

"Oomemians, of course. Damn darn it! I'd hoped the pair we encountered down below were the only ones pursuing me, but it now appears that others have been waiting for them. Up here.'' He leaned close over his console. ''Two ships, at least. Masked and waiting for us. I should have anticipated even though I did not see. We'll have to make a run for it.''

Kerwin swallowed as his stomach tried to fly up into his throat. ''Isn't that what we're doing?'' Even as he spoke the ship whipped upside down, avoiding another bright light, and dove close by the south pole of Earth's moon.

''Here, you'll see.'' Rail nudged another strip. A holographic projection of extraordinary complexity materialized in front of Kerwin's chair. There was an identical projection hovering in front of the lounge where Seeth had sought security.

Within the three-dimensional bubble he could clearly make out one vessel racing away from two others. From time to time a near wash of energy would wipe out the contents of the bubble, but the projection never collapsed entirely. Nor did the projected craft on which he realized he and his companions were riding.

''What are they shooting at us, anyway?''

''Death. Not for Izmir, perhaps, but most surely for sure for us. We've got to get out of here.''

''Here? Where's here?'' Kerwin looked around wildly. ''Here's no place!''

''Exactly, and we've got to find someplace else. If I could but leave my position here I could try to defend us. There is a gun. We are not defenseless.''

''A gun?'' Seeth started bouncing around on his seat, making use of all the movement his restraining field would allow. ''Where?''

''A small energy weapon. It's set in a bubble atop the ship.''

"Go back to the hall and turn right?" The punk's excitement was palpable.

"No, that's the bathroom. Keep going until you see a door on your left. It will lead to a narrow chute at the end of which you will find the gunner's chair. Am I to assume you wish to try and make use of it?"

"You are to assume, yeah, right. Lemme at it!"

"The system will adapt itself to your requirements and—"

"Never mind, man!" Seeth was already out of his chair, trying to maintain his balance. "I'll work out the rest." He started stumbling and staggering toward the hallway. Evidently, the ship's internal compensators were having a hard time dealing with the evasive gyrations Rail was putting the vessel through. As Seeth passed Kerwin he pulled a small switchblade from a pocket sewn to the right leg of his pants.

"Here, man. If they board us, don't let 'em take you alive!" He continued out into the hall, bumping into Miranda as she emerged from the john. "No time now, babe. Maybe later."

For a change she didn't snap back, just blinked at him and stumbled to her seat. She had a dazed look in her eyes.

"Boy, that was *strange*."

Kerwin badly wanted to ask her why it was strange, but didn't have half the courage. Besides which, deep down he wasn't sure he really wanted to know. She kept talking anyway.

"I mean, a friend of mine had a bidet in her bathroom, but that you could figure out."

The ship shuddered in a new way. "Ah," said Rail, "your friend has found the gunner's chair. I fear he is more enthusiastic than accurate, but perhaps his very unpredictability will confuse the Oomemians. They will rely on their gunnery computers to reply, and they will have difficulty because they will be unable to ascertain a pattern in our defense."

"That's for damn sure," Kerwin told him. "Hey, you mean Seeth's actually firing the thing? And by the way, he's not my friend. He's a punk, a pest, and an antisocial freak."

"He's also not hitting anything," said Rail thoughtfully, "but if naught else, he's shooting a lot."

"Probably likes the noise. Me, I don't like guns much."

"All that matters is that he delay them slightly to give us a little more time. The preparations for the slipspace slide are nearly complete."

"What's slipspace?"

"Where things move fast, young male Kerwin. A lot faster than they do in normal space. When we slide there, we'll move fast too. We certainly can't outrun the Oomemians in normal space. There's just no place to hide in normal space, but in slipspace everything is distorted, including tracking devices. We should be able to lose them, if they don't fry us first."

"So shut up and concentrate on sliding!"

"It doesn't matter if I talk. The process takes time and you can't rush it. Sort of like basting a turkey with high-tech physics, is how I believe some of your people might put it. A quite normal if complicated business, rather like shifting from drive into low without destroying the transmission in the process." He paused for a moment to address what must have been an intercom.

"Do be careful cautious back there, Mr. Seeth. There is such a thing as overwhelming the safeties. That was our stern you nearly shot off a moment ago. I really don't think it's possible for you to do that, but a little more judgement on your part would be appreciated.''

"Eehah! Yowie! Wahoo!" came the reply.

Rail frowned, glanced back at Kerwin. "What means? I thought my English was perfect good."

"It's fine. He's the one who can't talk. When he gets like that nobody can talk to him. He doesn't really care if he does shoot the ship's stern off. Probably would think it looked neat."

"Hey, slow down up there, Railman. You're going so fast I can't hit anybody."

"Just keep firing, Mr. Seeth, at anything but us. You're doing fine as you are."

"I am, huh? Swell." The ship shuddered as the energy weapon resumed rapid firing.

"I guess we're too far out to get KDKW or like that, huh?" muttered Miranda. "I mean, I think I just saw Saturn or Uranus or one of those big gassy things go by on our right."

"I'm afraid the time delay would make reception impossible unreal at this distance." The ship quivered. "Mr. Seeth?"

"Hey, just Seeth, okay? I think I almost got 'em that time!"

"Keep it up going. You are doing well." Rail looked back toward Kerwin and Miranda. "He is, you know. Your friend's actions must strike the Oomemians as insane. He's being very clever."

"Cleverness has nothing to do with it. He *is* insane."

Rail laughed, a light, stuttering whine. "Ah, you humans and your sense of humor." He turned back to his instruments. "Truly they want Izmir back very badly."

"If there's anything you'll be able to count on, it's

Seeth's unpredictability." What's this, Kerwin thought, jealousy? What for? Seeth was probably pushing the firing buttons with his nose. He didn't know what he was doing anymore than the Oomemians did, which, if Rail was to be believed, was the best possible reaction under the circumstances.

"Oh, damn!"

Immediately, he turned in his chair to look back at Miranda. "What's wrong? Are you hurt?" The ship was rattled by another near miss, and this time even Rail flinched.

"I broke a nail. Can you believe that? After that rotten ride in the van and bashing through the woods without even stumbling, I sit on my hand and break a nail. I can tell you, I've about *had* it."

"Gee, I'm sorry. Maybe we should just stop, pull over and trade Izmir to the Oomemians in return for some nail glue."

She made a face and stuck her tongue out at him.

"Ready set?"

"Ready for what?" A disgusted Kerwin turned back to their pilot.

"To slide to slipspace. It can be upsetting to first-timers. You might want to close your eyes, though that doesn't really seem to make much difference."

"Whoa, wait a minute! Why doesn't it . . . ?"

Rail's right tentacle tips slid in unison down four thin metallic strips. When they reached bottom, the universe started to come apart. This included everything within Kerwin's field of vision: space outside the viewport, Rail, the interior of the pilot's chamber, Miranda, and, most disconcerting of all, his own body. His fingers appeared to be separating from his hand, his forearm from his elbow, his elbow from his shoulder, all in slow motion. Everything was drifting away from everything else—or maybe sliding was a more appropriate verb.

There was no pain. Only a feeling of light-headedness combined with a slightly droopy feeling. Then something solid swam into view. It seemed strange that Izmir the Astarach could hold his shape. Oughtn't he to be coming apart also? The single blue eye stared blankly at him. Then Izmir flattened himself into a sausage shape that was alive with tiny internal flares of energy. A moment later he drifted out of sight.

"Hey." To Kerwin, his own voice sounded as if he were speaking through glue. "How long does this go on?"

Rail sounded equally lugubrious, though much more relaxed. Apparently everything was working properly, though how their pilot could tell with his instrumentation drifting all around the room, Kerwin couldn't imagine.

"It should be over soon. When we stop sliding we will emerge in a different section of space. I hope it will be the one I aimed for. I hope also we will not have company. Between my well-practiced evasive tactics and your friend's undisciplined but relentless defensive fire, we may have prevented them from placing a lock on us before we slid. Ah."

Kerwin's hand recovered its five errant digits. His strolling arms and legs reattached themselves to his torso. Something seemed to snap and he felt himself tumbling forward. The restraining fields held him tight and kept him from becoming an ornament on the interior of the port.

Then he found himself blinking. Everything looked normal again; the ship's interior, Miranda, himself. A voice made him turn moments later. Seeth was stumbling back into the room.

"Wow. Could you do that again? Talk about heavy hitting!"

"I could, but the need is not there." Rail was studying his console. "I think we succeeded in sliding clear of our friends."

"Aw, c'mon, man. You gotta do that again. That was great! I haven't had a high like that in months!"

Kerwin was breathing hard while his stomach was slowly settling itself. "You enjoyed sliding?"

"Is that what it's called? Felt more like flying to me. I mean, you talk about your out-of-body experiences." He glanced over at Miranda. "How 'bout you, sweetface?"

"It was okay. Nothing super. At least it was something different."

Kerwin released himself from the restraining fields and walked over to eye Izmir, who now hung from the ceiling like a fluorescent yellow globe. A series of glowing, pulsing black lines scrolled through his bulbous body.

"Something funny happened while we were sliding."

"Hey, now there's a news bulletin," Seeth said sardonically.

"It might be. It was Izmir. He didn't change. Everybody else changed, looked like they were coming apart, but not him."

"Really so?" Rail glanced up at the Astarach. "I must say I am not surprised. There is nothing like him. Another of his unique properties. You are certain of this? Piloting, I never had the chance to notice this before. Perhaps you imagined it."

"No. Everything else looked wild, but not him. He kept his shape throughout the whole slide."

"Fascinating. I will be most interested absorbed to see what our research people find when they are given the chance to examine him. On this ship I naturally have neither the time nor the equipment nor the education to commence such a study.''

"Hey, I don't care what you find out," said Seeth excitedly. "Nothing's gonna top that shooting match. I thought arcade guns were fun, but wow."

"It was a real gun," Kerwin reminded him somberly. "You were shooting at real people."

"Oomemians ain't real people, Jack."

Rail sounded approving. "You will be popular on Prufillia, my young friend."

"Say so. They were the bad guys, that's all that matters. That and the fact that I didn't have to keep putting quarters in. I mean, slipspace is *cool*."

"The first people from our planet to go faster than light, and all you can say about the experience was that it was 'cool'?" Kerwin shook his head.

"Hey, what do you want me to say? I'm no college boy. I ain't into complex semantics. Hey, lawn-face, can we do it again?"

"There is no reason to slide just now. I think we have accomplished what we set out to do."

"How are we doing, anyway?" Kerwin pressed him.

"I am running a final reassurance. The Oomemians can be deceptive as well as direct. They would like nothing better than to convince me I have thrown them off our track before swooping down on us."

"You got anything to eat in this dump?" Miranda was standing lazily next to her lounge chair, smacking her gum. "I'm starving." She extracted a small hand mirror from her purse and began studying her reflection, flipping a perfect blonde curl back into place. "You know, like, no matter what I do, I just can't get this mascara right."

"Nobody looks quite right in slipspace," Kerwin pointed out helpfully.

"Yeah, sure, that must be it." She put the mirror away. "How about that food?"

Rail's tentacles were moving feverishly over the controls. "At the moment I am more concerned with striving to insure our continued existence."

"Me too. I need food to preserve my continued existence."

"Oh, all right," the alien said crossly. "At the back of the room you'll find a small adjustable headband hanging from the end of a flexible metal support. Strap the band around your forehead, taking care to make sure the contact is tight all the way around, and then touch the blue strip on the wall to the right of the small recess. Think of what you wish to consume. The ship will do it's best to synthesize the food you're thinking about."

"No shit?" said Seeth.

"Only if you want it."

"Can it synthesize anything else?" There was no mistaking the eagerness in the smaller man's voice. "Like, drugs, maybe?"

"No, only food. What you require would involve the use of the medicinal synthesizer, which is located—"

"Don't tell him," Kerwin said quickly.

"Hey, get lost, man. Who asked you?"

"He's not sick." Kerwin moved a little closer to Rail. "He's only interested in getting high."

"Ah well, I'm afraid I can't permit the use of the medicinal facilities for recreational purposes. Besides which, I am not in favor of the effect such chemicals have on the human nervous system."

Seeth glared angrily at Kerwin. "Right, Jack. I'll do you a favor sometime, too."

Miranda had strapped the sensing band around her head, and now looked back toward the console. "Do I close my eyes or anything?"

"That's not necessary, unless you feel it helps you to focus in on the image."

She straightened slightly. "How long until it works?"

"The machinery will *beep* when it has received a strong enough image to comply with the request."

"Okay." She closed her eyes anyway. Kerwin thought it made her look like the sleeping beauty of legend.

A soft musical tone sounded behind the wall. Miranda blinked and unfastened the strap. The recess in the wall was glowing faintly. There was no protective screen, so Kerwin reasoned that the radiation had to be harmless. Not that anyone with half a brain would go sticking their hands inside, anyway. As the glow faded, the room was filled with a familiar, sharp aroma.

"That's more like it." Miranda reached into the recess and withdrew a large plate piled high with french fried potatoes buried beneath half a pint of ketchup. The recess also yielded a large chocolate malt and, perhaps as an afterthought, a bag of Doritos. Exactly the kind of food that would produce in a normal young human being by-products like fat and acne. The Mirandas of the race, however, were quite immune to such bodily distortions. Kerwin hadn't the slightest doubt Miranda could survive perfectly well on such a diet, and that neither her face nor figure would suffer in the slightest.

Since there were no table and chairs, she returned to her lounge seat, sat down, and began munching away happily.

Kerwin stared in dismay at the high-fat, heavy cholesterol feast.

"How can you eat that stuff? It's nothing but fat and grease."

"Fat and grease are very healthy."

He turned and gaped at Rail.

"Oh yes, our nutritionists found out long ago that such saturated fats are vital to the development of intelligence and good health. Grease in particular is most important for the proper development of the cognitive faculties. Why, among my people there are those who are known to take grease pills in hopes of increasing their IQ."

"That's crazy," Kerwin stammered.

Miranda delicately wiped ketchup from her full lips. "You think I could get a hot fudge sundae for desert?"

"An excellent choice," said Rail approvingly. "Calcium and sugar, not to mention the added stimulatory benefits inherent in the chocolate."

"Miranda, don't you think you should have something just a little more sensible?"

"Hey, who asked you?" Seeth was eying the synthesizer appraisingly. "You're such a health food nut, what are you gonna conjure up to eat? Sunflower seeds and soya extract?"

The odor of freshly cut, crisp french fries was overpowering. Kerwin found he had to keep swallowing back the saliva. "Uh, no. I was thinking more along the lines of steak, peas and onions, and a baked potato."

"Real health food," Seeth sneered.

"Okay, and what about you?"

"Me? I'm not hungry yet. When you don't have a lot of bucks you learn to get by on a little. Anyway, I ain't real picky. So long as it's edible, I'll be happy. Maybe I'll try and invent something.''

The ship lurched sharply sideways and Miranda had to scramble to keep her malt and grease platter intact. Kerwin frowned.

"That didn't feel right. Not that I'm really conversant with the way interstellar craft normally perform, but—"

"Your instincts are correct. It was not right." Rail's eyes were scanning a series of blinking strip sections. "We have certainly slipped away from the Oomemians, but in so doing it would appear we have sustained some damage. So I cannot look for another lower-shelf world like Earth. We're going to have to go somewhere with yard facilities where I can have the damage properly fixed. There are a number of neutral worlds in this quadrant." A holographic projection appeared above his console and he began studying it thoughtfully.

"We'll have to pick the nearest and hope we can remain inconspicuous. The Oomemians have observers everywhere. We'll just have to cross our zanzees and hope we can duck in, have the repairs made, and get out again before they can locate us.''

Miranda shrugged, plopped another french fry into her mouth and licked the tomato paste and grease from her perfect fingers. Something about the position of her head struck Kerwin as familiar.

"Hey, I do know you! I thought that first name rang a bell. You were one of the finalists for homecoming queen last year, weren't you?"

She favored him with a slight smile. "That's right. So?"

"You didn't win. I didn't understand why you didn't

win. I still don't. You were much prettier than any of the other finalists. You still are."

"Of course I am, but see, like, you have to do this talent thing also. You know. Play an instrument or dance ballet or stand up there and recite a poem or something. Now, I can do all that stuff, but it's like a drag, you know? Besides, somebody asked me to go skiing that weekend. So it was either the contest or the skiing, and I mean, like, the choice is obvious, isn't it? I'd always rather go up to Colorado than win some silly old contest. Why? Would you have voted for me?"

"As many times as possible," he replied admiringly. "But I wasn't eligible last year. Only juniors and seniors can vote for homecoming king and queen and I'm still a sophomore. You're a junior, aren't you?"

"Yes."

"Well, that's only one year."

"No." She smiled unapologetically. "That's an eternity."

"I guess that means you wouldn't go out with me if I asked you for a date, right?"

"Right."

"Hey, sister, you're out with him now. You're out with me, too, far as that goes." Seeth was practicing his leer again.

She glanced over at him, then back to Kerwin. "If you're trying to think of this as a date, forget it. I don't go out with freaks and wimps."

"So I'm still in?"

Seeth looked over at the older man. "Hey, buddy boy, that last appellation was for you, denso."

Kerwin frowned at him, looked uneasily back toward Miranda. "Hey, I may not be on the football team, but that doesn't make me a wimp."

"Nothing personal," she said sweetly. "I mean, he's a freak," and she nodded toward Seeth, "and he's an alien," a gesture in Rail's direction, "and he's a," she glanced up at Izmir the Astarach, who eyed her curiously out of his single blue eye, "well, nobody knows what he is. And you're a wimp. It's nothing to get upset about. Like, we all are what we are.

"Me, I'm a princess. That's just the way it is. Princesses don't go out with freaks, aliens, undefinable things that change their shape, and wimps. They only go out with Prince Charmings."

Seeth was picking at his teeth with a ragged fingernail. "Did Prince Charming take you skiing?"

"You never know if he's a real Prince Charming unless you try."

"Then how do you know I'm not Prince Charming?" Seeth asked her slyly, "or that wimpo Kerwin here ain't Prince Charming?"

"Don't call me that," Kerwin muttered darkly.

"Call it instinct," she murmured. "My perception tells me that neither of you is even half a prince. Like, I think I'd be closer to the mark with Izmir."

At this, Izmir let out what sounded like a burble of delight, grew four wings and promptly fluttered wildly around the room, his color changes running through the entire spectrum of visible light, and possibly the invisible as well. It was doubtful if this could be construed as a reaction to Miranda's comment.

"At least somebody's happy." Seeth nodded toward the plate in her hands. "Think I could have a few of those fries?"

"Help yourself." She extended the plate in his direction. "When they're gone I guess I can always imagine up some more. I want that sundae anyways.'' She pushed a bag in Kerwin's direction. ''Want some Doritos?''

''No thanks,'' he replied stiffly. ''I think I'll hold off until I feel like some real food.''

She wasn't insulted in the slightest. ''Suit yourself.''

When she and Seeth had finished the fries, she used the synthesizer to produce a double-scoop hot fudge sundae, complete with whipped cream, nuts, cherry, and sprinkled cinnamon and nutmeg, all of which she proceeded to down in a surprisingly short time. Even as he got queasy watching her, Kerwin found time to wonder how her body managed to maintain that magnificent figure on such a diet.

It was exceedingly unfair, he thought, and he said as much to Rail.

''Of course it's unfair. Why would you imagine it otherwise? The universe is profoundly indifferent to individual beliefs and desires and philosophies. On Prufillia we believe generally in Arch Noy Plasna, which, colloquialisms aside, translates roughly as Nothing Gives a Damn. Life is far too brief, existence is meaningless, and the universe has no purpose. That's the way it is, folks.''

''Pretty grim philosophy,'' Kerwin commented.

''The universe is a pretty grim place, my young friend. As I think you are having the opportunity to discover. But that doesn't mean it has to be dull boring. Each of us is here for a comparative instant and then we are gone. The universe doesn't notice us when we're here and certainly doesn't miss us when we're gone. We're all nothing but unified arrangements of atoms and particles, drifting around, enjoying consciousness every now and then for a second or so before splitting up to become bits and pieces of trees and stars and french fries.

"As long as we're not transformed into energy, those of us who are companion particles continue drifting through the cosmos, enjoying a kind of fragmented immortality, one with the everything. When you clump together, more or less accidentally, it might be as part of a rock or another person."

"Or a french fry," said Seeth as he finished the last of Miranda's fat-saturated hoard.

"Somehow, that's not what I think of when I consider the possibility of reincarnation," Kerwin muttered uneasily.

"I'm not talking about reincarnation," Rail said. "I'm talking about what your component atoms become part of when you cease to exist as an intelligent being."

"Hey, he did that when he turned six," Seeth put in.

"Blow it out your ear." Kerwin turned, disconsolate, and walked to the back of the room. Strapping the food synthesizer sensor around his head, he defiantly ordered a banana split.

Rail glanced back and smiled approvingly. "Now you're beginning to get the idea."

Kerwin dug into the mountainous concoction with blind enthusiasm, relishing every cool, gooey swallow. Even the bananas tasted fresh. He wondered at the sophistication and skill of a civilization that could synthesize something as complex as a banana split simply on the basis of his thoughts. But then, maybe compared to faster-than-light travel it wasn't so difficult after all.

"You might want to balance yourselves, please," Rail told them. Kerwin frantically tried to gulp down the last of the ice cream as he stumbled back toward his seat. "We're slowing to sublight speed. At least, I hope we are. Because of the damage we incurred while fleeing the Oomemian ships, we might have a problem or two."

"Like what?" Kerwin asked uncertainly.

"Well, when we emerge from the threshold we could possibly break up. For real this time."

Seeth began humming nonchalantly, "Breaking up is hard to doooo!"

✄ VI ✄

Kerwin found himself moaning softly, finally couldn't stand it anymore. "Will you shut up! Didn't you hear what he said? We could all die." His fingers tightened on the sides of the lounge seat.

"Nonsense." Miranda followed this completely confident assertion with a very loud belch, looked embarrassed, and added, "We're not going to die."

"Why not? How can you be so sure?"

She smiled over at him, radiantly beautiful, save perhaps for the slight ketchup smear dribbling from the left corner of her sensuous mouth. "Because I'm not ready to yet."

At which point the universe turned upside down. When it and Kerwin's stomach had righted themselves once more, the view out the port was dominated not by empty space but by the blue, white and brown of an inhabitable world. You didn't need a degree in astronomy to ascertain immediately that it wasn't Earth. The triple polar ring system, thicker than that of Uranus, was evidence enough of that.

Just as he was starting to relax, the ship spun wildly. He closed his eyes and swallowed, listening as Rail shouted a string of alien obscenities into an audio pickup. More surprisingly, a hidden speaker filled the room with a reply. The tone and words were utterly unintelligible to Kerwin. It sounded more like a buzz saw than a voice.

This exchange of interspecies insults rose briefly in volume before halting completely.

"We're here. We've made it," Rail informed them.

"Where's 'here'?"

"Nedsplen. A neutral world and a most successful and prosperous one. A pleasant place for those who live here as well as for the harried traveler. You should find the atmosphere and gravity to your liking. A very commercial people, the Nedsplenites. Their world is something of a crossroads for this section of the galaxy. As it's a logical place for us to visit, we should be on the lookout for Oomemian observers. Still, it's so busy and active and crowded that, with any luck, we will be able to lose ourselves for a while."

Kerwin tried to melt into his seat. The surface was rushing toward them at breakneck speed.

"No point in heading for one of the suburban ports." Rail seemed awfully casual about making an approach. "As long as we've come to an obvious world, we might as well land in the most obvious place."

Much to Kerwin's relief, they finally leveled off, skimming a long, shallow sea that formed an enormous harbor or inlet. Then they were flying over forests and agricultural regions and, soon after, an endless metropolitan area in which buildings and structures looked like the sucked-out carcasses of insects caught in the spider's web of transportation lines.

"The capital city of Nedsplen," Rail informed them. "Alvin."

Kerwin frowned. "The capital city of this important world is called Alvin?"

"What did you expect? Imperial Realm? Seat of Power?"

"I don't know. I just thought—it probably means something important in the Nedsplenian language, right?"

"As a matter of fact I don't think it means anything. I have no idea why it's called Alvin." He bent over his instruments. "We won't land at the central port. Too much traffic anyway, and there are plenty of smaller ports scattered throughout the city where we'll be less conspicuous setting down."

They came to a halt, hovering several thousand feet up in a parking pattern. While Rail waited for clearance, Kerwin and his companions were able to observe an astonishing variety of vessels and aircraft zipping back and forth in front of the port. Off in the distance, towers of metal and plastic and more exotic construction materials rose toward the sky. Despite their already rarified height, several appeared to still be under construction.

Rail spoke into his pickup and they began to descend. Slowly, this time. Metallic canyons rose around them, shutting out the sun. Kerwin had been down the Grand Canyon once. This experience was similar, the walls gradually closing in around you until even the upper canyon vanished. Except that these walls were artificial. A few minutes later they touched down. Kerwin gratefully freed himself from the restraining field.

"Feels good to be back on the ground."

"But this isn't the ground. Merely the landing field for this particular port. The actual ground lies far below us. Nedsplen's an old world, quite built up. Much as new cities were constructed on the foundations of older habitations on your own world, except that here the lowest levels are still in use.''

He didn't have time to ponder the significance of this because Rail was leading them outside, where the profusion of alien sights and smells was overwhelming. Kerwin had always considered himself someone of broad imagination. But it was one thing to deal with a couple of aliens like Rail and Izmir, quite another to emerge into a monstrous hangar of unfamiliar design where members of dozens of different races were congregating. It was a measure of how far they'd come that whenever he noticed the neatly manicured green skull of another Prufillian, he experienced a shock of recognition.

There were no humans to be seen.

Everything else imaginable, though, and much that wasn't. The smallest of the port's busy inhabitants stood barely eighteen inches high, while the largest topped out at over eight feet. These giants had skin like parchment that sloughed off at regular intervals. When the skin struck the pavement it dissolved like crystalized honey.

There were mammalians and reptilians, insectoids and water-breathers compelled to move about clad in suits full of liquid. They jostled with methane breathers, everyone walking, gliding, sliming, slithering, scuttling or flip-flopping on their way to obviously important destinations.

''Too much, man.'' Seeth looked like he was in seventh heaven. ''Hey, check that out.''

He pointed toward a creature resembling a two-foot-tall rabbit, complete to oversized pink eyes and long incisors that overhung the lower jaw. The long ears pointed forward instead of straight up. Each was hung with a dozen jangling earrings.

Seeth walked straight toward it. "Hey, Jack, where'd you get the jewelry? That's neat stuff."

The leporine alien spat harsh bunny noises at the human, then glanced past him and jabbered at Rail, who replied in something other than English. It appeared to satisfy the leporine, who hurried on by.

Rail turned to Seeth. "He said that you were an impertinent hairless biped speaking an uncivilized tongue, and that if I couldn't keep my pets under control they should be leashed."

Seeth's eyes narrowed. "Did he now? Maybe he'd like a few more holes in those ears." His switchblade appeared magically in his right hand.

"Are you crazy?" Kerwin grabbed his wrist. "We're already in the middle of one interstellar war. We're not here two minutes and you want to start another one."

Seeth continued to glower, but allowed himself to be led away. Meanwhile, Rail's eyes checked every recess and corner as they proceeded toward the downshoot.

They saw several Oomemians, but none spared a glance for Rail and his companions. Civilians busy with their own activities. If they were official observers they were exceedingly subtle. But, as Rail reminded them, not every member of the Oomemian race was attached to police or military authorities.

The downshoot was a transparent elevator. There was no cab, no container of any kind. Just an open cylindrical space twenty feet in diameter, containing a responsive repulsion field. Kerwin halted at the edge, staring dizzily down a hole several hundred stories in height.

Rail demonstrated by stepping out into nothingness. Seeth smiled and executed a swan dive. Miranda simply stepped out as though she used the shoot every day.

"C'mon, man," Seeth taunted him. "You ain't afraid, are you?"

Kerwin swallowed again, then took a deep breath and leaned forward.

A soft, invisible hand caught him and they began to descend together, Rail somehow controlling their speed. Izmir ignored the field as he transformed himself into a flat, almost two-dimensional form that was too thin to show more than his blue eye. He fluttered freely around them like a lost, highly-colored page from Audubon's elephant folio.

"You see," Rail said, "he can defy a shoot field as well. That he is possessed of remarkable qualities there can be no question, but whether he can be of use to the Oomemians or anyone else remains in doubt. Of course, I am no scientist. It will be their job to figure out what he is good for, besides casual entertainment."

Brightly lit levels continued speeding past them. It would take years just to explore what lay within walking distance of this single dropshoot, Kerwin knew. And in a city the size of Alvin there must be thousands of similar shoots linking its hundreds of levels.

"I can see him defying this field," Kerwin called out to Rail, "but look at his body. How does he do stuff like that?"

"I do not know. Perhaps he can readjust the composition as well as the arrangement of his atoms. It would not surprise me if he simply vanished altogether."

They began to slow. Seeth shot ahead, drifted back to rejoin them, though whether he'd managed the trick himself or with Rail's connivance Kerwin couldn't tell. Miranda came to a halt and walked out of the shoot without so much as a hair out of place.

Down under, Alvin resembled nothing so much as an endless shopping mall. There was plenty of foot traffic and Kerwin didn't see how a few humans and one Prufillian could be noticed among such an assortment of outrageously shaped creatures. That didn't prevent Rail from hugging the walls.

There were such things as hotels, and he quickly ducked into the one nearest the dropshoot, securing a room that was exactly that: a single large room. It was quite spacious, with furniture simple and straightforward enough to serve quite a variety of differently shaped torsos.

One wall was occupied by a massive holographic projection unit. It was programmed with a seemingly infinite variety of selections, which were controlled and adjusted by waving your hands over one corner of the wall. The hygienic facilities were hidden by part of another wall, which appeared as solid as all the others but which could be walked through as easily as mist. The barrier was sound and sight proof, for all that it was composed of nothing more than heavy illusion.

"What about my shopping?" said Miranda, getting down to serious business.

"That will have to wait." Rail was heading for the door. "You should all be comfortable here. This is more than I can really afford, but I'll find some way to justify the additional expense. I feel as if I owe you something You probably did save my life."

"Hey, no probably about it, man." Seeth was studying the holowall. "Those Oomyboomies would've wasted you in a minute if we hadn't intervened." Leaving the wall, he jumped on the second of the two large circular pads that occupied the middle of the room. It caught him half an inch above the actual surface and held him there, suspended.

This is something else. Sleeping on air.''

"Relax."

The door materialized out of the wall as soon as Rail got within a foot of its actual location. "There's a communicator between the beds. If you need anything, just call room service."

"How do we do that?" Kerwin wondered.

"The unit will connect with a universal translator. This is a fairly sophisticated establishment."

"Can they translate foods? I mean, like your synthesizer? What happens if I ask for a well-done steak?"

"The steak may not be beef, but it will be quite indistinguishable from the actual thing, I assure you. But please do exercise some judgement."

"How do you mean?"

Rail smiled gently. "Don't order anything well-done." The door opened for him.

"Where are you going?"

"Not shopping, I bet," said Miranda cattily.

"There are arrangements to be attended to, the repairs to my ship, and some contacts I ought to make as long as I am here."

"You really have to leave us?" Kerwin asked him.

"It will be safer this way. Safer for you and safer for me. As I've mentioned, you are rather conspicuous."

"Us, conspicuous? On the way in we passed something that looked like a tarantula with spectacles and spats. And you say we're conspicuous!"

"You are primates. In the hierarchy of galactic races, primates are uncommon. They usually manage to exterminate themselves before they achieve a level of civilization high enough to qualify them for admittance to the social life of the galaxy. Not always, but usually. I don't want you getting into trouble. I couldn't intercede on your behalf because that would mean revealing myself to local authorities, whom I'm sure the Oomemians have long since briefed. For all Nedsplen's sophistication, I don't think you'd find the local lockup any more amenable than those on your own world.''

"Izzat so?" Seeth rolled over on air. "Lemme tell you, there's nothing worse than the sheriff's jail in Albuquerque. I mean, it's full of wetbacks and dopers.''

"Similar problems exist here.''

"Yeah? What's a Nedsplen wetback look like?''

"There are several, depending on which water world they originated. For example—but why am I telling you all this? We are wasting time we don't have. I must get the ship fixed and us away from here as soon as possible.''

"You lied to me." Miranda leaned up against the other bed and pouted. "There is no shopping.''

Rail sighed, left the open door and spoke into a grid set into the wall. "There. I have opened a modest line of credit—modest, mind you—with a local general store. You can order via the communicator between the beds. Please be circumspect. No large jewels or anything like that.''

She exhibited some real animation for the first time since Kerwin had seen her in the back of her boyfriend's van. "Hey, I know how to shop. I mean, like, it's kind of like my profession. How do I get started?''

"Just speak to the communicator and say 'shopping.' Your purchases will automatically be credited to the room's account. One other thing. I'm going to leave Izmir here with you.''

The Astarach hovered near the ceiling. It had assumed the shape of a solid block of black granite lined with glowing white stripes. The blue eye moved from one side of the block to the other.

"Guard him with your lives." Rail exited rapidly.

"Hey, wait a minute!" But Rail was already gone. Kerwin didn't press the alien for two reasons. First, he was pretty sure Rail meant it when he said he had to move fast, and second, he didn't have any idea how to open the door, which had become part of the wall once again.

"Man, is this a great place or what?" Seeth stood and jumped as high as he could, landing on his backside on the bed. The thin suspension field caught him gently as a giant hand.

Eminently practical, Kerwin mused. A field could adapt itself to any shape. Speaking of adaptability, Miranda had already managed to conjure up a procession of exotic attire on the holowall. He wondered how the store representative, be it alien or machine, had managed to figure out her species and size. No doubt the wall scanned as well as broadcast.

As he stared, a portion of the screen seemed to leap out into the room to envelop her standing form in glowing red light that molded itself to her body. For the first time in his life he found himself envying a shaft of light. A moment later the light fled. Thereafter everything that appeared on the screen was exactly her size and shape. She was able to try on the various outfits simply by making a verbal request, whereupon a solid-looking, projected duplicate of the clothing in question would appear surrounding her form. The wall would then helpfully become a four-sided mirror, showing her how she looked in the attire from front, back and sides.

"I wonder if it's okay for her to submit herself to so many projections."

"Hey, leave the girl alone. Can't you see she's died and gone to heaven?" Seeth rolled on the bed.

Kerwin sat and watched the show for quite a while before commenting. "Uh, remember what Rail told us. You don't want to go over his limit."

"No sweat. Besides, he never said what the limit was. I bet I can keep ordering until we hit it and then the screen will just stop offering me stuff." She turned to face him. "How about this one?"

He stared. She was wearing what appeared to be a dress fashioned of thinly sliced rubies held together with ruby thread. The sliced stones varied in color from blood red at the bottom to a light pink near the neck. All of it no doubt artificial and whipped up as ordered. Such a dress made of real corundum would have been unbearably heavy. Kerwin had no doubt that the actual material was light and comfortable.

Ruby being a semi-transparent stone, each section was like a little red window.

"Your tongue's going to crawl out of your head." He blinked, saw Seeth leering at him. "Better watch it. I bet this joint's got individual room cleaning. Suck your tongue right into the trash. Have one of these."

There was a small container atop the communicator. It held what looked like a basket of napkins, but as Seeth had discovered they were actually flat white containers of a delicious, ice-cold syrupy liquid. Having drained one, he dumped the empty container on the floor.

The carpet rippled uncertainly for a moment. Then the individual fibers, like so many hands, began moving the debris to the right. Kerwin had to jump out of the garbage's way, though it probably would have gone around him if he'd held his ground. When the debris reached the far wall, a hole materialized in the floorboard. There was a small suctioning whine and the empty container vanished into the opening.

Kerwin looked uneasily at the substance beneath his feet. Was it some kind of charged or programmed material, or was it actually alive? The tiny fibers suddenly looked uncomfortably like green cilia. He walked over to sit down on the other bed, treading gingerly. The carpet didn't protest.

"Great place to party. Drop any chips and the floor cleans itself up." Seeth sucked another of the white containers dry and flung the empty aside. Once again the hundreds of tiny fibers shifted the trash toward the wall.

He jumped off the bed and blocked its path. The carpet hesitated, began shifting its burden to the left. Again Seeth moved to intercept. Kerwin watched until he could no longer restrain himself.

"Look, here we are on an alien world no telling how many lightyears from Earth. We're the first of our kind to experience stuff like this, and all you can do is tease the carpeting?"

"Whatever's fun, man." He finally stepped aside to let the floor complete its clean-up work.

In the meantime, boxes that looked like giant, solid-sided baggies had begun to accumulate beneath an opening in the opposite wall. Kerwin saw the ruby dress inside one of the transparent containers.

"Don't you think you ought to get some ruby slippers to go with that?"

Miranda considered. "No. I think maybe yellow. With a yellow something for my hair and something yellow for my wrist. That'd be sharp."

Obviously, she'd missed both his reference and sarcasm

completely. "Tell me something. How do you manage to stay in school?"

"Oh, I'm a *B* student. I guess I could manage an *A* average if I wanted to, but studying is like, a real drag, you know? I'm only in college because Mom and Dad positively insisted on it. We had, like, a real fight about it, and I would've put my foot down but then they would've cut off my allowance and that would've been an even bigger drag. So I figured why not give it a try. Now I've only got a year left to go and they've finally quit bugging me.

"Besides, I thought it'd be a great way to meet some cute guys."

"Have you?" He tried not to sound too hopeful.

The anticipation was wasted. "Not yet."

"Oh."

"I mean, Brock was all right but he was like, kind of an airhead, you know?"

"Why'd you chose UNM?" He was reluctant to end a conversation in which she was actually participating, it apparently being possible for her to successfully concentrate on two things at the same time so long as one of them was shopping.

"I like skiing. Besides, Houston, which is where I'm from, is so boring, and the weather there, well, it like sucks. I didn't want to go too far from home, and we do have good friends outside Hobbs. They have the *biggest* ranch. I mean, it's just awful for cattle but there's oodles of oil under it, and Uncle Joe told me he'd be happy to fly me back down to Houston anytime in his plane. So it's not such a bum deal." She pointed.

"What do you think of that silvery thing, the one on the far left?" She was gesturing toward something fashioned from tin foil—or maybe it was woven platinum.

"I can't say. I'm not much for fashion."

She shook her head sadly. "Honestly! You boys. Sometimes I just think you've no idea what's really important."

"Is that so?" He was miffed and tired of trying to hide it. "Sure. Let's find out what's really important, okay?" He walked over and spoke self-consciously to the communicator. "Hey, whoever's down there! Can you answer a question?"

The communicator replied in rough but quite good English. "I have access to the city library. I can answer *any* question."

"All right then. I want to know what's 'really important.' I mean the most important activity there is. Anywhere. In the whole civilized galaxy. What really matters? What's it all about. What's life really *for*, anyway?"

"One moment, please." The neutered voice went silent. Kerwin wondered what it was studying, what ancient sources, what endlessly debated philosophical tracts. General questions were always the most difficult to answer. He'd asked it almost in jest. Now he realized that a casual difference of opinion might result in him being the first human being to learn one of the great secrets of existence.

The voice spoke again. "Your question has been processed. It has long since been determined that the most important thing in the civilized galaxy is—shopping."

Kerwin's lower jaw sank toward the floor. Miranda simply smiled smugly. "See? Now, I want to try that silver thing on."

"Yes, miss,' said the communicator dutifully.

Slowly, Kerwin walked over to sit down on the other bed. Seeth eyed him pityingly.

"Hey, don't take it so hard, man."

"It can't be. It's a joke," Kerwin mumbled to himself.

"It's got to be a joke. Rail's got it programmed somehow. I never trusted him anyway." Suddenly he brightened. "I know! She's buying stuff like mad, so naturally the hotel or the store or both would want to encourage her to keep doing so. That's why it answered the way it did. Yeah."

"Right, buddy boy. You just believe that." Seeth sat up. "Hey, sweetcakes, how about ringing up the men's department for a while?"

"Okay. I don't like this outfit anyway." The holographic duplicate of the platinum dress rejoined its wall-bound brethern.

Seeth hopped off the bed and walked over to stand next to her. "Leather. I want the leather department. Or whatever you call it around here. And studs. Lots of studs, and make 'em, if it's not too expensive, gold. Yeah, gold studs."

"Yes sir," said the communicator. Static filled the wall. Kerwin muttered something under his breath.

"Hey, man, why don't you trade in those old jeans?"

"These old jeans are perfectly satisfactory," Kerwin shot back. He walked over to the communicator and helped himself to one of the syrup containers. It chilled instantly.

It was absurd, of course. Shopping was not the most important thing in the universe. He stood there pondering this inanity until something like a cross between a tuxedo and Robin Hood's jerkin appeared on the wall. At that point something went blotto inside his brain. The destruction was localized enough for him to turn and speak coherently.

"Wait a minute. Let's see if they've got that in *my* size."

⚡ VII ⚡

Hours later Kerwin still wasn't ready to credit shopping with being the most important activity one could indulge in, but it made for a nice diversion. It was pleasant for all three travelers to be functioning on the same wavelength for the first time since they'd been thrown together, to feel a part of the same thing even if it was nothing more than catalog sales. It didn't quite link them on a serious emotional level, but it did show that they had something in common besides age, language, and species.

Nor was the communicator restricted to clothing. They were able to order up ample food and drink, all of it synthesized as it had been on Rail's ship, and all of it equally delicious and satisfying. Kerwin was even able to solicit a mild compliment or two from Miranda because of his skill in explaining those nutritional requirements that the communicator couldn't quite translate. They even tried a few alien dishes, daily specials compatible with their physiology. Some of the consequent taste sensations were exhilarating.

When Miranda finally decided it was time to stop shopping and try on some of the clothing she'd actually purchased, Kerwin and Seeth discovered that the holowall could be entertaining as well as useful, a real mixed-media entertainment center—though some of the media was so mixed as to be unrecognizable. Eventually Kerwin found watching Miranda more absorbing. This left Seeth free to play with the unit until he found he could order up musical instruments as easily as clothes.

He gleefully ran through a seemingly endless catalog of devices, from synthesizers no bigger than a harmonica to drums the size of an earthmover.

"I'm gonna forget the band, man. With a couple of these gadgets I can be my own band."

"Don't get carried away." Kerwin indicated the communicator. "Don't you think it's about time we started trying to use this for some serious purposes? For instance, we're in the middle of a trans-galactic war. Maybe it's time we tried to learn something about it, like how it got started and how long its been going on. Maybe we can make a difference, somehow. Technically, we're neutrals. What do you say?"

Miranda shook her head. "Can't do that. At least, not now. Something more important to take care of first."

Kerwin looked back at her. "Like what?"

"Oh, come on. You mean you can't see it?" She indicated the small mountain of packages. "I mean, shoes. Like, I'm short half a dozen pairs for the outfits I've bought and there's no way, I mean *no way*, I can wear them without the right shoes."

"Right," said Kerwin tersely. "Never mind. Forget I said anything. I give up, I quit." He walked over to the big bowl of exotic candy that the communicator had produced and dug in angrily. He was munching what tasted like a cross between chocolate cream and raspberry trifle when the door appeared in the front wall to admit someone from the hall beyond.

It wasn't Rail. The human-sized rodent had an extremely long tail ending in a furry pad that the owner used to stroke his head and pat his shoulders. It was dressed in a stiff brown suit decorated with isolated gold stars. The face was flat and oddly humanoid, buck teeth and whiskers and projecting ears notwithstanding.

He glanced quickly around the room, not missing the piles of food and clothing.

"Geez, don't you people ever knock?" muttered Seeth.

"Don't have to knock." The rodent adjusted the headset he wore. Portable translator, Kerwin decided immediately. "I am Taumun, floor manager for this section of the hotel, and I have something for you. Compliments of the management."

"Great, another present." Seeth sat on the edge of the bed. "What is it?"

By way of reply, their visitor held up a long strip of what looked like Scotch Tape. As it twisted slightly in the air conditioning, Kerwin thought he could see what might be some kind of writing imbedded in the otherwise transparent material.

"Your bill, people." Taumun's attitude was nothing if not correctly formal. "You have gone way over your credit limit and the hotel therefore is within its rights in requesting that you bring it up to date before additional sums may be charged to your room account."

Seeth looked over at Kerwin, who shrugged, then back to the rodent. "I don't understand, whiskers. I thought our credit rating had been established."

"So it was, but," and Taumun flipped the tape so that it rolled itself into a coil, "you have long since exceeded that rating with your multiple orders to the kitchen, the confectionery, the bar, and various outside shops.''

''Not much leeway, is there?'' Kerwin was desperately trying to stall for time.

''That's your business, people. Now, which of yous would like to bring this account up to time of moment? Whence done I will depart and leave you to your enjoyment. Well?''

Kerwin continued praying for the help that was not forthcoming. ''I don't understand. See, the guy you need to talk to is Mr. Rail.''

Rodent eyes narrowed. ''Whom?''

''Rail, Arthwit Rail. The Prufillian who brought us here. It's his credit rating you're calling into question.''

The manager's whiskers twitched and his muzzle retracted slightly. ''No Arthwit Rail is registered to this room or this entire hotel.''

''That's impossible. Who established the credit rating we've been using?''

''The level was automatically registered when you took possession of this room. I assume it was yous who did so.''

''No, no, there's some confusion here,'' Kerwin went on worriedly. ''See, this fellow Arthwit Rail, he set us up here in this room and told us he'd be establishing credit for us to make purchases with. I'm sure he'll be back any minute and we can clear this up. By tonight, at least.''

''Is already tonight,'' said Taumun primly. ''Deadline for ordering your account has been several hours passed already.''

''So what's a few hours?'' Kerwin told him lamely. ''What's the big deal?''

''The big deal,'' replied the manager, as the translator

134

demonstrated its facility with colloquialisms, "is the tab you've run up. Expensive clothing, candies, drinks, all manner of luxuries. This matter needs be settled now or there will follow consequences."

"I'm sure Rail will be back soon."

The rodent's muzzle contracted. "Who is the Rail you keep referring to? If any of you would care to bring your account into balance, I will retire happily. If not. . . ."

"Wait, wait a minute." Kerwin walked over and dragged his wallet from his pocket. It took him a minute to find his Visa card. "How about this?"

Taumun took it in one furry hand, examined both sides and, before Kerwin could stop him, took a bite out of the plastic. He passed it back with a corner missing, sounded thoughtful. "Tasty, but not very nutritional, I'm afraid. You cannot bribe me with a cookie."

"What can we bribe you with, ratso?" asked Seeth casually.

"You are impertinent. Which fact I will overlook, if you pay up."

"We don't have any money," said Miranda. "I mean, I've got my American Express but I guess that won't be any better, huh?"

"Maybe it'd taste better," Seeth suggested.

"Thank you, but I am not hungry," the manager said primly.

"What do you guys use for money here, anyway?" Seeth asked him.

"There are any number of recognized credit chips and lines. I don't suppose you have contacts with the Ferrif of Placon?"

"Hang on, I'll check." Seeth strolled over to whisper to

Kerwin. "Come on, you're supposed to be the bright boy here. Think of something."

Kerwin glared at him, looked back at the manager. "What about using our belongings as security?"

Taumun looked dubious. "What sort of belongings?"

"Our clothes, I guess."

"If you refer to the attire currently in use, that would not secure a drink of water in this establishment. If you refer to the items already purchased, those will be held until such time as your hotel bill has been paid."

"Hey, you mean I spent all that time shopping and I don't even get to keep anything?"

"Life's a bitch, sugarlips," Seeth said.

"Besides which," Taumun continued, "we are in the hotel business, not retail sales. I can only accept recognized credit."

Kerwin sat down on one of the beds. "We're all just going to have to wait until Arthwit Rail returns."

"Au contraire, sir. I have no proof that your mysterious Mr. Rail even exists. I am very much afraid I am going to have to ask you to vacate these premises."

"Leave?" What had begun as confusing had suddenly turned serious. "We've no place to go. We're strangers here and we don't have any money. If we did, we'd give it to you."

"Your personal difficulties are not my concern."

"Just a few hours. I'm sure Rail'll be back by then."

"Hang tight, I've got an idea." Seeth turned toward the back of the room. "Hey, Izmir, come on over!"

The Astarach had been hugging the ceiling. Now it spread itself wide like an ambulatory parasol and drifted toward them. Seeth put a comradely arm around the nearest portion of the fluttering mass.

"This here's Izmir the Astarach, the most valuable—"

"Seeth!" Kerwin said warningly. "We can't. . . ."

The smaller man glared at him. "We can't what, man? This Rail dude whips us halfway across the galaxy, dumps us here, disappears, and when we're about to get kicked out in the street he ain't nowhere to be found. So, screw him." He looked back at Taumun and smiled. "This Izmir's maybe the most valuable thing in the whole universe, see? How's that for security?"

The rodent twirled a whisker and glanced sideways at the suspended enigma. "He doesn't look particularly valuable. The levitation trick is neatly done but hardly unique."

"Tell you what," Seeth continued, "you keep him as security on this room until our old buddy Rail gets back."

"I am sorry. Personally I should like to help you out, but as I said, we are not in the barter business."

Seeth removed his arm from Izmir, who promptly drifted back up to the ceiling. He hovered there, surveying the goings-on below out of his blue eye, as Seeth leaned back onto the other bed.

"Tell you what, then, bignose. We're just going to stay here, and there's not a damn thing you can do about it. So you might as well go back to your nest, or whatever it is, and we'll all keep calm until Rail returns."

"I must ask that you leave now."

"Leave? You mean, like, get out?" Miranda asked him.

Taumun frowned at his translator headset. "I thought that was what I said."

"Sorry, cheese-eater, we ain't movin'." Seeth crossed his arms and leaned back, luxuriating in the softness of the suspension field.

Five minutes later they were standing on one of the mall-like boulevards fronting the hotel, watching morosely

137

as well-dressed guests moved freely through the entrance. Seeth would have gladly given Taumun a fight, but the manager had unsportingly called upon the assistance of a couple of ursine types just small enough to squeeze through the hallways—provided they advanced one at a time, in single file. This pair of intelligent mammoths had gently deposited them outside the hotel, though not before quietly assuring them that next time they wouldn't be handled quite so politely.

The Terran trio were left with the clothes on their backs and the few small articles they'd been able to hastily cram into their pockets prior to their summary ejection. Seeth lamented the fact that they'd been removed before he had a chance to swipe one of the hotel towels—assuming there were any towels to swipe.

Kerwin wished now that, instead of letting himself be drawn into the flurry of useless shopping, he'd taken the time to shower and brush his teeth. Feeling dirty as well as discouraged, he sat down on the smooth, almost slick pavement. It looked like pink foam. Seeth leaned back against the wall, balancing himself on one foot while regarding the passing crowd.

Miranda crossed her arms. "Well I don't think it's very nice of them, not very nice at all. What a way to treat people! Back in Houston they wouldn't rate a single star."

"I'm sure the entire company is trembling in their collective shoes," Kerwin muttered.

"All those beautiful clothes." She sighed. "You'd think we weren't going to pay, or something. I've never been so insulted in all my life."

"I just want to see our buddy again." Seeth was repeatedly, methodically slamming a fist into an open palm. "Our *friend* Arthwit Rail. Our good neighbor. Our rescuer. I'm going to smash his funny little teeth down his funny little throat.''

''Save it,'' Kerwin snapped at him.

Izmir the Astarach had twisted himself into a crude parody of Seeth. He likewise leaned up against the wall, long blue legs extending from a black body. He was slamming a blue fist into a blue palm while yellow lines of force climbed up and down his limbs. Each time quasi-fist met pseudo-palm, lightning flared at the contact point and miniature thunder rumbled along the wall, disorienting the occasional hotel guest.

''He'll be back,'' Kerwin reminded his companions. ''Izmir's with us, remember?''

The Astarach glanced over at him at the mention of his name. Folding arms and legs up into his body he assumed a pyramidal form, turned upside down and began spinning like a giant top.

''Man, are you *dumb*.''

Kerwin looked up in surprise. ''What are you talking about?''

''Dumb. D-u-m-b. Read my lips, college boy. What if he ain't coming back? So we got Izmir here. What if our good buddy Rail's decided Izmir's not good for anything after all? Remember, we don't know how much of what we've been told is for real and how much was invented inside of golf-course-head's brain. We've got only his word for everything we've heard. Maybe he made it all up to save his own skinny neck. Maybe Izmir's like nothing more than a religious token or something.

''Maybe they can track this Izmir after all. He can put out a lot of energy when he wants to. These Oomemian guys have been tracking him somehow. All those little rings and lines of energy exploding out of him all the time.

Think about what this Rail's done: gone and brought us to this Nedsplen place where you can't talk anybody else's jive without a machine to translate, stuck us here broke where nobody even knows where Earth is, and put this Izmir thing onto our necks.

"For all we know he's halfway back to Prufillia by now, laughing all the way because the Oomemians are going to come down hard on us instead of him. Tell me, Jack, what happens when those Oomemians find us, huh? You think they're gonna want to listen to the explanation and excuses of a bunch of us primate primitives? They didn't stop to listen back in Albuquerque, they sure as hell aren't going to be patient here. So I'll tell you what they're gonna do. They're gonna blow us away and take this idiot whatsis back with them to dear old Oomemia and get medals pinned all over whatever it is they use for chests, while the last mention of us on this plane of existence is going to consist of a couple of lines in the morning paper. 'New Mexico Students and Brilliant Local Musician Vanish in Mountains Overnight.' "

"What about Brock's story?"

Seeth made a rude noise. "You kidding? If he's stopped running he might tell somebody we stole his van. I don't think he'll mention the bit about the Oomemians or good ol' Arthhalfwit. The cops'll assume we went joyriding and trashed it or crashed it or sold it to buy drugs or something. Hell." He kicked at the pink foam underfoot, was unable to scratch it. "A budding career in music nipped in the bud."

"What musical career?" Kerwin had tired of the punk's rantings.

"Mine, Jack. I'm good. On keyboards and percussion, and I can handle bass guitar when I have to."

"Now who's jiving who? I've heard you play. You can't do two choruses of 'row, row, row your boat' without a numbered key chart."

"Hey, so I'm just getting started. Everybody improves with practice. Great rockers aren't born, they're made."

"I'm hungry," Miranda said prosaically. "Let me have a piece of that candy you swiped."

"Sure thing, sweetcakes." Seeth handed her a foil-wrapped square. She touched the top of the package and it responded to her body heat by unwrapping itself. Looking glum, she bit the square in half and chewed slowly.

Since the busy pedestrians continued to ignore them, Kerwin mused, maybe the local cops would also. And there were plenty of local cops. That much of Rail's tale they could believe. It was starting to get dark as the artificial illumination above the street dimmed.

"Wonder how cold they let it get down here?"

"Only cold enough for aesthetic purposes, man. This is an advanced civilization, remember? They got climate control and everything. They don't have to put up with junk like rotten weather." Seeth glanced toward the dropshoot. "I'll bet it stays like paradise all year 'round."

Two hours later they found themselves huddling together beneath a storefront overhang while rain dripped down through the city's multiple levels. The precipitation was damp and chilling. Even Seeth was subdued.

But not for long. There was too much energy rushing through the punk for him to stay quiet for more than an hour. "It's late. This stuff ought to go away soon. I'll bet they don't run the faucet all night long."

The rain dribbled through the openings formed by grates and drains, as though someone had roofed-over Manhattan. Miranda hugged herself and muttered disconsolately, "I'm still hungry."

"What," said Kerwin bitterly, "you mean there's something more important than shopping after all?"

"Don't get me wrong. I'd like to have all that stuff I ordered. But it's not, like, vital. The fun's in the looking and buying, not in the having."

"Sometimes I wish I'd stayed with anthropology for a major. Dead people are so much easier to understand."

"Not to mention more predictable," said Seeth. "Look, we've got to eat, right? So we've got to make some bucks." He gestured at Izmir. The Astarach had twisted himself into a screen and was making a show of supporting their shielding overhang. "Nobody's stopped in their tracks to offer us a fortune for the wonder of the universe, here. That means it's up to us. I know all about survival. I spent a whole summer in Winslow once. Here, each of you take one of these."

From a deep pocket he extracted three tiny, flexible headsets. The right tip of each glowed a soft pink.

Kerwin perked up at the sight. "What are those? Where'd you get 'em?"

"Man, you really think I've got nothing between my ears but haggis? They were in a slot at the base of the big communicator in our room. I swiped 'em when you were arguing with ratface. They weren't tied down or nothing. Maybe they're complimentary. You know, like back home where the fancy hotels give you soap and shower caps and crap like that."

Kerwin screwed the receiving end of his own translator into his left ear. "These are miracles of miniaturization." He looked around nervously. "They must be expensive as hell. Hotel security's probably looking for us already." He remembered the hirsute spectres that had dumped them out into the street. He had no desire to meet them again.

"Don't mean they're expensive here," Seeth countered. "With all these different types strolling around, hundreds of different races, I'll bet this is one of the most common devices on the market. Everybody's gotta have one to talk to his neighbor. I'll bet they're real cheap. Disposable, even."

Miranda finished adjusting hers. It blended perfectly with her attire. Naturally. "Wish they had them in yellow and gold. What do we do now?"

"The best we can, honeyhips." Seeth gazed thoughtfully at Kerwin. "He's a student, so he's useless."

"Hey, easy."

"He's right, though. You are useless."

He looked at her. "What about you? I mean, you're beautiful and all that, but I don't think you'd appeal to any of the locals."

"I sure hope not. What about you, Seeth? What can you do?"

"Well, I've been known to borrow stuff now and then without asking, but I'm not what anybody'd call a professional thief, and I'll bet they've got anti-burglary machines here so sophisticated we wouldn't recognize them even after the cops came and picked us up. So that's out. Anyway, we don't need a lot. Just enough to rent a place to sleep and get something to nosh. For now, anyhow."

"A lot or a little, it doesn't matter. We've no way to earn any money."

Seeth grinned at him. "Pockets ain't empty yet, Jack. Check it out." He proudly removed two more devices from inside his leather. One resembled a cross between a UHF antenna and a flute. One side was lined with buttons and there were three mouthpieces. The second device looked like a closed flower until he touched a concealed control. The top promptly splayed open, revealing six petallike appurtenances, each of which boasted four strings running from the outside rim down into the center of the ''flower.''

''What are those?'' Miranda asked him.

''Don't you remember? When you finished buying out Hong Kong I started blinking through the instrument section. I put these away the same time I borrowed these headset translators.''

''Why these two?'' Kerwin wondered curiously.

Seeth shrugged. ''They were the only portables—the only ones that folded up.'' He touched another switch and the flower petals lit up from within. Fingers run along one set of strings produced a delicate, bell-like tone.

''No guitar, but a little practice and I ought to be able to do even better than row, row, row your boat.''

Kerwin felt a little sheepish. ''Sorry about that. I was upset.''

''Forget it. Never happened.'' He turned to Miranda.

''Don't look at me. I can't play a thing.''

''No sweat. We'll handle it.'' He passed the flute-antenna to Kerwin. ''Think you can do anything with this?''

Kerwin examined it with interest, finally placing his lips over one of the mouthpieces. It was too small for his jaws, but then so was the mouthpiece for a bagpipe. A querulous puff generated a sound of astonishing depth and resonance. He began experimenting with the buttons set in one side, finally removed it from his mouth.

''Might be able to. What are we going to do? Give a concert?''

''Hey, why not? You see any signs banning street musicians?''

"No, but I don't see any street musicians, either. Not that we'd be able to read any signs."

"So much the better. We'll be a novelty. Our music sure will."

"I have to confess I don't have any better ideas. I don't guess you know any Mozart?"

"Mozart schmotzart. Are we gonna play real music or what?"

"All right," Kerwin said tiredly. "I knew it was probably too much to ask and I don't want to argue about it. You start with something and I'll try to follow, okay?"

Seeth did just that, his hands roaming in circles across the top of the flower petals. As for the flute-antenna, Kerwin found it surprisingly simple to get the hang of. Before long the two of them were jamming away like mad in the rain and cold, wondering if the sounds they were fashioning were even comprehensible, much less appealing, to the few remaining passing pedestrians.

After a while the rain ceased, not gradually, but as if someone had turned off a faucet far above. More pedestrians began to appear. Stores and shops began to reopen along the walkway, which was soon alive with nocturnal strollers. Kerwin would have put a beckoning hat on the pavement if they'd had one.

Miranda's boredom was replaced by a growing interest in the music the two young men wove on alien instruments. She started by nodding her head, then smiling, then moving sensuously in some private universe of her own. Soon she was dancing and twisting in time to the eclectic rhythm, swaying and kicking like a lost line escaped from its oscilloscope.

It was all Kerwin could do from then on to concentrate on his pseudo-flute. The girl could *move*, though whether

her supple gyrations would appeal to non-humans was a matter for contention. But when Izmir joined in, lighting up like some atomic-powered Christmas tree, changing shapes and colors while bleating incomprehensibly, they began to attract the attention of many of the passersby.

Miranda slipped out of her shoes and danced barefoot. The pavement was pleasantly cool and drying rapidly. Soon her abandoned footgear began to fill up with an interesting assortment of metallic, plastic and ceramic shapes. It looked like the debris gleaned from the depths of a child's toychest.

Izmir grew several long legs and tried to dance with Miranda. Failing to keep in step with her or the music, he abruptly transformed himself into an extensive sashlike sheath of glittering gold and copper, the alternating bands rippling like fluid metal. Electric discharges crackled in the air as he wrapped himself around the girl. It worried Kerwin for a moment, but she assured him she wasn't feeling a thing and that this new Izmir-form weighed next to nothing.

The Astarach seemed content to be treated like a piece of clothing. Miranda easily whirled him through the air, spinning him above her head like a Spanish dancer. Throughout it all the single blue eye drifted amidst the gold and copper, mournfully surveying its surroundings.

It was a presentation sufficiently exotic to stop even sophisticated alien travelers in their tracks. A crowd grew as many lingered to watch. Kerwin tootled on, keeping a wary eye alert for anything that looked like a policeman. He had the feeling a cop was recognizable as a cop no matter how many limbs or eyes he possessed.

No representatives of local authority showed themselves, however, and for all they knew such sidewalk performances were perfectly legal. If not, none of the onlookers voiced any complaints. In a city the size of Alvin, it was conceivable that police responded only to reported violations of the law and didn't have the time to go hunting them up. Just to patrol it you'd need a force the size of the French Army.

The performance finally ended when Kerwin ran out of breath and Seeth's fingers were starting to turn raw from his constant strumming of the flower machine. Kerwin collapsed his flute and Seeth folded up his musical petals. Miranda looked askance at the two of them.

"What's the matter? You're not tired already, are you?" She looked as fresh as a marathon runner after a month's time off.

"Not entirely," Kerwin wheezed. "Dead tired'd be more like it."

"Come *on*." She snapped her fingers. "That music was like, totally rad." She spun a circle, tresses flying.

"Pack it in, sugarthighs." Seeth was leaning back against a wall, wiping sweat from his forehead and the shaven sides. "What do you run on, fusion?"

"No." She looked down the well-lit street. "But now that you mention it I am, like, you know, kind of hungry. Remember?"

Seeth slung his portable onto his back. There was no strap, but the instrument clung to his leather jacket as if both surfaces had suddenly acquired a Velcro overlay. Maybe it just liked leather. Then he bent to examine the bizarre contents of her shoes.

"Coins?" Kerwin wondered aloud.

Seeth sniffed one shoe. "Looks like garbage to me."

"Maybe they were rendering their opinions."

"Yeah. So it's garbage or money." He squinted at the

boulevard lights. "Only way to find out's to try and spend the stuff."

Miranda needed her shoes back, so each of them took handfuls of the booty and stuffed it into their pockets. She slipped the right shoe on, then the left, frowned and removed it again, turned it upside down and gave it a shake. Something that looked like a mouse-sized copper barbell fell out, clanged on the pavement. Like much of what their audience had deposited, it was covered with indecipherable writing. Some of the specimens pulsed with internal light while others were merely softly luminescent. Kerwin pocketed the barbell and joined his companions as they headed down the street.

They found the restaurant by smell rather than sight, since they couldn't read any of the various inscriptions on the buildings. Same went for the extensive computerized menu. Fortunately it was duplicated verbally and their tiny headset translators worked wonders.

In exchange for a pair of silvery thimbles and half the length of a spool of gold-colored wire, the restaurant supplied them with three enormous platters piled high with what resembled shelled lobster meat, some kind of steaming purple vegetable that tasted like an impossible mix of strawberries and asparagus, a single, monstrous loaf of seed-filled bread that popped when it was cut or broken, twelve different kinds of spread to apply to it, and tall glasses of drinks that laughed as fizz broke their surfaces, each bubble containing a miniature giggle in a different language.

They approached this alien repast with some trepidation, which lasted only as long as the first few bites. Everything was new and wonderful. Kerwin didn't see how they could finish half the colossal meal, but he hadn't reckoned with their accumulated appetites. Traveling and slipping and fighting and running and shopping and dancing were hard work.

He had a little trouble with the lobster-meat legs that lined one side of the platter because they bore more than a passing resemblance to the limbs of a quartet of aliens seated two booths away. The food was in plain view, however, and since it didn't seem to bother them he knew he oughtn't to feel as though he was snacking on some of their distant relations. Come to think of it, what would an arachnoidal alien make of a human eating monkey meat?

They offered Izmir a choice from the cornucopia, but he ignored it all. Assuming the shape of a chair, he looked on blankly, only occasionally producing a soft, meaningless mumble. The blue eye gazed blithely from the back of the seat.

"He doesn't sleep and he doesn't eat." Kerwin shoved breadstuff into his mouth. "Wonder if he breathes?"

"Not if he's a machine, man," said Seeth.

"He doesn't look like a machine." Kerwin shrugged. "Doesn't look like anything, actually."

Miranda was munching on a chunk of bread that was decorated with at least four different kinds of spread. Each time she took a delicate bite she emerged utterly unsmeared. Kerwin had grease all over his face. So did Seeth, but it didn't trouble him.

"You guys play pretty good together." Green jam dripped off the edge of her bread. Kerwin held his breath, but no law of nature was about to be contravened. The jelly tumbled to the floor as she gestured casually with her hand. "Almost like you'd, you know, done it together before."

Kerwin looked away, slurped a sip from his laughing

glass. "We kind of used to fool around with stuff together. Piano, drums, anything we could get our hands on when we were younger."

"Yeah," agreed Seeth, "but that was a long time ago."

"Long time ago." Kerwin found himself nodding. "We don't get together much anymore. Kinda gone off in different directions."

"Hey, that's, like, sad. I mean, it's nothing to me, but it's like the stuff you see on TV; childhood buddies not getting along anymore, stuff like that."

Seeth let out a single, sharp laugh, as much bark as anything else. He grinned nastily. "Childhood buddies, hell." He nodded at Kerwin. "That Yuppie jerk is my brother."

Kerwin glared across at him. "Who you calling a jerk, joke? Look at yourself. You don't even look like a human being anymore. You fit right in with all the other aliens."

"Hey, buddy boy, I don't need definitions of what's human from the likes of you."

Miranda's eyes darted from one young man to the other. "No kidding? You two are really, like, brothers, huh? I mean, same parents and like that?"

"Can't you tell, sweetnails? Ain't it obvious?"

She frowned uncertainly. "Not really."

Kerwin let out a snort of disgust. "This little twerp could've been something. Lawyer, doctor, engineer—his SAT scores were out of sight. Back before he fried his brains with that music and started hanging around with animals."

"That's me, man." Seeth leaned back in his chair and grinned proudly. "I was gonna be a lawyer, but I got saved."

"Sure you did. Born again ape-man."

The grin vanished. "Shut up, Jack. Just shut up. I do what I want when I want to. People take me as I am. I don't have to wear any phoney suit-and-tie uniform so's I look nice and safe like everybody else. I don't have to kiss—"

"That's enough, guys," Miranda interrupted. "I mean, I just wanted to make sure you were really related. Besides, you're upsetting Izmir."

Both men glanced in the Astarach's direction. Izmir continued to hold his chair shape.

"He doesn't look any different to me," Kerwin told her dubiously.

"Well, it's just like, I mean, I can almost sense stuff inside him. Not like he's got a mind or anything. Just sorta like vibrations and things. I thought I sensed something like that just now. I don't think he likes arguing and dissension. I think he likes neatness and order."

"Sure he does," said Seeth. "That's why he changes his shape every ten minutes."

"But each new shape is ordered."

Seeth patted her hand reassuringly. "It's all right, good lookin'. This is probably more complicated than anything you've ever had to deal with, right? So it's only natural you'd be feeling a little weird about stuff." When she didn't object to his patting her hand he tried to pat her shoulder. She frowned at him disapprovingly and edged away.

"Watch the hands, I mean, like, this is a public place and all. They probably have laws about stuff like that."

"Like what? You putting me on?" He gestured at the street. "What's public about this? We're the only chimps in this circus. We could probably do it here on top of the table and nobody'd even blink. They probably wouldn't even know what we were doing.''

Kerwin probably should have kept his mouth shut, but he didn't. ''Give it a rest, Seeth. Besides, we've got enough of this money-stuff to last us for a while. We don't need to do any more exhibitions. If we got any kind of reaction out of these creatures from the sight of your naked body it'd probably be laughter.''

Seeth went for his throat, right across the table. Izmir skittered aside on his three chair legs while Miranda just sighed and leaned clear. Dishes, bread, jams, spreads, meat, drinks and alien silverware went flying. None of it touched her, of course. A few fortunates like Miranda were born encased in invisible force fields. Stains and slop never soiled them. One of the miracles of natural physics that even Einstein couldn't explain. Like color and taste and weak forces, it was right up there with the most esoteric nuclear theories. The dirt repellers.

A chunk of lobster—maybe—went flying past her. She didn't even bother to duck. Might have mussed her hair.

Neither Kerwin nor Seeth had time to observe this unique phenomenon because the two of them were now rolling across the floor in the company of numerous individual components of their dinner. A few alien patrons looked on with casual interest, but soon returned to their own meals.

The only ones who expressed more than a passing concern were three very short insectoids. Save for the obvious intelligence in their faces and postures, they might have been giant aphids escaped from some barnstorming entomological carnival. They wore identical, intricately woven capes of black and purple material, which rose to form high collars behind their heads and served to conceal most of their bulbous, pear-shaped bodies. Moving gracefully on four hind legs apiece, they approached the dinner table recently abandoned by Seeth and Kerwin Ransom.

Kerwin extracted himself from Seeth's grasp and nodded at the alien trio. "Look, dummo. People even shorter than you are." Seeth responded by trying to flatten his older brother's nose.

Actually, they'd been so closely entwined that next to no damage had been done.

One of the aphid-things turned to another and buzzed. The other two buzzed back, gesturing with their antennae instead of their hands. As the brothers were about to resume their sibling altercation, the aphids calmly picked Izmir off the floor and ran like mad for the restaurant egress.

Miranda rose. "Hey, they're trying to swipe Izmir!"

The two men separated, eyed each other warily. "So what's it to us?" Seeth was carefully rearranging his bike chain.

Kerwin headed hesitantly for the exit. "Come on. You heard what Rail said. We're supposed to guard him with our lives."

"Guard him with your life, clown." He brushed food from his Mohawk.

"We can't let strangers take Izmir like that. He's as helpless as a puppy." Miranda rushed past Kerwin and out onto the street in pursuit of the kidnappers. Or were they thieves? It all depended on what Izmir was.

"Can you believe that, man?" Seeth shook his head. "Dumb squeeze."

Kerwin couldn't reply because he was being verbally assailed by the proprietors of the restaurant. His translator kept up with their rapid-fire speech easily. Not that translation was necessary. Someone was going to pay for the mess they'd made. They had Kerwin up against a wall and were berating him unmercifully. Several of their accusations didn't translate at all.

Being marooned on Alvin without female companionship, however indifferent it might be, was worse than chasing after Izmir. Seeth tossed a couple of pieces of plastic ruler at the restaurant's owners. This appeared to placate them instantly. Then he and Kerwin lit out after the would-be homecoming queen.

They found her staring over a flimsy-looking rail that encircled a bottomless pit. Kerwin drew back from the abyss, sucking in his breath. Flickering lights marked the descending levels of the city. It was like staring down into a vertical infinity mirror.

"Far out," said Seeth.

Miranda pointed. "They went over that way."

They followed her around the pit until the rail ended, whereupon she jumped out into nothingness. Another dropshoot, Kerwin noted nervously as she began to descend, only this one had no walls.

"Time waits for nobody, man." Seeth jumped in after her.

No time to think, anyway, Kerwin told himself. He closed his eyes and stepped over the brink.

⚡ VIII ⚡

Falling rapidly, but not accelerating, Kerwin opened his eyes, promptly closed them again. His body told him everything was under control but his mind saw him smashing noisily against a solid surface far below, blood and guts flying, bone shattering. A hand wrapped around his and he opened his eyes again to see Miranda smiling confidently at him. She gave his fingers a slight squeeze, then drifted away with swimming motions.

They slowed and exited the shaft thirty levels below the one that had grown almost familiar. In aspect and atmosphere this one was very different from the one they'd left. There was trash lying in the street and the storefronts looked considerably seedier than those above. Miranda pointed.

"I saw them stop and go that way when they left the shoot." They followed her up the street. Sure enough, three squat figures could be glimpsed trundling a fourth shape between them. Izmir's abductors were not fleet of foot despite the fact that each possessed an additional pair.

"How can they run at all with such short legs?" Kerwin said, panting as they pursued.

"Hey, lay off the short jokes." Seeth was having a difficult time keeping up with Miranda, who seemed to flow effortlessly across the pavement.

As they drew closer they could hear the aphids buzzing among themselves. As Kerwin wondered if they knew they were being followed, one of them turned, pulled something from inside its cape, and leveled it at the three humans. Seeth grabbed Kerwin with one hand and gave Miranda a shove with the other. Together they tumbled to the street behind a pyramidal tower that might have been a restroom or trashcan. Something that sounded like a berserk dragonfly slammed into the other side of the tower, making it ring like an out-of-tune church bell.

Seeth rolled, looked up the street. "Right, let's go. Bastards."

As they scrambled to their feet and rushed around the tower, Kerwin saw that the opposite side had been blown open. Twisted metal groped at air.

"How'd you know that was a gun?"

"C'mon, brother. Use your pinhead. What do you think somebody you were chasing would point at you? A feather duster?"

They were starting to run out of breath. A sharp pain was running up Kerwin's side (he'd drunk too much at dinner), and even Miranda was starting to slow. But they'd closed the distance between themselves and Izmir's captors, who weren't possessed of inexhaustible energy either.

Two of them held onto the apparently unperturbable and indifferent Astarach. They were huddled in front of an abandoned storefront that dominated the end of a cul-de-sac. Save for the presence of one feeble streetlight set in the roof overhead, they might all have been on some isolated moon.

Seeth slowed, stopped, still breathing hard. "Right. That's our property. Turn him loose or we're gonna take your little bug heads off, comprende?"

"Hey, wait a minute." Kerwin was looking around anxiously. "Where's the third one?"

A high-pitched buzz brought his head around and answered the question at the same time. The third member of the insectoid trio appeared from behind the concealing bulk of a transformer housing. He was pointing what looked like a pen and pencil set that had been fused together. He was aiming it at Kerwin's stomach, which began trying to shrink into a small, hard ball.

"Darn." Miranda looked down at herself. "These just *aren't* the right clothes to be buried in."

"Maybe we can reason this out." Kerwin extended both arms, palms exposed, and took a step toward the armed aphid. "Look, we really don't know what's going on here. We're strangers, we don't want to get involved, and if we could just sit down and talk maybe we could. . . ."

Somebody hit him in the head with a hammer. He felt himself falling, accompanied by Miranda's scream. It wasn't loud, but he nevertheless found it personally as well as perversely gratifying that the first real emotional reaction they'd extracted from her came about as a result of his being shot.

Distantly, he was aware of additional explosive sounds, muted and faint. Seeth yelling. A crackling in the air. Miranda screaming far away. His consciousness was rapidly fading.

At least, he mused, I get to die on a full stomach, even if I don't know what my stomach's full of.

It didn't seem that he was out of it for very long. He found himself staring up at familiar faces—Seeth, close by, looking almost concerned, and Miranda, for a change looking relieved instead of merely bored. Surprisingly, there was also a third face—a green one full of whorls and swirls that seemed to wriggle as he stared at them. As his vision cleared, they slowed down and finally stopped.

Arthwit Rail straightened to look at Seeth. "Well, your friend is alive."

"Lucky," Seeth responded. "Damn lucky. Always been damn lucky. He's smart, but he ain't got the common sense of a turnip."

"I heard that." Kerwin was delighted to discover that his voice functioned.

Seeth glanced down at him. "Good. Means your ears work. As for your mouth, I never worried about that failing. Sit up, dimwit."

Kerwin complied, put a hand to his forehead. "What happened?"

"What do you think happened, man? You got shot."

"I thought I got dead."

"Just grazed you," said Rail. "I am not sure graze is the proper right word. The shell the Falarian fired at you exploded prematurely. You were knocked down by the concussion. The shell was intended to explode once it had penetrated your skull, but the Falarians are not renowned for the precision of their manufactures."

Kerwin rose shakily to his feet. The cul-de-sac was gone. They were at an outdoor cafe in a gloomy, grimy, rundown area. Everyone sat down at the empty table nearby. A few other aliens were enjoying the dubious delights of this establishment. They didn't look nearly as prosperous as those who strolled the streets thirty levels above. One or two glanced casually in his direction before looking away.

"What about the Follar—Falarians?" His head still hurt.

"Fertilizer now," said Rail calmly. He sipped something from a tall, narrow-mouthed vessel.

Seeth's eyes were shining. "Rail here got two of 'em and I busted up the third myself." He made a face. "Got green goo all over me."

Rail shook his head. "You primitive primates and your propensity for violence."

"*Our* propensity? Don't play the high and mucky with me, greenface," said Seeth. "You fried two of 'em and I don't see you moaning and wailing."

"It was necessary, not desirous. Why did you leave the hotel? I agonized for some time while I searched you out."

"We didn't leave." Kerwin gently supported his head in both hands as he leaned over the table. He felt sick. "They kicked us out. We—we kinda overdid the shopping, I think."

"I warned you about that. Still, you should not have been summarily ejected."

"Why not?" He looked up. "The manager said no Arthwit Rail was registered in the hotel."

"Did you expect that I could so openly declare myself in a public place? Alvin is alive with Oomemians and their agents, all intent solely on locating myself and Izmir."

"Izmir." Kerwin's eyes opened wide. "Hey, where is Izmir?"

"Oh, I'm sitting on him." Miranda moved slightly. A blue eye winked at Kerwin. "I think he likes the chair shape." She settled back down. "Kind of tickles."

Seeth was about to say something, but Kerwin threw him a warning look and for once his younger brother kept quiet. Rail was still talking.

"I didn't think you could have gone far, not being familiar with this world, but you had progressed farther than I believed possible. You have apparently managed to cope quite well."

"Yeah, my brother's the resourceful type," Kerwin told him.

Seeth looked surprised and pleased. "Scavenging's one of the highest art forms of human civilization. What about those bugs? Why were they trying to swipe Izmir?"

"The Falarians are prime allies of the Oomemians. I think, though, that they meant to keep him for themselves instead of notifying their friends. Otherwise we would have been captured by now."

"Great allies."

"There will be others." Rail sighed. "Clearly the word is out that we are about. I had hoped for more time."

"They must really want that chair. I mean, Izmir."

"I told you as much." Rail took another sip of his drink. "I am glad I was able to find you again."

"Yeah, us too. So why don't we skip this scrapheap and dally elsewhere?"

"I wish it were that simple. Unfortunately, the Oomemians have located my ship and placed it under surveillance. I was extremely fortunate to discover this before revisiting the vessel. We dare not even return to the port. If we tried to leave by that means they would have us in an instant. And now we are responsible for the deaths of three Falarians. They will have their own reasons for wanting to find us."

Seeth made a face and wiped his palms on his sleeves. "Hope they don't. I don't think I'll ever get all that goo off."

"You do not comprehend the seriousness of the situation. With deaths involved, the Alvinian police will be dragged into this."

"Are they Oomemian allies too?" Kerwin asked him.

"No, no. As I said, Nedsplen is rigorously neutral. Her inhabitants have no love for either us or the Oomemians. The police will look for us when they discover that a crime has been committed."

"How do the Nedsplenites view human beings?" Seeth inquired.

"With massive indifference, I should think. As primitive visitors you would not be worthy of attention were you not in my company."

"That's just what I thought, man." He looked over at Kerwin. "So why don't we dump this guy? Maybe if we go to the papers or somebody, they'll get the Oomemians to lay off us."

"How would we get home?" Miranda wondered.

"Are you kidding, sweetcakes? You saw the bread we made in a few hours. We could probably find ourselves a full-time gig, maybe in some major club." He began snapping his fingers. "Make some real money. Buy ourselves tickets home, or rent an interplanetary limo, or something."

"No thanks," said Kerwin. "The novelty of our music might wear off fast. I wouldn't want to chance being stuck here. So we have to stick with Rail until he can get us home."

"I am grateful for the thought." Rail looked apologetic. "I know you have no reason to help me, or even to like me. I have caused you nothing but trouble difficulty thus far."

"You can say that again, man," griped Seeth.

"I have caused you nothing but trouble difficulty thus

far. But if you will continue to help me I can promise you that when we reach Prufillia you will be richly rewarded by my government, and that transportation will be provided to return you to your own world.''

Seeth considered. ''I'd rather play music than get shot at by people who look like something the exterminators found in my Aunt Heida's basement.''

''You're liable to get shot anyway,'' Kerwin reminded him. ''Remember how the Oomemians work?''

''Yeah, there's that. I don't like it, but—okay. We'll hang around a while longer.''

''Thank you, thank you!'' Rail's gratitude was as genuine as it was effusive. ''You will not regret this.''

''I'm regretting it already, Jack, but like brother-mother says, we don't have a whole lot of options. So, what do we do now, if we can't hang around here and we can't get to your ship?''

''We must find another means of leaving Nedsplen. I have contacts here.'' He eyed them unsurely, as if pondering how best to continue. ''In fact, the only ones who can help us now are the human beings.''

Kerwin's reaction was anticipated. ''Wait a second. We're human beings.''

''No. I mean the real human beings.'' Rail looked uncomfortable.

''I *am* a real human being!''

Seeth smiled easily. ''That's debatable.'' Kerwin glared at him as Rail strove to explain.

''You do not understand. You will. I probably shouldn't be doing this: giving away the secrets of the ages is frowned upon by the general judiciary. However, we don't have much choice, since these people are about the only

162

ones on Nedsplen I can trust.'' He pushed back his chair and rose. ''Come.''

''Where we going?''

''Down.''

Kerwin leaned back as they passed beneath a low-slung ventilation shaft, found himself staring up at a hundred subterranean levels of city. A few droplets of moisture from the evening's preprogrammed precipitation still clung to black metal and slick plastic, dangling precariously like jewels loose in their settings. Everything smelled of damp metal and machine oil. Like a Mexican bar.

''You mean there's more 'down'?''

''Oh yes, a great deal more,'' Rail assured him. ''Alvin is quite a substantial city even by galactic standards, though it is of course by no means the largest.''

''Of course.'' Kerwin saw they were heading for a different dropshoot. ''Which is the biggest?''

''I am not certain. It's hard to keep up with such things, you know. I would say that Hatanga on what used to be Youseekia is the largest.''

''Why do you say 'on what used to be'?''

''Because it's all Hatanga now. You can't find any of the original Youseekia. It's all been built over. The city covers the entire planet, except for what's left of the oceans. The city's built out into the continental shelves, everywhere. That's where the power plants are located. They use the heat from the planet's core. Have to. You can't run a planet-wide city on batteries, you know. Alvin's impressive, but Hatanga's an old place while Nedsplen's comparatively new. That's why the city isn't any larger than it is. Ah, here we are. Be so good as to follow me closely. I wouldn't want to lose any of you to an intersecting horizontal transportation shaft. There are a lot more of those down here than up above. You know how to use one of these?''

''Sure,'' said Seeth. ''You step off into nothing, close your eyes, put your head between your legs and. . . .''

''Give us a break, Seeth.'' Kerwin requested tiredly.

''Why? You know, I get the feeling that the deeper you go into the city the more profanity is appreciated. What do you say, Arthwit old sod? You like a good dirty joke now and then.''

''Every race does, though as I said before the Oomemians are prudes. It is, however, difficult to convey meanings even with the assistance of translators. Scatology does not travel well between individuals whose physical points of reference are quite different in construction. Sometimes one person's joke is another's anatomical impossibility. This renders many devoid of humor or meaning.''

''That's cool,'' Kerwin told him, nodding toward his little brother. ''He also has neither humor nor meaning.''

Seeth was looking around. ''If I can find something portable and heavy, I'm gonna bust you in the teeth.''

''Please, forebearance and restraint. We have no time for extended personal squabbling.'' They'd reached the rim of the dropshoot. It was as black as a country well on a moonless night.

Taking Izmir by an extruded limb, Rail swung the Astarach through the air. Izmir hung in the center of the dropshoot field, waiting for them to follow. Apparently he was also capable of neutralizing or otherwise somehow defying the field. Another potentially useful talent? Kerwin didn't know and didn't want to spend the time considering. He was much more interested in finding out who the real human beings were.

Rail jumped into the field and began to descend. His

human companions followed, while Izmir spiraled lazily around them, circling, rotating on various individual axes, babbling incessantly and incomprehensibly.

They didn't descend all the way. That would have dropped them into the service and maintenance levels, Rail explained. It seemed to Kerwin that they ended up mighty close, however.

Lighting at these depths was entirely artificial. No sunlight penetrated from the distant surface. He studied their fellow urban spelunkers with interest.

They didn't appear poor or downtrodden as much as they did secretive. Everyone here talked in whispers and murmurs. Despite the fact that the street Rail led them out into was as spacious as any they'd encountered higher up, the pedestrians hugged the walls and made obvious efforts to avoid the light.

"A lot of those who live and work here do so to avoid notice," Rail explained unnecessarily. "They're here so they can avoid attention."

"This is sure the place for it," Kerwin commented.

"I don't like it." Miranda's voice was firm, like the rest of her. "It's icky."

"Sweetthing, you sure have a way with words." Seeth clucked his tongue in mock amazement. "Boy, if I had that command of vocabulary there's no telling what I could do."

"You think you're so smart, mister street punk? I'll bet you don't even have a credit card, much less a platinum one."

"You're right, bright eyes, I don't have a credit card. I don't have a gasoline card. I don't have a draft card. My wallet's as bare as old Mother Hubbard's cupboard. Except for this, of course." He excavated a handful of mixed alien currency.

Rail's eyes bugged. "Where did you get that?"

"Song and dance." Seeth looked smug. "Me and my idiot brother jived some of the local yokels out of a few spindles and cubes and spools. Don't even know how well we did."

"From the looks of what you hold in your hand, well enough." Seeth repocketed the money. "I did not know you two were brothers, though now I admit to being able to see the similarities."

"Say what?"

"He means that our bone structure and like that are similar," Kerwin told him while uneasily watching an alien the size of a small hippo duck to clear the ceiling. Small oval eyes peered challengingly back at him, and he was glad when the creature had disappeared, even though it hadn't looked anything like an Oomemian.

This wouldn't be a good place to be lost and broke, he decided.

When it seemed like they'd walked halfway around the planet, Rail turned into a large, commodious store whose shelves, support and containment fields and ceiling were stocked with an assortment of unrecognizable goods. The place was fascinating nonetheless.

Miranda tried to examine something that resembled a bejeweled purse and received a mild electric shock for the attempt. The proprietor had been assisting a customer who was all eyes and mouth. Now he shuffled over to greet them. A four-foot-long neck rose from a two-foot-high body mounted on six legs. It enabled him to peer easily over the thin plastic counter, but not reach it with his hands, which were attached to three-foot-long arms. Except for a pair of long ears fringed at the edges, the head looked horsey. The ears twitched incessantly as he talked.

"Yess? Ssomething I can help you with?"

Miranda stood sucking on her knuckles. "That thing bit me."

The creature smiled, showing thick, squarish teeth. "All of our expenssive goodss are protected. I can unlock it for you if you wissh a closser look."

Rail stepped forward. "My friends are not familiar with certain modern devices."

"Modern devicess?" The owner looked confused. "Thiss sstore iss two hundred yearss old."

"What kind of place is this, anyway?" Kerwin asked him. Rail replied before the proprietor could.

"The nearest equivalent on your world would be a second-hand shop. A pawn shop, I think is how you call it, though the analogy doesn't quite hold." He turned back to the horsey-head. "I need to speak with Yirunta."

"He'ss in the back." The proprietor eyed them curiously out of naturally bulging eyes. "I'll go get him. Who sshall I ssay iss here?'"

"He'll know me." Rail smiled.

The six-legged giraffe-thing turned, then halted in his tracks. Izmir the Astarach had assumed the exact size and shape of a complex modern sculpture that rested against the far wall. The only difference between them was that the original was jet black while Izmir had selected a bright cobalt blue, except for black bands that rotated rapidly around his exterior. The shop owner was fascinated.

"You would not want to sell that mimic, would you? It is a wonderful toy. Or is it a free individual?" The proprietor peered harder, as unable to decide that intriguing question as Rail and his human companions had been. "I cannot tell what it is."

"Neither can anyone else," Rail told him, "but it doesn't matter. Whether *who* or *it,* he's not for sale."

"Should you ever reconsider. . . ." The giraffe-thing vanished into a back room.

Meanwhile Seeth, Kerwin and Miranda walked through the mass of what probably passed for junk on Nedsplen, any portion of which would have been priceless on Earth. Well, maybe not priceless. As Rail pointed out, junk was junk no matter its world of origin.

Eventually a massive, bulky shape trundled out of the back room. Across his eyes he wore a pair of elaborate magnifying glasses with built-in programs for determining the true age of antiques, the clarity and origin of gems, and various other useful bits and scraps of knowledge. A dealer's tool. His attire was less imposing: silvery pants and matching tank top.

"Arthwit Rail! Heavens, but it's been a long time."

"Too long. Good to see you again, Yirunta." The Prufillian and the human being embraced while Seeth and Kerwin gaped at the newcomer. Not Miranda. She could have cared less, engrossed as she was in her intense examination of the shop's stock of bracelets and necklaces.

Yirunta pulled back from his old friend. "Now what brings you . . . ?" At which point he caught sight of the shop's other occupants. "Oh my heavens; good gracious. Cro-Magnons." He looked back at his friend. "I know you've been involved in some pretty disreputable goings-on, Arthwit, but really! Cro-Magnons?"

Rail looked away. "It was unavoidable. They saved my life."

"Did they? Well, I suppose even a Cro-Magnon is capable of the occasional, isolated civilized act, no matter what the histories say. What do you mean, saved your life? Why was it in danger, pray tell?"

168

"Because of that." Rail gestured toward Izmir, who had abandoned his sculpture in favor of imitating a floor fan, complete to the intricate motion of its interwoven blades. "The Oomemians value him highly. Highly enough to put out a general alarm for him and myself when I borrowed him."

"Borrowed, huh? You always were a great borrower, Arthwit. Only this time, may we assume, you have sort of overborrowed?"

"That's about the extent of it. I had run to the world of my friends here, and after they saved me from the Oomemians I felt something of a sense of responsibility toward them. Had I left them behind, the Oomemians would have killed them. Besides which, things happened too fast for careful contemplation of possible alternatives."

"I guess they're harmless enough, surely." Yirunta was gazing thoughtfully at Kerwin. He moved down the counter. "I must say they are somewhat less gruesome in person than in the texts. Not much, though. The basics are still present; the puny features, the shrunken skull, the attenuated skeletal and muscular structure."

"You're no pretty-boy yourself, Jack," said Seeth.

"The crass, crude method of communication," Yirunta concluded.

"But—but you're a Neanderthal," Kerwin sputtered.

That's exactly what Rail's friend was. The massive upper body and arms, the sloping forehead and prognathous jaw, the presence of considerable body hair all identified Yirunta immediately. Only the jeweler's glasses, now pushed back to rest on the low forehead, seemed out of place.

"What else would I be? At least everyone knows what everyone is here." He turned back to Rail. "Pray say, have they made any progress at all?

"I wasn't on a sociology field trip. I really couldn't tell you. It seemed like a pretty primitive business, this Earth. That's why I went there. Place is still classified as uninhabited, you know."

"Poor old Earth." Yirunta was shaking his head sadly. "Every so often I get the urge—never seen the place, of course. No human has for thousands of years. That was part of the deal."

"Wait a minute, wait a minute." Kerwin was gesturing anxiously. "What do you mean, no human's seen it? What about my friends and I?"

Yirunta pursed thick lips. "I suppose in your own minds you count yourselves as human, but then you can't help that. You're prisoners of a long-established historical socio-cultural fixation."

Kerwin was getting tired of this fellow's condescending attitude, friend of Rail's or not. "Fixation, hell. We're the superior species. You're the ones who became extinct, not us."

"Became extinct." Yirunta laughed delicately. "How droll. You Cro-Magnons always were amusing in your clumsy way. We didn't become extinct, young primitive. We left. Moved. Changed our address. Took up new residence."

Kerwin frowned. "I don't follow you."

"Well, that was the idea, of course. You really don't know what happened? No, of course you don't. How could you? Living on a proscribed world you wouldn't have access to your true history. Well now, I've been out of school for quite a while, but I'll try to bring you up to date a bit."

"I don't know if that's wise," Rail put in worriedly. "What happens when I return them to their home?"

"No one will believe them," said Yirunta easily. "That's

170

a traditional Cro-Magnon trait and one that I doubt has changed. They tend not to believe anything unless they're responsible for it themselves." He looked back at Kerwin. "The story is a simple one, cousin. You correct me if I slip anywhere, Arthwit."

"Not me. I don't know much Prufillian history, much less that of the outer regions."

"Then I'll just have to keep it as simple as possible."

"Just tell it straight, beetle-breath, and we'll muddle through somehow," Seeth assured him.

"Very well. As was true of many worlds where intelligence developed, the primitive Earth was under observation for some time by the Isotat."

"Always nice to be popular," Seeth commented.

"Whoa," said Kerwin. "Who are these Isotat? Have we passed any of them in the streets?"

Yirunta smiled, an extraordinary explosion of lips and teeth. "No one has ever seen an Isotat. Not a Prufillian, not an Oomemian, no one. We've only seen their moon-sized ships. No one knows where their home world is, or, indeed, if they even still bother with one. They may have dispensed with planetary life in favor of a nomadic existence aboard their immense vessels, which are considerably faster than any other known mode of transportation. Sometimes they tell us things. Such conversations are always one way. They do not respond in any way to queries or questions. They are friendly but aloof, concerned yet distant.

"The only occasions on which they are known to interfere in the affairs of another sentient race is when they choose to assist developing species that are on the verge of achieving civilization. They are either curious, empathetic, or both.

"Anyway, as the story goes, in studying Earth they naturally observed the burgeoning conflict between human beings such as my people—Neanderthals, if you will—and your ancestral Cro-Magnons. Apparently this was most unusual, two offshots of the same common simian ancestor developing intelligence almost simultaneously. The Isotat determined that the Neanderthals were likely to be wiped out by the more primitive but far more aggressive and numerous Cro-Magnons."

"You really consider yourselves the superior branching," Kerwin said.

"Oh, gracious no—we didn't consider ourselves anything of the kind. We aren't subject to racial conceits like you Cro-Magnons. I imagine our ancestors weren't, either. As to who is the superior, you'd have to consult the Isotat and that, of course, is quite impossible.

"However, it is not always the superior form that dominates. We were far more peaceful and contemplative than you warlike simians. Where we were open and accepting, you were treacherous and clannish. Where we were truthful, you were sly and deceptive. The Isotat were quite right. Against such instinctive subterfuges we wouldn't have stood a chance. Individually we were stronger, but in matters of war we were clearly outclassed. Besides, Cro-Magnons breed like flies.

"So it was decided that while both peoples were deserving of further development, they were not compatible. The Isotat determined that the more artistically inclined, more sensitive Neanderthals would be overwhelmed by the army-antlike precision of the Cro-Magnons."

"Everything you say is open to debate," Kerwin argued.

"Not the historical part, I'm afraid. The Isotat stepped in and resolved any debate before it got started. About sixty thousand years ago they brought several of their enormous vessels to Earth and resolved the conflict by simply moving all of my ancestors they could find to another empty world. I understand the original decision was to move the Cro-Magnons, but by the time the Isotat could make the necessary decision and arrange the complex logistics, there were already so many more Cro-Magnons that it was easier to move us than you.

"So you see, it was a practical business, not a question of who should have dominion over the planet that spawned us. Moving involved no actual trauma, since my ancestors and yours were too primitive to have developed the notion of Earth as home. Home was the local cave. We've settled in quite comfortably and qualified to join the galactic community. We regard House, the world which the Isotat gave us, as our home planet now. There's no question of jealousy arising, no reason we should ever want to visit Earth, except on matters of anthropological curiosity. Unfortunately we can't do even that because Earth is still classed as uninhabitable, uncivilized, unsocializable, and otherwise unsuitable for travel." He nodded toward Rail. "But I guess he told you that much."

"I had to. The Oomemians were on top of me and I owed these three who'd saved me an explanation."

Yirunta nodded understandingly. "No need to worry. As I said, no one will believe them if they choose to speak of their travels upon their return home. It has happened before. The travelers are always laughed at and ridiculed."

"What makes you think," Kerwin said, "that the Isotat weren't just handing you a line about your supposed superiority in order to get you to move?"

"They didn't have to mention it. Remember, we're talking tens of thousands of years ago, real primitive peoples. When the gods come down from the sky and offer to move you to Paradise, what primitive is going to resist? Of course, a few did. They were fast enough and clever enough to escape the Isotat ships. So there were a few remaining for you Cro-Magnons to beat up on. Didn't you ever wonder why we 'died out' so fast?'' He looked back at Rail. ''I don't suppose they've changed their habits yet?''

''Fractious as ever, I'm afraid,'' said Rail disappointedly. ''I really don't see them becoming part of galactic culture any time soon. They've had atomics and fusion weapons for a while now. It's only a matter of time.''

''Says you,'' said Seeth. ''We're gonna settle our problems, you'll see. A few changes of opinion and government in the US and USSR and we'll get everything under control.''

''I certainly do wish you well,'' said Yirunta. ''Every new race has something to contribute to society. Perhaps we might even sponsor your application. You know, helping out the idiot brother, the missing-link relationship.'' Seeth started to say something and Yirunta forestalled him. ''Please, I am not insulting you. Merely stating the facts as I know them.''

''Well, your facts are screwed.'' Seeth was only partly mollified. ''I'll bet you don't even have rock and roll.''

Yirunta's enormous brows drew together as he turned to Rail.

''A current form of popular music,'' the Prufillian explained. ''Really nothing more than a variant on earlier themes that I imagine could be traced back to their very beginnings. The younger portions of certain dominant populations now consider it an advanced form of expression. What is amusing is that they fail to realize that it is the very connection with their ancient past which gives it relevance.''

"Then I imagine we don't have it." Yirunta appeared curious nonetheless. "We have moved quite a way from our primitive modes of expression. I would like to hear it. Who knows what ancient feelings it might stir up?"

"Listen to him," said Seeth sardonically. "And they think they're advanced! He probably thinks Bon Jovi is a Country-Western group."

"Look, we're discussing the history of the entire human race here," Kerwin told him. "Couldn't we leave rock and roll out of it for a minute?"

"Hey, Jack, no way can you discuss the human race and leave out rock and roll."

"How much is this?" Miranda was pointing to a glittering bauble that was intended for a much larger neck than her own, or for a portion of an alien anatomy that bore no relation to a neck. It glistened and glittered. As she pointed, Izmir drifted close and promptly turned into a perfect if far larger duplicate of the necklace.

"Most extraordinary." Yirunta was staring at Izmir. "What else can it imitate?"

"Just about anything," Rail told him. "Leastwise, we've seen no suggestion of limitation as yet. He can also levitate freely in all directions, including within a dropshoot. The strength and direction of the field seems to be irrelevant. I am certain he also has properties and characteristics that we haven't begun to explore. My facilities, as I've told my human friends, are limited."

Yirunta was nodding. "I begin to see why the Oomemians valued him so highly. Perhaps they've no idea of his capabilities or potential, either."

"They must suspect." Rail ran fingers through his green fuzz. "If they did not, they wouldn't be pursuing me so intently. One problem with Izmir is that he appears quite indifferent to the activity surrounding him. He will drift off with whoever beckons to him. I don't know what his name means or if it's some kind of Oomemian code.''

"What's in a name?" Yirunta murmured. "Well, I've no love for the Oomemians. They're a rude, uncouth lot. And I do owe you a favor or two. So we'll help. As for my distant cousins," and he surveyed the three humans in his shop, "never let it be said that we didn't look after poor relations.''

"Thanks, I guess." Kerwin stepped up to the counter and extended a hand. Yirunta took a step backward and waved lightly.

"Nothing personal," he insisted, trying not to sniff ostentatiously, "it's only that your body odor is, well, different.''

"Hey, brother ape," Seeth said, "we all stink together."

"He must mean you," Kerwin put in. "When's the last time you had a bath, little brother?''

"Don't call me little brother, man. Don't call me brother at all. I've been trying to live down the relationship since before I was born. Besides, what makes you think it's me? Maybe I smell to you but not to him.''

"You all smell more or less equally." Yirunta was telling the truth as much as he was trying to make peace. He looked over at Miranda. "That's forty-six yora, plus tax.''

Miranda had draped the necklace around her neck. "Is that a lot?''

Yirunta forced himself to hide a smile. "Not a proper question to ask a bartering businessman.''

"What the hell's a few yora?" Seeth dug into a pocket and dumped a handful of marbles, spools, glowing sticks and cubes on the counter.

Yirunta's brows lifted. "So much cash obviously locally acquired. Have the Cro-Magnon advanced more than I've been led to believe?"

"Some of us are more adaptable than others." Seeth pushed the collection toward him.

Yirunta chose a pair of cubes from the assortment of currency, took them apart and returned the outermost shells.

"Your change."

"You mean that's all there is to it?" Miranda smiled at Seeth. "Thanks."

He shoved the rest of the money back into his pocket. "No thanks required, honeyskin. The bucks belong to you, too. You did the dancing."

"Sure, but it was, like, you know, your idea. The music bit."

An uncomfortable Kerwin was starting to feel left out. "We all contributed. That's only right. We're all in this together."

"Ooooo, profound!" Seeth bugged his eyes in mock astonishment.

"I'd like to run some tests on this Izmir," Yirunta said to Rail.

The Prufillian became suspicious. "What kind of tests?"

"Easy, old friend. Nothing damaging."

"I'm not sure you could damage him if you tried, but I don't want him altered in any way."

"I give my solemn promise. Bring him into the back."

While Yirunta, Rail, and Izmir disappeared through a rear portal and the giraffe-thing attended to business, the three humans continued their inspection of the store and its contents. Eventually they wandered back to see what was going on.

A few of the devices that Yirunta was applying to Izmir

looked awfully sophisticated to Kerwin, sufficiently so that he found himself wondering if the Neanderthal might be something more than just part-owner of a low-level pawnshop. After he concluded his hour of testing, they had to wait again while he chatted into something unrecognizable to persons unseen and unknown. When he'd had enough conversation, he rejoined them.

"You've got a deal, Arthwit. We'll help you get off Nedsplen with this Izmir and your Cro-Magnons without attracting the Oomemians' attention."

"Thank you. I wasn't entirely sure you had access to such resources any more, old friend."

"You'd be surprised at the kind of resources I still have access to." He was staring past Rail at Izmir. "Extremely interesting, your Izmir. I just took some readings, you know. I can't interpret them. Not my specialty. But I relayed them to some people who could understand the numbers and they are very, very interested in conducting a much more exhaustive examination."

"Oh, oh, this sounds familiar. Am I correct in assuming that your intention isn't to take us straight back to Prufillia?"

Yirunta put a hand on the skinny shoulder, spoke quietly. "Now look here, old friend. Without our help you haven't a chance of getting within a thousand light years of Prufillia and you know it. By now the Oomemians have scrambled everything they can get into space, short of putting themselves on a full-scale war footing. You couldn't smuggle in a toothpick to Prufillia or any of its satellite worlds without the transaction coming under intense scrutiny. Your people, I understand, are yelling, but since no actual hostilities are involved, everyone's just waiting for it to die down and go away."

"I don't know," Rail sounded dubious. "This wasn't the kind of deal I had in mind."

"You wouldn't be taken to House." Yirunta was trying to soothe his friend's obvious anxieties. "If the Oomemians spotted you going in, or even found out what was going on, then we'd be in formal violation of our treaty of neutrality with both Prufillia and Oomemia. But there's another place where you can be safe from them, where some of our own people can, shall we say, assist you in learning of Izmir's possibilities without outside interference."

"I'm going to have to think on this a minute," Rail told him bluntly. "My whole purpose has been to get him to Prufillia."

"Not entirely. From all that you have told me, your primary intention was to deny the Oomemians access to him. That you have done, and that we shall continue to help you to do."

"Hey, what about us? Remember us?" Kerwin said plaintively.

The two aliens ignored him as they continued with their discussion. Kerwin didn't mind being called primitive, but extraneous was something else.

⚡ IX ⚡

"Take it easy, buddy boy." Seeth had come over to chat. Yirunta and Rail were still arguing, still bargaining. Kerwin had begun to grow bored listening and had returned to examining the contents of the shop. "Can't you see we don't matter here? We're just excess baggage. Hey, they might even forget about us and we'd be stuck here." He looked thoughtful.

"You know, I don't think I'd mind that. I mean, Alvin sure as hell's a lot more interesting than Albuquerque. I might be able to get a real gig somewhere, form a side band from some locals. We could start a new trend. I bet in a place like this, where everybody has access to everything, a new idea, new music, new anything would be worth its weight in cubes and marbles. I might do better here than in New York, even. This could be my big break!"

"Are you totally out of your mind?" Kerwin looked at him askance. "This isn't home. This isn't even Earth. Suppose you stay here? What happens when you want a chocolate shake or TV?"

"First off, man, these food synthesizers can probably do

chocolate like anything else. As for the other, you don't really think I spend my valuable time watching the bozo box, do you? I bet the entertainment systems here are a lot slicker.'' He looked past Kerwin to Miranda. "How about you, sugarhips? Wanna be in my band?"

She put a finger to her perfect lips. "I don't know. It sounds like it might be fun, but Mom and Dad might worry about where I am."

"No way. We'd get a letter to 'em or something. Whatever the local version of Fed Express is. You don't have to tell 'em exactly where you are. Just say you've switched to another school in another town and that everything's going swell. If we hit it big here, we could probably make enough of this garbage," he jiggled the currency weighing down one pocket, "to hire a ship to take you home for a visit. Same way our buddy Rail's been doing it."

"I still don't know. Like, I mean, I'll have to think about it. But the shopping here *is* neat. I'm sure there are stores I can't imagine that carry clothes like nobody's seen. Of course, clothes aren't any fun unless you've got other people around to admire them."

"Gee, that's strange," Kerwin muttered. "I thought their function was to keep you warm and out of the elements."

"Don't be silly," she chided him. "That's why we have air conditioning and central heating."

"Yeah. Get with it, dummo."

Kerwin glared at Seeth. "I've had just about enough of you for one day, little brother."

Seeth's expression hardened. "I told you not to call me that, man."

An instant later they were rolling around on the floor again, flailing away and doing more damage to their own hands than to each other. Yirunta glanced down briefly and shook his head.

"The Isotat certainly knew what they were doing." He raised his eyes to Rail once more. "You've had time enough to think things over, goodness knows."

The Prufillian let out a resigned sigh. "Then it is agreed."

"Don't look so disappointed. It's really the best thing for you at this point. No one will challenge a neutral ship departing Nedsplen. You will have succeeded in denying Izmir to the Oomemians, which was your main concern, and you'll travel in comfort and with the protection of an armed ship. Your friends," he added as an afterthought, "will be properly cared for and returned to their own backward world as soon as possible."

"It's not that. All the arrangements sound satisfactory okay. It is just that I was rather hoping that, patriotic duty aside, I might be able to clear a few thousand on this trip. After all, I've hardly had time to sleep, have nearly had my head shot off on numerous occasions times, and—"

"I understand." Yirunta smiled knowingly. "That problem has already been addressed. My people assure me that they will draw up a formal contract for the use of Izmir just as soon as they can settle on a proper definition for what's being done, not to mention a definition for Izmir himself. If and when research discovers a practical use for him, you'll share in any profits. Keep in mind that were you to take him straight back to Prufillia you'd likely receive nothing except effusive thanks and maybe a medal you could hock."

Rail brightened visibly. "True enough. Applause is all very nice, but it's better to receive something more concrete for one's efforts than an expression of appreciation."

"That's settled, then." Yirunta clapped him on the

shoulder, his huge hand nearly spanning the narrow clavicle. He nodded at Izmir. The Astarach had molded himself to the door frame. Brilliant lights all crimson and gold were running around the door's circumference, a whirlpool of color that surged freely around the single blue eye above the frame. "How do we move it?"

"Like I have said, Izmir's mood seems to vary from the cooperative to the indifferent. He's nothing if not docile. He will follow me as he has in the past. As to how he will react once your scientists begin experimenting with him, that is not my concern. Once I've turned him over to you officially, my involvement is ended."

Yirunta was nodding appraisingly. "Fair enough." He looked back down at the floor. "Now, if you would be so good as to assist me, we'll separate the two animals and utilize the simplest possible terms to explain things to them."

Yirunta chose Kerwin, since he was the larger of the pair, lifting him easily off the ground and pinning his arms at his sides. Rail had a little more trouble with the hyperkinetic if smaller Seeth.

"Just keep him away from me, that's all!" Kerwin glared furiously at his brother as Yirunta gently let him go. "Keep him away from me and everything will be all right."

"Yeah, everything's cool, man." Seeth slipped out of Rail's grasp, tugged his jacket into place and brushed at his disheveled Mohawk. "But if he calls me 'little brother' one more time I'm gonna kick him down a shaft where the field's been turned off."

"I wish you wouldn't fight." Miranda pursed her lips and smiled warmly at both of them. Warmly enough to melt stainless steel, Kerwin thought.

"We'll try," he told her. "I'm sorry if we upset you."

"Oh, you didn't upset me," she said brightly. "It's just that you were making a scene, and I don't like being embarrassed in front of people no matter what they look like."

"Details?" Rail asked Yirunta.

The Neanderthal leaned over the counter. "You will remain here for the rest of the night and on through tomorrow. You'll be safe here, goodness knows, and you can rest and recover your strength. Tomorrow night some of my friends will come for you. They will take you to a ship, not at the main port, goodness knows. Too many Oomemians and their lackeys about. You'll travel via subsurface transport from Alvin to Nophia, one of the capitol's satellite cities. The port there is just big enough to accommodate interstellar shipping.

"If we can get all of you off-world before they realize what's happened, they'll continue concentrating their search here for several days at least. By that time you'll have made enough slipspace slides to lose them completely."

"I wish I could be as confident. It sounds good, but you don't know the Oomemians as I do. They could track through Chaos itself."

Yirunta was nodding. "They are a determined folk, I agree, but I still think we can slip you out unnoticed."

"I thought I'd done that a dozen times this past year."

"Yes, and each time they tracked you down. Haven't you ever wondered how?"

Rail looked baffled. "I thought they had good search patrols after me."

"I'm sure they do. Gracious, you mean it never occurred to you that they might be tracking Izmir instead of your ship?"

Rail just stared, then turned his triple gaze on the Izmir-doorway. "Tracking him? I thought the radiation he puts out was strictly localized."

"Radiation? Oh, *gross.*" Miranda made a face.

"It's not the kind that can be accurately measured with the portable instrumentation I have here in the shop," Yirunta told them, "but he's definitely generating a field of some kind."

"Then how come I never picked it up?" Disbelief colored Rail's query. "If it's strong enough to be tracked over spatial distances, I sure as moodals should have detected it inside my ship."

"For one thing, he doesn't seem to put it out consistently. It comes and goes. For another, he projects it. It rolls around unconstantly. If it was a steady-state kind of thing the Oomemians would have caught you a year ago. You wouldn't have been able to hide at all."

"What kind of field?" Kerwin asked him. "What kind of radiation?"

"Oh, you wouldn't understand, I'm afraid." Yirunta tried not to come off as condescending, but failed. "Don't let it concern you because I don't pretend to understand it either. It's a subnormal field, not in slipspace but something else."

"What else is there besides normal space and slipspace?" Seeth wondered. "And if it ain't in either of those, how can you detect it?"

"There are secondary field manifestations. Extrapolating from these, one can hypothesize the existence of the other. As I said, you wouldn't understand. The physics are very complicated. What is most interesting is that the field is evenly dispersed. It appears to maintain its strength over considerable distances. It isn't strong but neither does it fade.''

''What kind of distances?'' Rail asked him.

''Oh, as near as I can calculate, each pulse spreads out in a sphere approximately thirty thousand light years in diameter.''

Kerwin swallowed. ''That's pretty big, isn't it?'' He looked over at Izmir with a newly appreciative eye.

''That's enough to cover half the galaxy. How can he generate that kind of energy?''

Yirunta shrugged. ''Beats me. As I said, I'm doing a lot of hypothesizing here. We're dealing with unknown dimensions, impossibilities, another spacetime that may be larger than our own.''

''Zen physics,'' Kerwin murmured.

''What?'' Seeth made a face at him.

''Zen physics. Measurements of what shouldn't be but is.'' He looked at Yirunta. ''How much larger?''

''I have no idea, cousin. My instruments aren't calibrated for near-infinities. All I have is portable equipment. We're talking an area at least ten to the eighty-third parsecs across. That's where my calculating unit just sort of gave up.''

All of them stared silently at Izmir. Except Miranda, who'd found the earrings.

''Look at that thing.'' Yirunta was pointing toward the doorway where Izmir held sway. ''You don't know what it's made of, it defies dropshoot fields, it changes its shape at will, levitates silently, and seems to enjoy duplicating sculpture and doorways and jewelry. No wonder the Oomemians want him back.''

He vanished into the back room, reappeared shortly in a brown vest shot through with green metallic thread, and a matching cap that formed two points on one side of his head and a third on the other. Thus clad he looked like a cross between Robin Hood and King Kong.

"Come with me. I'm taking you all out to dinner. You'll be cooped up here for a day as it is. We have much to talk about, goodness knows." He put a comradely arm around Rail's shoulders.

"Maybe we should stay here now, like you said." Kerwin was looking out into the dark street.

"As you must realize by now, young Cro-Magnon, Alvin is quite large. I doubt we will encounter any Oomemians right away. They'll be concentrating on the main spaceport, Arthwit's abandoned ship, and the travel centers. Besides, they're following you by tracking Izmir's occasional pulses. Whether we go to a favorite dining place for food or remain here will not alter their means of finding you."

Yirunta left his six-legged partner with instructions and then led them out onto the seedy boulevard, heading for the nearest upshoot. His assurances couldn't keep Kerwin from glancing nervously at every passing alien face.

"Why does he generate these energy pulses, anyway?" Kerwin asked him.

"Who knows? They appear to be quite random. I thought for a moment they might have something to do with his physical changes, as for example when he went from imitating that piece of sculpture to duplicating the necklace your female is now wearing."

"Hey, I'm not anybody's female," Miranda told him warningly. "Not that I'm, like, heavy into women's lib or anything, but I just kind of, you know, belong to myself."

"That's another thing about Cro-Magnons, particularly the women," Yirunta said conversationally. "They talk all the time without saying anything. I think they are fascinated by the sounds their mouths make.'' Without stopping, he spoke to Kerwin.

"Anyway, I saw no correlation between these elsewhere energy pulses and shape changing.''

"Anything that can put out even a weak energy field that maintains its strength over thirty thousand light years must be capable of producing incredible amounts of power,'' Kerwin mused aloud.

"Hey, now there's a clever observation.'' Seeth grinned casually at the Neanderthal. "All Cro-Magnons ain't equal, you know.''

"Gracious, I'm certain that's so. Some of you must be dumber than others. However, your friend and relation is correct. The question is, what are his limits, and can he generate anything stronger?'' He was staring at Izmir, who trailed them several feet above the street. The Astarach had become a tall, twisting spiral, rotating around an imbedded flashing globe.

"Not to mention how he does it,'' Kerwin added.

"We've never even seen him eat nothing, for cryin' out loud.'' Seeth kicked at a piece of debris that the street-cleaning machines had overlooked.

"How could he eat?'' Miranda eyed Izmir pityingly. "He hasn't got a mouth.''

"Anything which can generate energy without converting it from mass defies known physics,'' Yirunta observed. "That would be reason enough to regard him as immensely valuable. If he is not producing the energy from local sources he must be drawing it from elsewhere. I wish I had taken more math and spatial cognition. It must have everything to do with this hypothesized other space.

If he can tap into such a source he may be capable of generating much more than these weak if expansive pulses."

"You calling an energy pulse that covers thirty thousand light years weak?" Kerwin asked him.

"Everything is relative, cousin. I call it weak, gracious me yes, but only compared to what his potential may be. What if instead of spreading this pulse over such an immense region he could concentrate it in a smaller area? Direct it? We are talking, my friends, about unknown and hitherto inconceivable amounts of energy." He looked at Rail.

"Haven't you ever considered, my friend, how much energy is required simply to change shape and substance, to generate those beautiful colored lights that run across his surfaces? Not to mention what is involved in levitating or countering the effects of a dropshoot field. Such fields manipulate tons of freight. They were not intended to be countered, yet he resists their pull without visible effort. Energy is involved, goodness yes! Incalculable energy."

"We saw him drift through the shoot fields several times," Kerwin admitted.

"As he pleases, or so friend Rail claims. Without strain or effort, without producing heat or any other byproduct."

"None we could detect," Rail agreed.

"Then something quite extraordinary is in our midst, friends. Something I am not clever enough to analyze. Something which defies natural law."

"Maybe he doesn't defy it." Seeth and Kerwin turned to gape at Miranda. She was mildly embarrassed. "I had freshman physics. It fit my schedule. Got an A, of course. Actually I thought it was kinda boring. I mean, like, all that stuff about quantum mechanics and subatomic particles. When they started talking about 'color' I got interested, but only until I found out what they meant. I thought it had something to do with matching paint to fabrics. But this goofy stuff about bosons and quarks and anti-pi-mesons, I mean, like, who needs it? Besides, it's all so obvious.''

"Do tell," mumbled Seeth.

"What about Izmir?" Kerwin tried not to make it sound like a challenge but couldn't help it. "Is he obvious?"

"Oh no. Mr. Yirunta's right about that. It's just that he's kind of like, you know, overwhelmed by the physical evidence as well as the philosphical implications and as a result his initial judgements are emotionally clouded.''

"Goodness gracious me," Yirunta murmured softly. "Please do tell me, cousin, what you mean when you claim he does not refute known natural law."

"It's like—this is so totally obvious, I mean—he's not contravening accepted physical principles, he's only manifesting them in a new way. The mathematics are solid and stable. It's our inadequate perception that's confusing the issue. Like trying to find something to go with gold lame that isn't gold lame, you know?"

"Interesting." Yirunta looked back to Rail. "Are the Cro-Magnons still dominated by the male children?"

Rail nodded. "But this may be changing. Remember, I wasn't on Earth to do a sociological study."

"The sooner they shift to a matriarchy the sooner the species will be ready to integrate into galactic society. The old tales always did say the Cro-Magnon women had more common sense. At least they knew enough to come into the caves out of the rain.''

"Yeah?" said Seeth belligerently. "Then how'd we end up with a male-dominated outfit?"

"Aberration of nature." Yirunta shrugged. "Who knows?

With Cro-Magnons anything is possible.'' They had slipped off the shoot and were walking down a brightly lit, busy street. ''Here is my favorite restaurant. I think you will find it to your taste. I have opted for good quality and quantity rather than risk unsophisticated palates on gourmet cuisine.''

''No sweat, Jack.'' Seeth eyed the softly lit establishment eagerly. ''I mean, gimme a burger and fries and some ketchup and I'm fine.''

Kerwin wondered how their headset translators would handle that claim, but Yirunta appeared satisfied with the reply.

''I thought as much.''

After a filling if strange meal, they returned to the shop and waited impatiently for the evening to come. Since Alvin functioned around the clock, Kerwin wondered what difference it made whether they tried to flee during daylight hours or at night. Yirunta replied that no matter how advanced the Oomemians' detection equipment, darkness still offered opportunities for some cover.

Miranda wasn't bored in the slightest. She had the whole shop to peruse in detail, and proceeded to do so following a four-hour nap. When Yirunta remarked on her staying power, Kerwin commented that shopping seemed vital to her continued good health. Not as important as breathing, but close.

When she grew bored with the shop's contents, it was decided that she could safely patronize some of the other stores nearby. She returned as the evening rain was descending with her arms full of plasticine boxes. Yirunta eyed them askance.

''I thought you meant to go shopping in the philosophical sense.''

She frowned. "What's that? There's, like, no such thing as shopping in the philosophical sense."

"You cannot take that all with you." He was firm, immovable.

Kerwin made sure he wasn't caught between them.

"What do you mean?" she said tightly. She looked over at Seeth. "He gave me the money." She indicated the boxes. "It's all paid for, in cash. I'm not taking any of it back."

Yirunta tried to be patient. "Listen to me, madame. If we are to remove you safely and quickly from this world without attracting the attention of the Oomemians, we cannot travel encumbered by superficials. We are trying to save your lives, to return you to your home world, to your own kind. This is not a shopping expedition."

"Of course it is," she replied determinedly, nodding toward Rail. "He said it would be. He promised me."

Rail swallowed. "What I promised and what I find I can now deliver are not necessarily the same thing. I'm sorry, but this isn't a game we're playing."

"Exactly. You think this was a game?" She indicated the pile of packages. "It took me simply *hours* to pick all this out. I'm not leaving without it." She sat down on the top container, which, despite its apparent fragility, supported her weight easily, and crossed her arms.

Yirunta leaned toward Rail. "Why don't we just sedate her?"

"You could probably do that," Miranda told him, demonstrating superior hearing along with everything else, "but you won't."

"And why won't we?"

She smiled triumphantly. "Because you're supposed to be the superior branch of humanity, like, and if you have to resort to violence of any kind you'd be denying your own claim.''

''A life-and-death situation and I'm arguing philosophy with an inferior cousin.'' Yirunta bowed slightly in her direction. ''You win—temporarily. I'll talk to Captain Ganun when he arrives and we'll see if he can't accommodate your baggage as well as your mouth.'' He smiled sweetly. ''Perhaps you'd like the ship that will try to carry you to freedom to make a few stops on the way back to Earth, so that you could pick up a few last items, complete any unfinished aspects of your new wardrobe?''

''Oh wow, that'd be super!''

The Neanderthal shook his head dourly. ''Is she crazy, or am I?''

''For what we're doing trying we all qualify,'' said Rail. He indicated Izmir the Astarach, who had transformed himself into a Wirmasian music box. Solid colors like animated mercury were crawling along his flanks while he played a soft, waltzing tune.

A half-dozen of Yirunta's friends came for them when everything but the all-night shops had closed down. Every one of them looked like they could have stepped into the starting offensive line for the university, including the two women in the group. They wouldn't have won any beauty contests back home, but then Kerwin knew he was judging them by different standards. No doubt Yirunta and his colleagues found Miranda unbearably skinny and fine-featured.

One of the women gave Seeth the once over and whispered to her companion, ''Look at the fighting monkeys.''

''Watch your lip, blubberbutt.'' Seeth shot back.

The woman growled at him. Actually growled. ''Blubberbutt? How'd you like to be a smear on the wall, monkey?''

The one known as Captain Ganun stepped between them.

"Less than a minute and the Cro-Magnons have you fighting," he told her. She looked properly abashed. "The histories were right. Goodness gracious, you should be ashamed of yourself."

"I am, sir." She stepped clear, turned her back on Seeth and mumbled, "But I will not tolerate insults from an inferior species."

"Who you calling inferior, with a body like that?" Seeth demanded to know.

"That's enough!" Yirunta was displeased. "It is only through Ganun's good graces that you are coming along at all. Our only real concern lies with Arthwit and Izmir. You travel on sufferance. We could easily leave you behind."

"Suits m—"

Kerwin stepped forward hastily. "He didn't mean anything, sir. He's just nervous, like the rest of us."

"Who's nervous?"

"Tell her," Kerwin told his brother sternly, "you didn't mean anything by what you said."

Seeth ran a hand across the shaved side of his skull. "Yeah, right, Jack. I didn't mean anything by it. Sure. But if she calls me a 'fighting monkey' again. . . ."

Two of the other members of Ganun's crew were whispering to one another. "What do you think?" said the one with the blue haircut. "Ten druzins apiece. Think they'd fight each other? That would be something to see! A real bit of history, goodness knows."

"I don't think it would matter." Rail had overheard. "They are brothers."

"I never heard that it made any difference to Cro-Magnons. I hear they even fight their parents." They were staring in fascination at the three visitors from Earth.

"Ugly things," said the other crewman, gazing at Miranda. "I mean, look at the female. There's nothing there and what there is, why gracious, it's all unbalanced."

"I said that's enough!" Ganun snapped. "These are our guests. They are contemporaries despite their peculiar racial characteristics, not ancestors dredged from an ancient past. I don't expect you to embrace them fondly, but the least you can do is be polite. You will treat them like the guests they are." He glared at Seeth from beneath enormous eyebrows.

"And you, sir, will comport yourself like a guest."

"Yes sir, aye-aye sir, right on, Captain sir!" Seeth snapped to attention and ricocheted a salute off his forehead. "And if you need any help flying your ship around the Oomemians, just ask my idiot relation here. He's ROTC." Kerwin's lips formed an obscene word. Seeth merely grinned.

"Right. Let's get a move on." Ganun was eyeing his chronometer uneasily. "From all that you've told me, it's only a matter of time before the Oomemians close in on you because of the radiation or whatever it is that this creature is putting out." He nodded toward Izmir.

"That's right so," said Rail. "Though, because the energy is low-level, they may have a difficult time picking it up again here on Nedsplen. Too much background stuff."

With Ganun's crew leading the way, they began to exit the shop. One of the crewman curiously shook the boxes he was carrying. "What's in here? Emergency supplies? Special food for the Cro-Magnons?"

Oh boy, here it comes, Kerwin thought nervously. Mutiny, or worse.

"No," Miranda told the Neanderthal. "I've been shopping."

"Oh, well, that's all right, then." The crewman made sure he had a good grip on the packages. "First things first, right?" He waddled carefully out the door.

Miranda smiled at Kerwin. "See, I knew there wouldn't be any trouble. These people *are* superior. They know, like, what's important." She followed the crewman out the door.

Kerwin followed too, muttering that something didn't make sense. He didn't quite know what it was, but one of these days he was going to figure it out.

Instead of continuing down the main boulevard, the procession soon turned into a back service way. Only technicians from the city were supposed to have access to this concealed labyrinth, but for the professionals in Yirunta's crew it was a simple matter to break the electronic locks and then reseal them once they'd entered. Horizontal shoots carried them across the metropolis, sometimes ascending at gentle angles, so that by the time they reached the city's outskirts they were back on the actual surface. Kerwin and the others knew it was the surface because they could smell fresh air and growing things and see stars overhead.

A low-slung air-suspension vehicle was waiting for them. It carried them down an enclosed tube at a speed nothing short of breathtaking. Soon they were traveling the sublevels of another city, which to Kerwin's eye appeared every bit as extensive as Alvin. The machine plunged down a sheer drop and leveled off in a subterranean transport tube, briefly accelerating once more. When they finally cruised to a halt, the doors parted to admit them to a lush, open square lined with brightly lit fountains that floated in midair like watery dandelions. Though they walked directly beneath the powerful sprays, not a drop of water fell on them.

"It's all timed," Rail explained. "Programmed to evaporate after it's traveled a specified distance. The moisture is then sucked back up through those cones hanging from the ceiling, where it's recondensed and piped back to the aerial fountains. We have similar devices on Prufillia."

"Outstanding," Seeth murmured. "Psychotic rain."

Their Neanderthal escort led them into an upshoot. The crew kept their fingers close to their sidearms, but no Oomemians materialized to challenge them.

They were deposited on a level not far below the surface. Another pair of journeys via horizontal shoots took them to a vast spaceport. A small car was waiting to transport them across the tarmac. With its recognizable wheels and straightforward seats, it might almost have been manufactured in Detroit.

They barely had time to examine their new surroundings when the car slowed to a halt outside a bulbous, silvery hull. Scrambling out of their seats, the Neanderthals exchanged hasty greetings with waiting crewmates. With Izmir docilely tagging along, the refugees were hustled inside.

Each was assigned to a tiny private room that opened onto a much larger common room. There were restraint lounges set in a circle and Kerwin lost no time slipping into his. Assuring them everything was going as planned, Captain Ganun departed for the command center. Moments later the floor quivered. There were no loud rumblings, no impressive chemical eruptions. Lift-off was indicated only by a gentle feeling of motion.

"Man, they ain't waiting around," Seeth observed.

"Like they've been ready to take off as soon as we got here." Kerwin was inspecting the walls of the room.

Rail was relaxing in one of the spacious chairs. "Yirunta knows his job work. This has gone well. There has been no chase pursuit and it may be we have escaped undetected. The journey to House may be relaxing." Off in a corner, Izmir was hugging the ceiling. He moved easily aside as Yirunta rejoined them.

"All's well so far, my friends. I haven't seen House since I was a child and my parents emigrated to Nedsplen, so I am looking forward to this visit as much as anyone. It will be good to look upon a real ocean once more instead of these pond patches, which are all that remain of the seas of Nedsplen. Most have been covered by city or machinery."

"I was impressed with how clean everything was," Kerwin told him. "The air, the water, stuff like that."

"One can build a livable city without pollution and slums. It is mostly a matter of will and responsible government. This requires responsible individuals. People who are willing to put the general welfare above personal gain and ambition. People who are willing to work for others, who take pride in their accomplishments instead of personal advancement. Something I believe you Cro-Magnons have not been able to achieve."

"Only in isolated cases," Kerwin admitted.

"That still don't make us 'fighting monkeys'," Seeth muttered.

"I am afraid that is what you are known for." Rail swiveled his chair around. "While I was on your world I observed a sport which, like so many things you do, is nominally illegal but practiced nonetheless. Two small birds were armed with short sharp knives on their legs, and then placed opposite each other in a restricted venue. Those surrounding them placed bets on which animal would survive the incipient battle and which would do the most damage.''

"Cock fighting, yeah. A lot of that goes on in New Mexico.''

"The feeling seems to be,'' Rail continued, "that if you take any two Cro-Magnons, arm them, muss their feathers a little and put them in close proximity they will try to kill each other. I suspect a lot of betting will take place if and when you do try to join the galactic community.''

"Maybe we'll have matured by that time.'' The analogy embarrassed Kerwin.

Rail shrugged. "Difficult to pass up a chance to make money. We'd have to do it without the knives, though. Most of the civilized peoples have outgrown blood sports.'' Noting that his friends found ongoing discussion of the subject disagreeable, Rail rose and moved to the far wall.

"Wouldn't you like to see where you've been?'' He touched a hidden control.

No curtains parted, no drapes rolled up. No blinds clattered toward the ceiling. The entire end of the room vanished. Kerwin found himself grabbing wildly for his seat. They were a thousand feet above the sprawling suburban metropolis that housed the spaceport they'd just left, rising slowly and steadily toward departure orbit.

"We'll accelerate go faster presently,'' Rail informed them. "There's a lot of traffic in this area. We're still relatively close to Alvin.''

Exhibiting no symptoms of vertigo, Seeth promptly walked right up to the edge of the illusory sheer drop. "Hey, this is great!'' He put a hand out toward nothingness. "Feels kind of rubbery. Not like glass.''

"The effect is accomplished by actually altering the composition of the ship's hull. If one wanted to spend enough money on the required necessary equipment, I suppose one could build an entirely transparent vessel, but this would inconvenience those individuals who are subject to—"

"Fear of heights," Kerwin moaned, finishing the sentence for him as he clung weakly to his chair.

"Fear of heights?" Seeth looked back at him. "That still bother you, brother boy? This wall's solid, man. There's nothin' here to be afraid of. Come on over and take a look. Ain't never gonna see a view like this again."

While Kerwin demurred, Miranda sauntered over and peered out.

"Neat. Like when Uncle Joe flies me to Houston."

Yirunta put a steadying hand on Kerwin's shoulder as he eased him out of his restraints. "It's quite all right, dear cousin. There may look to be nothing there, but it's every bit as solid as the rest of the hull."

"I know, I know." Kerwin wiped sweat from his forehead. "It's all mental. I know that."

"Then here is an excellent opportunity for you to conquer an unreasonable fear."

Kerwin forced his eyes open. There was Seeth, smirking at him. Miranda stood nearby, looking down while questioning Rail. All three of them were standing inches from cloudland. So what was he, the intellectual superior of his two companions, doing standing frozen to the spot, unable to move? Was he that terrified of an illusion?

With Yirunta helping, he moved a step at a time toward the transparency. Soon the time to look down arrived. He did so, and swallowed.

They were ten thousand feet above the city. Except for

the slow crawl of clouds, there was no feeling of motion. A slightly redder sun than he was used to was just rising over the far horizon as day returned to this part of Nedsplen. The pale, ghostly crescents of twin moons were fading into blue sky. He forced himself to stand there. Somewhat to his surprise, he did not faint.

The magnificent panorama gave him something to focus on. The city of Nophia spread out in all directions, individual structures gleaming as they were touched by the rising sun. Off to the east, a green belt separated the smaller metropolis from greater Alvin. Except for the green belt there wasn't an open patch of ground to be seen. Most of the parks, Rail informed them, lay beneath underground domes. Along with air and water, sunlight was simply another commodity to be piped in.

Rapid movement, dimly glimpsed, caused him to lift his head. It was not a cloud. It had long, sharp teeth and brilliant little nasty eyes that were locked on him like gunsights, and a wingspan the size of a Cessna, and it was coming right for him.

It wasn't vertigo but another type of sensory overload that finally caused Kerwin to pass out.

◢ X ◣

"I think he's coming around."

Something cool on his forehead, accompanied by a soft hissing. Cool mist bathed his face. Opening his eyes, he saw Yirunta nod, put something in his pocket and step back. Rail was there too, and Seeth. No sign of Miranda.

He found her when he sat up. She was still standing against the transparent wall, outlined against the firmament. Space was alive with streaks of moving color, a Jackson Pollock painting in slow motion. Shifted stars, Kerwin mused, or another effect he had no name for.

"What happened? That thing . . . ?"

"Prestral bird," Yirunta explained.

Seeth's face was animated as always. "Man, you should've hung around for the end. Splattered itself all over the hull, which looked transparent to it, too. You must've had evening meal written all over you, brother. It never slowed up."

"It was gross." Miranda spoke without turning from the galactic palette. "Totally gross."

"You must not be ashamed or angry at yourself," Yirunta told him gently. "Gracious sakes, you're not used to flying, much less such a perfect transparency. It was just bad luck that it dove as you approached.''

Seeth was still rambling on. ''Like a bug on a windshield at seventy miles per, man! I don't know if it was trying to pull up or what. You wouldn't think one bird could have so many guts.''

''Happens all the time,'' Yirunta continued. ''Nedsplen remains rich in large-scale ornithological species. They do have a tendency to run into ships as they are departing.''

Kerwin blinked at the far wall. It showed no sign of any impact. ''What happened to the. . . ?''

''The guts?'' Seeth said cheerfully. ''They burned off when we really started moving.''

''Pity it couldn't have been an Oomemian,'' Rail murmured.

''Where are we now?'' Kerwin stood. Perhaps it was because he was still dazed, but he found that the transparent wall no longer troubled him. ''Where's Nedsplen?''

''Oh, long and far behind us.'' Yirunta looked pleased. ''We're well on our way to House. You were unconscious for quite a while and, knowing little of Cro-Magnon physiology beyond the fragility of the system, I was reluctant to turn you over to the ship's infirmary. Your friends assured me you would recover, and so you have.

''We should arrive in a few days. Meanwhile, you are free to enjoy the facilities of the ship. Captain Ganun believes in treating his guests well.''

''I don't suppose that means—'' Miranda began.

''I am sorry, Miranda, but this is a working transport vessel. There are no shopping facilities on board.''

''Darn. Oh well, at least I got my stuff from Alvin with me.''

''Is that right?'' Kerwin muttered.

"Well, of course. I mean, like, those packages are kind of sacred, you know."

"Sacred shmacred. You can't take that stuff back to Earth. What would people say?"

"That they'd like to copy the designs."

"I don't mean the designs, dammit! What happens if somebody starts analyzing the materials?"

"I'll tell them that I bought them in Alvin."

"Right, sure."

"You upset yourself unnecessarily," Rail told him. "If it comes to that, your people will invent their own explanations. Anything to avoid dealing with reality. You Cro-Magnons are wonderful at rationalizing. Your collective obtuseness is of historic proportions.

"And while you do have the run of the ship, Captain Ganun suggests you remain in this meeting area whenever possible. There are individual cabins encircling this central room. If you stray outside you're liable to come in contact with the regular crew. In spite of the fact that everyone has been ordered to treat you as respected guests, there could still arise the occasional awkward confrontation."

"Don't worry, Jack." Seeth looked confident. "I'll stick tight. I got some music to play, I got something to eat, I've even got cash." He jiggled a pocket full of interstellar currency. "Got no reason to stray. I'm gonna squat right here and strum my toy." He displayed the compact, folded flower instrument.

"What about you, my friend," Yirunta asked Kerwin. "You have your instrument as well. Or would you prefer another form of relaxation?"

"If there are some books," Kerwin began, then thought better of it. "Naw. I don't guess you have books. Just computer screens and stuff, right?"

The translator struggled for a moment but soon made his meaning clear. "Of course we have books. We value them highly. No matter how much information you can pack into a single molecular storage cube it's never quite the same as picking up a book. You wouldn't be able to read any of them, though. Translators work with the mind and ears, not the eyes.

"With a cube playback you still won't be able to read any of the inscriptions or subtitlings, but your translator will be able to handle the aural accompaniment and of course you'll have no trouble with the visuals. What would you like to study?"

"Galactic history," Kerwin said promptly.

"Goodness gracious me. That takes in quite a lot of territory. You're talking millions of cubes. Anything in particular?"

"You bet. Anything recent on the Isotat and anything about their visits to Earth. Anything about the Neanderthal migration, your own history, and if I can get through enough of that, I'd also like to see a condensed update on the Prufillian-Oomemian War."

Rail turned proudly to his old friend. "There, you see? They *have* come quite a way since you were transported to House. They do have other interests besides fighting."

"It would seem so. Encouraging." Yirunta sounded sad. "What a shame they continue to waste so much time and energy on petty domestic quarrels."

By the next day, on-board activity had settled into a routine. The crew grew used to their prehistoric guests and, contrary to some initial worries, there were no recurrences of the ancient rivalry. The Neanderthals continued making comments about the presence of stinking fighting monkeys on board, but among themselves and in private, while for their part the two Cro-Magnon men kept their opinions about ape-women to themselves.

Kerwin couldn't read nonstop. When he and Seeth weren't jamming with their newly acquired alien instruments, he managed to cajole his younger brother into trying a game that resembled chess played with a child's building blocks. The idea was to complete your architectural construct before your competitor. When this was accomplished to the satisfaction of the game's computer, lights flashed and a musical tone sounded repeatedly.

They were halfway through one such contest when Yirunta stuck his head into the communal room. "Sorry to interrupt, goodness knows, but Ganun wants everyone in the war room."

"War room?" Rail put aside the miniature viewer that had been clipped to his chin. "What's wrong?"

"Ain't it obvious?" Seeth abandoned his construction, which promptly collapsed, and rose. "Something's wrong with the ship's plumbing and we need to have a conference to figure out what to do about it." He started pacing and waving his arms.

"Why would we be asked into the war room unless somebody's after us, man! Can't you figure out when somebody's after us? Does everybody's brain except mine work in slo-mo?"

"I can see how you acquired your name," Rail said primly. "It derives from the English word meaning 'to fume'. You're angry all the time, isn't that right?"

"That's me, Jack. All the stupidity and venality I see in the world, I just can't settle down and take it easy. Tough. So I'm a hardcase, so what?"

"Actually," said Kerwin quietly, "his real name isn't

Seeth. It's Seth. He's named after an uncle who lived in Iowa.''

Seeth-Seth glared at his brother. "You're supposed to keep that private, man. You promised."

"This isn't Albuquerque. I don't think you have to worry about it getting around."

"Yeah, maybe. Just watch it, okay?"

Yirunta observed this exchange uncertainly, decided to ignore it. "Listen to me, dear cousins. This vessel is now on a war footing. Ganun sent me back to inform you because he feels you deserve to know what is going on." He looked past them. "Where is the female?"

Kerwin sighed. "Parading around the ship in one of her new outfits. She seems to be laboring under the impression that some of the crew might find it interesting. She doesn't realize they'll be laughing at her behind her back."

"They may not. Clothing is clothing, no matter the wearer. Style is everything."

Seeth stepped close. "So who's chasing us?"

Rail was despondent. "I had so hoped that the Oomemians would not be able to track us."

"So did the Captain," Yirunta admitted. "We aren't sure the Oomemians are involved. Actually, I don't know quite what's happening. It's all very confusing and remember, I'm not part of this crew. I'm a guest like you. It could be that, in attempting to avoid the attentions of the Oomemians, Ganun has inadvertently intruded on someone else's space. Please follow me, that we may be enlightened together."

He led them through the ship. They met few crew on the way. Already at their battle stations, Kerwin thought uneasily.

They entered a luxurious, oval room. The lighting was

soft and indirect. Holographic sculptures drifted freely, while three-dimensional murals lined the curving walls. Glowing bubbles bounced against the ceiling. Deep, comfortable chairs were scattered haphazardly across the floor. Automatic servers moved easily between them, dispensing food and tall, cool drinks.

Yirunta looked grim. "Here we are."

"Wait a minute." Kerwin was shaking his head as they moved further into the room. "This is the war room?"

"Of course. What did you think it was?"

"I dunno. I guess I expected something, well, something a little more Spartan."

Ganun sat in the biggest, softest chair in the center of the room. Other crew members occupied similar seats. One wall was dominated by a single, curving transparency that provided a sweeping view of stars and nebulae. Off to one side, several members of the crew were crowded around a door-sized viewscreen. Its depth of field was astonishing.

"Hey, this is my kind of war room!" Seeth threw himself into an empty chair and snuggled down into the cushioning depths. He was nearly swallowed, since the furniture was intended to accommodate much larger backs and backsides. He slid his fingers across the arm controls and an autoserver promptly appeared in front of him.

Kerwin studied the occupants of the room. "Nobody looks very tense. Where are the battle screens and gun turrets? It looks like everybody's getting ready for a party, not a fight."

"I like it," said Miranda not unexpectedly. She walked over to examine a tower of pure white glass while Kerwin muttered under his breath. "This is neat. You know where I can get one?" she asked Yirunta.

"We're about to have a battle, maybe get blown into vacuum, and all you can think about is the decor?" he snapped at her.

"Well, I mean, sure." She ran perfect fingers along the pyramidal tower.

"I believe that is a mobile, self-setting, full-spectrum radionics sensor," Yirunta informed her.

"Wow! One of these would just look simply *great* out in front of the sorority house."

"Instead of a lantern-holding jockey, no doubt," Kerwin growled, more upset at the situation than her indomitable indifference to reality.

She walked around the device. As she did so she looked down at Seeth, comfortable in his oversized chair. "Your brother says your real name is Seth."

Seeth's gaze narrowed and he sat up straight, putting his fresh drink aside. "I warned you, man. I'm gonna kill you!"

"You may not have to." Yirunta stepped between the brothers. "In any case, restrain your play, please. The situation is serious."

"You could fool me." Kerwin was looking toward the curving port. "How the hell are you supposed to tell this is serious?"

"Ganun said so. Ganun does not overstate."

"Don't worry." Miranda smiled down at Seeth.

"I ain't worried. We'll make spacedust out of 'em, whoever *'em* turns out to be."

"Oh, I don't mean that. I mean your name. I think Seth is kinda classy."

"You do? No shit?"

"Sure. I mean, like, that's a real solid old-timey American name. Real frontiersy-like. Cute. Sociologically rad."

She sighed. "I mean, these days every guy thinks he's cool if he's named Jake or Jules or Brock or Matt, or something like that. There's no warmth in those names, no naturalness. It's like, you know, they think they're engraved in granite or something." She got a dreamy look in her eyes.

"I've always fantasized about meeting a *real* guy. Somebody named Ezra or Isaiah or like that."

What Seeth said was, "No kidding?" What his eyes said were, "Man, this chick is *weird*." What he said next, still not quite sure if she was putting him on, was, "My uncle raised hogs, too."

"For real?" Miranda's eyes got very wide. She knelt down on the carpet next to his chair and leaned one arm close to his. "For sure? That's just the ultimate to the max. Like, he actually slopped the pigs and dug up the ground and all that real organic stuff?"

"Uh, yeah, organic, right." Seeth wore the expression of a casual traveler who'd unexpectedly stumbled across the trail that led to the pot of gold but still wasn't sure of the signs. "And, uh, we were real close, too, Uncle Seth and me."

Kerwin glared down at him. "That's funny. I seem to remember you saying Uncle Seth was the only person you ever knew who made a profession out of shoveling pig—"

"Shut up, man! I mean it, shut it down!" He smiled warmly back at Miranda. "Like I was saying, cinnamonlips, that's why I was named after him."

"A farmer." The dreamy expression deepened. "I mean, that's like so, you know, so *real*."

"Right, real. Can you hear me okay? I mean, it's kinda noisy in here bein' on a war footing and all. Ice cubes clinking and video players going. Come a little closer and I'll tell you all about Iowa.''

Miranda settled into the chair next to him. There was enough space to accommodate them both, but not so much that Seeth's blood pressure didn't start rising toward triple digits. The fact that they might be annihilated at any moment by a still unrevealed enemy didn't seem to be bothering either of them in the slightest.

It was too much for Kerwin, who turned away and headed toward Ganun's command chair. Surely she was putting all of them on. All this breathless mooing over realness and fertilizer and farm dirt didn't go with the twisted, silvery, off-the-shoulder alien gown she was wearing, or the air-repulsion shoes that enabled her to glide along a hundredth of an inch above the carpet, or the necklace that instead of falling from her neck climbed in a series of tiered rainbows to form a sweeping arc slightly to the left of her head, which rose and fell according to her mood, which perfectly set off her. . . .

He forced himself to focus on the Captain, who was sprawled with his legs across one arm of his command chair, munching on something sweet while gazing at the small viewer that extended from one arm of the chair on a flexible tube. Yirunta and Rail were already standing nearby.

"Good," the Captain commented on seeing Kerwin. "Where are your companions?"

"Otherwise occupied," he confessed reluctantly.

"Well, you can convey the necessary information to them. Briefly, we find ourselves in a very dangerous situation here." He popped a few more pieces of whatever he was snacking on into his wide mouth.

"Yeah, I can see that," Kerwin muttered. "I just don't understand your attitude.''

212

Enormous brows knit together. "Attitude? What's wrong with our attitude?"

"I just mean it doesn't look like you're getting ready to *fight* anybody."

"We're not getting ready to fight. We're fighting already."

Kerwin glanced toward the viewport. "I don't see any maneuvering ships. I don't see any laser beams or missiles being fired. I don't see any explosions. And this doesn't look like a war room."

"Gracious me, I don't see your problem, young cousin. Everyone is at their station doing their job." Realization struck him. "Oh, *now* I understand. You're talking about a primitive conflict where you actually see your opponent and attack him physically."

"Isn't that the way it's usually done?" Kerwin responded confusedly.

"Heavens no. Not in deep space. We're talking about individual vessels that are traveling at speeds measured in light minutes. Not only can you not see your opponent, but even if you possessed the fastest biological components in existence and fired a weapon that traveled at the speed of light he would have moved a million amrits by the time your beam reached the place where he'd been. Interstellar battles are far too complex to leave to mere organics like you and me. It's strictly the province of machines."

"Our computer against their computer," Rail added for good measure.

"I see. The computers figure out when you're going to be in position to shoot and then you fire based on their predictions."

"No, no, no. Goodness no. You don't understand at all." Ganun turned in his chair, setting his drink aside.

"We are trying to travel from point *A* to point *B*. Our pursuers seek to prevent this. They instruct their battle computers accordingly. Our computer then tries to predict what their computer is going to do and programs our evasive action in turn. Instead of a highly wasteful exchange of destructive energy the actual conflict becomes, well, a sort of stately dance across the firmament. No shots are fired.

"Eventually one vessel secures a superior tactical position over its opponent."

"*Then* you open fire," Kerwin said.

Ganun was shaking his head sadly. "No conception of what modern warfare is about, absolutely none."

"Go easy on him," Rail advised. "Remember, they still employ hand-to-hand combat on his world."

"Yes, I'd forgotten." The Captain looked up at Kerwin. "Before anyone can fire, the respective battle computers have analyzed tactical position, ship size, armament, likely crew levels, and a thousand other factors. They get in touch with each other and exchange this information. If our pursuers earn the superior rating, we'll surrender. If not, we'll escape. No need for actual death and destruction."

"What kind of battle is that?"

"A civilized, practical, and economical one That's the trouble with conflicts among you primitive types: messy and wasteful." He took a sip of his drink. "So there's really no reason to let your blood pressure rise. There's not going to be any shooting. Oh, it happens once in a while, when the opposing predictions are too close to be decided sensibly. But that's rare."

"What if the pursuing ship gets the upper hand and decides to go ahead and blow you out of existence?"

"Nothing we could do to prevent it. But that's not the

way things are done. You see, if it was found out such a thing had happened, we might blow one of their ships out of existence next time. Nobody, not even the Oomemians, goes around blowing up ships that have already surrendered. Interstellar craft are expensive.''

"What about people doing it for the personal satisfaction of seeing their enemies go up in smoke?''

Ganun smiled and wagged a finger at him. ''Don't impose your own sociocultural aberrations on advanced peoples. What you refer to is strictly a primitive pleasure. We may not have outgrown conflict, but we've certainly gained control of our adrenal glands.''

"So if whoever's chasing us wins this battle of computer number-crunching . . .?''

Ganun shrugged. "We slow down and turn you and your friends and this Izmir thing over to them.'' He frowned, surveyed the war room. "Speaking of which, where is our precious freak of nature?''

Kerwin found the telltale blue eye up among the floating lights, pointed.

"Oh yes,'' said Ganun, "I see it now. Anyway, that is how this will be decided. Hopefully it will be our computer that will prevail. We have the advantage of a head start and a good ship.''

"I can't say I'm surprised,'' Rail muttered. "It has to be the Oomemians. They've managed to follow me to every world I've visited.''

A subaltern approached, handed the Captain a printout. Ganun's eyes roved over the script. When he had finished he looked up grimly.

"I'm afraid this time you're wrong, old friend. It's not the Oomemians who're after us. We are being pursued by Prufillians.''

Rail's three eyes widened to the point where they seemed to occupy most of his face. "Then why do we continue to run? Those are my people."

"Don't forget the deal we made." Ganun spoke evenly, unemotionally. "Izmir is to be studied near House by human scientists. That was the bargain. We were to save you from the Oomemians. That we've done."

"Yes, I know that, of course." Rail's unease was understandable, Kerwin thought. "But I made the agreement on the assumption that we wouldn't be able to escape the Oomemians any other way. That doesn't mean we have to fight my own people."

"We're already fighting them, as I've just finished explaining to my young cousin here. Both battle systems have been engaged for several hours." He glanced down at the printout. "I could just as easily have kept this information from you, remember, and told you it was the Oomemians who were after us. Yet I chose to tell you the truth. I felt you had a moral right to know."

"Well, I appreciate am grateful for that, certainly, but—"

Kerwin interrupted the distraught Prufillian. "What about our moral rights? We don't give a damn who puts Izmir under the magnifying glass; you, the Oomemians, or Arthwit's people. We just want to go home and mind our own business. It's been bad enough being caught in the middle of one interstellar conflict. We don't want to be in on the beginning of another."

"You have my sympathy, goodness knows," Ganun murmured apologetically. "You've placed yourselves in an awkward position and don't know how to extricate yourself from it. Unfortunately, at this point in time there is nothing I can do. Were I to interfere with the work of the battle computers it is highly likely we would quickly lose the fight. That would mean turning all of you over to Prufillia. I don't want to do that.''

"But what about me?" Rail looked utterly lost. "If you do lose the contest and they find me on your ship, they'll carbonize me as a traitor. Ganun, you can't do this! I risked my life for almost a year on behalf of my people, but they won't believe that if they find me on a human ship they've been forced to war track."

"Oh, piffle! Don't get so emotional. You sound like one of these Cro-Magnons. You are my guests. Guests can become prisoners with a twist of a syllable. If we lose I assure you I'll make it a point to inform the Prufillian officers that you're here against your will.'' He glanced up at Kerwin. "All of you. So you see, you've nothing to lose. Whether we lose or win this fight you'll be treated as heroes by the victorious side.''

"Well—that makes sense. I feel better. Thank you.''

"Mention it not. By the way, there appears to be more than one vessel engaged in pursuit. Considerably more, though we've no precise count as yet. More seem to be arriving all the time.'' He shook his head unhappily. "It seems your people received word you were in this region and decided to come looking for you. You may get your wish to rejoin them.

"As for you, young human, it may be that you will get your wish and that the predictions will be close enough to require actual combat. Then you will see all the pretty explosions and flashes of light and blood and gore your race is so fond of.''

"You've got me all wrong. We don't like war at all. We hate combat. It's just that we can't seem to settle our problems any other way, sometimes.''

"Dervil drap,'' said Ganun curtly. "Truth is truth and

fact is fact and nature is nature and you can't help what you are, so why try to deny it? Anyway, it probably will not come to that."

"If it does," Kerwin inquired, "you'll move to a real war room?"

Ganun was starting to sound bored with these stupid questions. "For the last time, cousin, *this is* the war room. You don't really think we'd entrust the operation of immensely powerful transspatial weapons to our own ridiculously slow reactions, do you? If it comes to actual fighting, the computers will operate our combat systems as well."

"All I can say is that it's a damn funny way to fight a war."

"You Cro-Magnons." Ganun looked sympathetic. "Everything has to be a hands-on experience with you, doesn't it? You don't even know how to relax when you're fighting."

The subaltern returned to hand the Captain what looked like a stick of cherry chewing gum. Instead of placing it in his mouth, Ganun slipped it into a small tube set into the side of his chair. The stick vanished. A holographic sphere instantly appeared in the air in front of his legs. It was alive with dots and lines and ciphered symbology that would have made Kerwin gasp in wonder if he hadn't encountered dozens of similar hallucinations during the past couple of days.

Ganun studied the sphere, rotating it slowly. "Well, things are getting complicated." He didn't sound especially upset. This projection was far more sophisticated than those Kerwin and his friends had previously encountered, as the Captain proceeded to demonstrate.

He stuck one thick finger into the drifting mass of stars,

and must have made contact with something within, because the view immediately zoomed in on one small spherical section, although the outer sphere remained the same size. Now the globe contained only a few stars. Moving among them were tiny glowing pinpoints of light. Ganun's finger touched one. It brightened briefly.

"That's us." His finger retreated to the edge of the sphere, though still not far enough for Kerwin's taste. "Here come your friends and relations," he told Rail.

The Prufillian's jaw dropped as he counted twelve, thirteen. . . . "There must be two dozen ships."

"Must be." Ganun was nodding sagely.

"But that's a full fleet. How did they muster a fleet so quickly in this region?"

"Obviously, your own people want this Izmir as badly as do the Oomemians."

"They're close. Too close. You won't be able to get away. Why not surrender now and eliminate the possibility of armed conflict?"

"I would, except that the situation is not that simple. Notice here." He moved his fingers within the sphere again. The field of view expanded slightly.

A swarm of dots were beginning to enter the projection near its northern axis. "Oomemians," the Captain explained unnecessarily. "Quite a few Oomemians. They followed us, as you surmised they might. They just took a little longer closing from a different direction. Our computers must find this interesting. Three-way battles are rare."

Kerwin stared into the sphere, fascinated by the moving dots. "Won't the Prufillians and the Oomemians fight each other and allow us to get away?"

"Don't be naive, cousin. Excuse me, perhaps I am

being unfair. It's unlikely you are compelled to consider the ramifications posed by an interstellar battle in and out of slipspace more than occasionally.''

''Actually, anything more complicated than algebra makes my head swim. Seeth was the one who was good in math, though he'd die before admitting it.''

''Regardless, you must see the complications. The Oomemian computers must decide not only whether they can overtake and defeat us, but if they can do so without being destroyed by the Prufillians, who have the same problem. It will take even advanced computers some time to compute all the possibilities and render decisions. Meanwhile, we can relax and be grateful.''

''Why?''

''Because this will delay both fleets. In the interim we may draw near enough to House for them to send some ships to our defense. I don't believe either the Prufillians or Oomemians would enter House-controlled space, if only because we could bring more firepower to bear close to home.''

''You're thinking logically. Don't,'' Rail warned him. ''This isn't your usual free-space confrontation. Izmir scrambles the equations. Both sides want him too badly. Someone might do something crazy, like override the recommendations of their computers. They might try shooting anyway anyhow.''

All eyes turned to the Astarach, who drifted among the illumination globes trilling atonal nonsense, blissfully indifferent to the fact that three major lifeforms were mobilizing awesome forces in an attempt to gain possession of him.

''Wait, I have an idea!'' Kerwin looked from Ganun to Rail excitedly. ''Why don't we just tell everybody that

Izmir belongs to *us* and that we're taking him back to Earth?''

''Because no one will pay any attention to you, young cousin, including me. In this matter, Earth and its desires count for very little.''

Kerwin tried not to appear crushed. ''It was just an idea.'' He looked across the room to where Seeth and Miranda were engaged in deep conversation: as deep as Miranda ever got, anyway. Seeth was doing most of the talking. Kerwin raised his voice.

''Hey! Don't you guys wanna know what's going on?''

Seeth barely looked in his direction. ''Naw! You take care of it, brother. Keep me posted. If we ain't gonna be obliterated in the next ten minutes quit bothering me, okay?''

Izmir drifted across the ceiling, a collection of glassy, glowing bubbles. As those below looked on, the bubbles coalesced into a solid sphere with the blue eye prominent on one side.

''Remarkable,'' Ganun observed quietly. ''The shape-changing ability, the levitation and heatless defiance of shoot fields, these enormous yet weak pulses of radiation—there are secrets behind that blue eye, gentlemen, secrets. I wonder what he really is.''

''Maybe he's just a pet,'' Kerwin commented. ''He acts like it, the way he follows people around.''

''What is the meaning of this dark spherical shape? Is he trying to mimic the battlezone projection?''

''Either that or he wants to go bowling again,'' Rail muttered. In response to Ganun's look of puzzlement, he added, ''A Cro-Magnon sport. It involves problems in velocity and mass.''

"Mass," Ganun murmured. "I wonder at its true mass. I don't suppose you've ever measured it?"

"Not accurately. He can vary that as well also. When we were doing this bowling sport he was a modest weight, but at other times he cannot be moved. Then he becomes light as air, as he was a moment ago."

"I can accept the levitation and all the rest." The Captain was leaning back in his command chair and staring at the floating enigma. "Alteration of mass is something else. He cannot be changing his mass. There must be another explanation for the phenomenon. Perhaps he is moving quantities of himself between the here-and-now and someplace else."

"That's the craziest thing I ever heard," said Kerwin before he could stop himself.

It didn't upset Ganun. "That's the craziest thing I've ever seen. We know next to nothing about it, my cursory examination notwithstanding. Consider that we still do not know something as basic as whether or not it is alive or simply a clever device."

"I lean toward device," said Rail.

"Why?"

"Some things not even a unique lifeform is capable of."

"You are holding back, goodness knows. Explain yourself. I am under attack by not one but two different war fleets. I have no time for guessing games."

"It's just that—well, watch." Rail moved beneath the bowling ball sphere. "Izmir, take a hike. Just a short one."

Without responding verbally, the globe expanded into a glistening sphere shot through with streaks of bright yellow.

"That's impressive," said Ganun.

"No, it's not impressive at all," Rail argued. "What's going to happen next should be impressive."

It was. It caused the most dedicated crew members to look away from their stations and stare.

The blue-eyed glowing sphere that was Izmir drifted slowly over to the viewport. Without hesitation it moved through the transparency, halting ten feet beyond the ship's hull. It hung there in the void, unaffected, floating alongside the ship.

"You're right," Ganun whispered. "That's very impressive."

"I don't have the slightest idea how he does it," Rail said, "but it just doesn't strike me as the sort of thing any lifeform, no matter how bizarre or adaptable, should be able to do. It's obvious he doesn't require the presence of an atmosphere. That much I've known for some time." He walked over to the port.

"That's enough, Izmir. Come back inside."

Obediently, the bubble repeated its trick, floating back into the war room through the solid viewport. Two members of the crew rose to check the window on infinity.

"Not a scratch, goodness knows," one of them reported. "No warping; no change at all."

"He went through it like an open door." Ganun couldn't take his eyes off Izmir.

"Yeah, he does it all the time." Rail sounded as much bored as bemused. "Solid walls, floors, anything. I'm sure it must be related to his shape-changing talent. Obviously he's malleable on the molecular level, perhaps even the atomic. He can adjust his space. Once he even slipped through my body. I didn't feel experience a thing, but it sure made me queasy. He does the trick with fields as well as solid obstacles."

Ganun was nodding. "Impossible to cage or restrain. Also impossible to lock out. Our weapons people will be very interested."

"Fortunately he has shown no inclination to harm anyone or anything," Rail went on. "I've tried, believe me, to get him to defend us against the Oomemians, but he won't. Whether it's a conscious decision or not I've no way of knowing, though he did once assume the shape of an emerald trapezoid and drift through an Oomemian assassin's head, which upset him sufficiently so that he forgot about trying to shoot me."

"This is quite beyond me. It's clear that we're dealing here with new physics and potentialities that no one has thought of. No wonder your people as well as the Oomemians are willing to send entire fleets in pursuit of him. How do you control him?"

"He seems willing to listen to just about anyone, but I think he has a special feeling for me. Don't ask why. I've tried to decipher his babble, but I'm beginning to doubt it has anything to do with speech. It may just be some kind of involuntary electronic emission."

"I'd take you bowling," Kerwin told the glowing sphere, "but we don't have any pins."

The blue eye shifted to stare down at him. It was extremely disconcerting and Kerwin found that sensation disconcerting in itself because there was no reason for him to be uncomfortable. He was unsettled nonetheless, perhaps because of the ability Izmir had just demonstrated.

"He's fond of this bowling, you say." Ganun looked thoughtful. "He likes to drift through solid surfaces. What else does he like to do? Move worlds out of their orbits?" He glanced at Rail. "I wonder if you have any idea what

224

you've been wandering around with this past year. I wonder if any of us really suspect what we're onto here.''

Kerwin had turned his attention to the battle sphere. ''If the Oomemians end up winning, we'll never have the chance to find out.''

''True enough, young cousin. The Oomemians can be disagreeable. However, we are neutrals.''

''That doesn't mean a thing when Izmir's involved,'' Rail reminded him. ''I really think believe they'd risk open war with House and its allies to get him back.''

''After that little demonstration I doubt nothing.'' The captain nodded toward the viewport, which was still being studied by the disbelieving crew members. ''At this point, nothing would surprise me.''

He was wrong, of course, but not for the reasons he imagined.

⚡ XI ⚡

The appearance of the Oomemian fleet complicated the Prufillians' pursuit, much as Ganun had suspected it would. By the time another day had passed, both fleets had drawn nearer to the fleeing House vessel, yet neither could approach within firing range because doing so would upset the delicate tactical balance being maintained between them. They were compelled to keep their distance from each other. The number of ships involved and the velocities at which they were maneuvering made Kerwin dizzy just thinking about it. He began to understand why interspatial combat was too complex to leave to mere organic brains.

Meanwhile, the computers did battle in rarified numberland and did not complain.

Ganun's crew occupied themselves with games and recorded entertainment, reading, and various other recreational activities as they awaited the outcome of the mechanical battle. It still struck Kerwin as unreasonable and he said as much to Rail, not wishing to risk Ganun's contempt a second time.

"It's the way things are done," the Prufillian explained.

"Hell of a way to run a war."

"A typical Cro-Magnon perspective."

Kerwin lowered his voice, tried not to sound like he was pleading. "Look, couldn't you call me and my friends humans, too? Please? I mean, I don't want to get into a fight about it. Not with these people. This is their ship, besides which they're all bigger than me, but I'm tired of being addressed like something out of an anthropology text."

"I am sorry apologetic, Kerwin, but consider that this is quite strange weird upsetting for me also. I do not wish to get involved in an interevolutionary squabble."

"What do you think's going to happen?"

"If something does not happen soon," and Rail gestured with a thin green arm across the floor of the common room to where Miranda was trying on two different pairs of shoes, "your female companion is going to perish of boredom."

"Yeah, it must be tough for her. Nobody's paying any attention to her except Seeth, and that'd be rough on anyone." He didn't see his younger brother and suspected he must be practicing his alien instrument in the privacy of his own small cabin. The soundproofing on the ship was excellent.

"But I meant happen to us."

"The possibilities are limited," said Rail thoughtfully. "If the Oomemians emerge the winners, they will take Izmir with them and execute the rest of us. If the Prufillians win, I don't think any of us will come to any harm. Prufillia has strong rules concerning the treatment of aborigines."

"I think I preferred Cro-Magnons."

"Sorry. As for myself, I will either be tried and executed or decorated and enriched, no matter what efforts

228

Ganun exerts on my behalf. Much will depend on the social status and personal politics of the fleet commander. If we succeed in reaching House's sphere of influence they will doubtless, as Ganun explained, send out a fleet of their own. We will then find ourselves in the midst of a multiple battle, because I do not think the Oomemians, at least, will give up.''

"All because of him." Kerwin sighed and pointed to where Izmir had transformed himself into three interconnected transparent poles, within which streaks of lightning were coursing up and down like so many markers on a video game.

"Yes. Because of him. Because he can do things that are impossible, like migrating without harm through the hull of a vessel traveling in slipspace."

"You know what would be funny? If, after all this, whoever ends up with him can't derive a single useful thing from studying him."

"The possibility had occurred to me also. As I've said, my main reason for taking him was not in hopes of learning from him but to deny such learning to the Oomemians."

That's when the alarms started singing throughout the ship. For the first time in days there was some real activity above and beyond an exclamation of delight when someone won a gambling bet. Ganus's people could move fast when they had to. Kerwin and his companions rushed to the war room.

Ganun himself was everywhere—giving orders, checking stations, absorbing and relaying information, reconfirming statistics. They caught up to him as he was bent over a complex, curving console manned by three high-ranking crew members.

"Gracious no, that's impossible. Check it again. Are you certain?"

"Yes, sir."

Kerwin turned as Seeth burst, shouting, into the war room. "Hey, all you hairy relations! I just came from the dorsal observation dome and you ain't never gonna guess what I saw!"

"Not now, Seeth!" Kerwin was trying to figure out what was going on, his brain and headset translator both working overtime to make sense of the multiple conversations taking place around him. "Nobody cares what you saw."

But he was wrong. Everyone did care. And in a minute they all saw for themselves as it hove into view outside the main port.

It got real quiet in the war room. Quieter than Kerwin had ever heard it. Nobody moved except Izmir, who drifted along the ceiling, indifferent as always.

Miranda finally put her hands on her hips, staring out the port like everyone else. "Oh great. Now what? This means, like, it's gonna take us a little longer to get home, right?"

There was a spaceship outside the port. Its approach hadn't been noted by any of the ultrasophisticated detection devices Ganun's vessel was equipped with. It had simply appeared, giving no time for evasive action, even though deep inside Kerwin sensed escape would have been impossible anyway. Whatever method of propulsion it employed, it was obviously radically different from the drive used by the Prufillians and the others. Perhaps it didn't even travel so much as simply appear. Kerwin had a hundred questions about it, and he was not alone.

"How big is that thing?" Ganun was whispering to his technicians.

The ranking engineer began spouting figures that were more than a little irrelevant. The visitor was beyond easy comprehension. Words like huge, monstrous, and vast simply did not apply.

Seeth's comments were supported by observation if not statistics. "I'd say it's about the size of China, man. Or maybe Brazil. Geography wasn't my best subject. I was more into auto shop."

The flanks of the irregular object were alive with lights. There were no visible weapons or engines, nothing else to mar the smooth metallic surface. It was just a great gray shape floating in space; an illuminated moon.

"I knew it." Miranda let out a tired sigh, looked resigned. "It's, like, my own fault for getting mixed up with people who can't do anything right."

"Sweethips, nobody's responsible for where we is right now," Seeth told her. "I don't usually spend my nights watching aliens war, you know?"

"Liar." Kerwin looked back into the war room, toward the holographic battle sphere drifting in front of Ganun's command chair.

The elaborately deployed Prufillian and Oomemian fleets were rapidly coalescing, abandoning their strategic alignments in favor of compact, easily defensible formations. The unexpected arrival of the gigantic alien vessel had made garbage of days of intricate maneuvering.

"Do you think we're about to be attacked?" Rail nodded toward the newcomer.

Ganun stared at the gigantic starhip. It was staying close without visible expenditure of energy.

"Neither your people nor the Oomemians are fools.

They will continue to track us but they won't come close so long as *that* is around. I don't think they'll attack unless they have some idea of who or what they might be attacking.''

''I don't think they'll keep *too* close, sir. Have a look at this.'' The chief technician adjusted his instruments.

Now everyone faced the battle sphere. Surrounding the minuscule green dot that represented the ship from House were six of the vast gray shapes, including the one visible through the port. Taken together, the six ships might enclose a volume as great as the Earth itself.

Rail swallowed. ''Who could build such a craft, far less six of them?''

''Only one people. I never expected in my time to see one of their ships. No one has seen more than one. Yet there are six. The Isotat.''

The lights fluttered in the war room, and for an instant Kerwin was certain they were under attack. He crouched behind a table. Miranda shook out her hair and fumbled boredly through her purse until she found her sunglasses.

Hovering in the center of the room, and generating as much radiance as several large spotlights, were two globes— each six feet in diameter. Faint pink lines crisscrossed their surfaces and appeared to move within. Each globe trailed two dozen three-foot-long pale pink tentacles from their cream-colored undersides. They had no eyes, mouths or other visible external features. Yet one could sense what was front and back, what constituted top and bottom.

''Sorry for the intrusion,'' the nearer globe said in a stentorian tone. Everyone in the war room clapped their hands to their outraged ears.

''Sorry for the loudness,'' exclaimed the other globe more quietly. ''You must be careful,'' he informed his spherical companion. "These are simple minds equipped with the simplest of detectors."

"In the excitement I had forgotten. I apologize." To everyone's astonishment, the first globe executed a slight bow.

It was a pure telepathic communication, Kerwin realized, but strictly oneway. The first blast of mental energy had overpowered everyone. Well, almost everyone. Seeth's brain had been dulled by attendance at too many concerts. He'd spent too much time down on the floor beneath giant speakers. His receptors were already numbed.

"Far out," he was murmuring. "Giant Christmas ornaments from space!"

"Shut up!" Kerwin said warningly. "They might not like being insulted."

"Hey man, what makes you think it was an insult? I thought it was like a compliment. Anyway, bugs like you and me, we're probably beneath their notice, right?"

One of the globes turned and moved toward them, drifting slowly above the carpet, the tips of its tentacles dangling a foot off the floor. It halted a yard from Seeth, who squinted into the brightness.

"No harm intended, fat boy, okay?"

Two tentacles reached out. They wrapped around Seeth's waist and lifted him off the floor. Kerwin took a step toward his brother but was held back by Rail.

"Don't, my friend. There's nothing you can do. There's nothing anyone can do."

The Isotat leisurely examined its prisoner. "Fairly simple water-based lifeform." It stuck another tentacle into Seeth's left ear. Seeth contorted, then went limp, his jaw hanging slack and drool dripping from his mouth. If not for the presence of the alien it would have been a perfectly normal pose.

"Some intriguing undeveloped neuronic potential," the globe went on while Kerwin gritted his teeth and held his ground. "Much of it misguided, I fear."

The tentacle slipped free and the creature placed Seeth back on the floor. His legs were shaky and he would have fallen if Rail and Kerwin hadn't grabbed him under the arms. They kept a wary eye on the nearby globes.

"You all right, kid?"

"Hey, I'm okay," Seeth responded thickly. "I took some pills made me feel that way once, Jack. Like your head's a ball bearing and the rest of you's a chrome wheelcover."

The globes continued across the room, examined one of Ganun's technicians, then turned abruptly toward Arthwit Rail. The Prufillian let out a moan and bolted for the exit. There was a slight crackling noise and he crumpled to the deck, momentarily paralyzed. The Isotat repeated their inspection procedure before withdrawing, leaving him groaning but apparently unharmed by the ordeal.

"Associate species. Related form," declared the second globe.

Now they headed toward Izmir.

"Uh-oh. Friday night at the fights," mumbled Seeth as he and his friends joined most of the war room staff in running for opposite corners. The Prufillian and Oomemian fleets could have swept down on them together now, but no one cared enough to so much as glance in the direction of the battle sphere.

The Astarach had traded his attenuated poles for a pair of intersecting black rectangles shot through with silver sparks. Kerwin held his breath. He had plenty of company.

One of the globes extended its tentacles toward Izmir.

"Amazing how we can hear them like that," Kerwin whispered.

"C'mon, man, use your head," Seeth said loudly. "They ain't talking to us. We're just picking up loose broadcasts. We're just ants to them. The only thing on this boat worth noticing is old Izmir there."

As he finished, the first Isotat wrapped several tentacles around Izmir and pulled. They could tell it was pulling because you could see the strain in the muscular pink limbs. Izmir continued to hover in place, unmoved.

After several minutes of this, the second Isotat joined the first. Their joint exertions were insufficient to budge the Astarach, who simply observed them silently out of his single bright blue eye. As they pulled he hummed to himself. Kerwin thought it a distinct melody, but didn't dare suggest the heresy to anyone within hearing range.

Eventually the Isotat gave up and released him, having failed to move him an inch. They hung close to one another and a low whine became audible in the room. High-speed communication, or something else?

"Why doesn't Ganun do something instead of just watching?" Kerwin spoke to Rail, who by this time had fully recovered from the trauma of his examination by the aliens.

"Do what? These are the Isotat. No one has ever seen one before. Only their vessels, remember? It is a measure of the importance they must accord Izmir for them to appear in person for the first time in recorded history."

"They're not all that impressive, really."

"They don't have to be." The Prufillian indicated the viewport, where the rest of the cosmos was obscured by the gigantic bulk of the Isotat ship. "They have that to be impressive for them."

235

"We still ought to be doing something."

"What would you wish like Ganun to do? Have them arrested? They teleported aboard, or were projected by mechanical means we cannot imagine. They could depart as easily. You can't threaten creatures who can teleport. Would you threaten them with weapons? I don't know about you, my friend, but for myself I've not the slightest doubt that all they'd have to do is look at you and you'd turn into a pile of dust. Besides, Ganun *is* doing something."

Kerwin looked toward the command chair. Ganun was drinking steadily and heavily from a long, green container. When in doubt, apparently, get drunk.

Well, he certainly was going to keep his faculties about him. He was the first human being to see such wonders and he didn't want to forget any of it, even if no one was going to believe him when he got back home. He'd keep these events frozen in his memory—assuming the Isotat didn't decide to clear them out like so many bugs infesting an instrument tray.

They were still too involved with Izmir to bother with the insignificant organic lifeforms who filled the war room. A glance at the battle sphere showed the Prufillian and Oomemian fleets hovering just within the sphere's boundaries, closely grouped around their respective flagships. He thought it unlikely either would actually attack. About all they could do was stay near and wait to see what the Isotat intended to do.

At the moment those inscrutable creatures were approaching Izmir anew. The Astarach had assumed the shape of an inverted black pyramid. Red and purple light flared from his sides and base.

One of the globes extended a long tentacle. Kerwin thought it was the same one that had been used to examine

Seeth, but he couldn't be sure. As for his brother, he didn't seem to have suffered any ill effects from the brief alien intrusion, but then, after years of pharmacological experimentation and constant subjection to hundred-forty-decibel rock music, it would have been difficult to tell.

Somewhat to everyone's surprise, the Isotat managed to insert the tentacle an inch into Izmir's surface. There followed a tremendous flash of light, which temporarily blinded everyone in the war room. The other Isotat shrank back, coiling its tentacles tightly up against its underside as it retreated as far as the viewport. Everyone else tried to duck behind the nearest solid object. The war room was rank with the sharp stink of ozone and another odor Kerwin couldn't identify. It was as if the world's largest flashbulb had suddenly gone off soundlessly in their midst.

He'd flung himself behind a console. He and Rail rose together, blinking spots from their eyes. Izmir hung in place, apparently unaffected.

Of the probing Isotat, all that remained was a smoking pile of tentacles, supporting what looked like a deflated dough-nut. You could hear the remains sizzling from anywhere in the war room. The alien had been fried like a cheese crisp. The peculiar second aroma that Kerwin had been unable to recognize was the burning of alien flesh.

Izmir turned himself into a series of connected rings, the eye moving easily from one ring to another as the rings twisted in the air to finally form a single, rotating, pipelike shape that unexpectedly sprouted a half-dozen blue wings. They flapped in slow motion, moving Izmir neither forward nor back.

Everyone held his breath as the surviving Isotat drifted across the room to hover close to its annihilated compan-ion. It moved a lot more slowly this time, Kerwin noted.

Not only were they the first people to see an Isotat in the flesh, they had become the first to view a dead one.

"Do you think they can bring it back?" Kerwin whispered.

"Not unless they're capable of full-scale resurrection." Rail stared as the intact Isotat carefully picked up the still smoking corpse of its companion in its tentacles.

"They won't blame us for what happened, will they? I mean, we didn't have anything to do with it."

"Obviously not." Rail was as nervous as his human friend. "But who knows how the Isotat think?"

"You think they know on the big ship what's happened here?"

"If they can communicate telepathically and teleport themselves, I find it hard difficult to believe they haven't been in constant contact with their fellows all along. They must be deciding what to do even as we speak."

"Captain?" A new voice, hesitant but determined.

Ganun glanced sharply at his navigator. "What is it, Irana?"

The navigator was staring not at his instruments but at the viewport. "Captain, the Isotat ship—look!"

Ganun complied. So did everyone else.

Something was happening to the exterior of the monster vessel. Portions of its gray skin were developing silvery blisters. Then someone let out a yell and pointed wildly at the battle sphere.

Objects were intruding from the eastern side. They looked like a handful of metal toothpicks. Kerwin counted eight when another flash lit the war room. This time it occurred outside the ship, and the viewport compensators automatically dampened the flare so that everyone inside wasn't permanently blinded by the tremendous discharge of energy. The surviving Isotat rotated sharply, still clinging to the body of its companion.

Something like a Mons Olympia volcano erupted on the far side of the Isotat craft, flinging into space a globe of energy thirty miles across. Looking back at the battle sphere, Kerwin could see similar dots of light being flung from the other five Isotat vessels in the direction of the approaching toothpicks. As if that wasn't enough, a moan made him look behind him.

Unshakable, unperturbable, indifferent Miranda was sitting next to a chair. She was surrounded by half-open packages, her exotic gown drooping across her slumping body, and she was crying.

"I wanna go *home*. I'm—I'm scaaaared. I want Mummy!"

"We all want our mummys," Kerwin told her gently, "but Mummy is halfway across the galaxy. We can't even see our star from here." Something shook the ship and everyone reached for a handhold as the deck rang like a gong. The lights flickered.

"I don't care!" She rose and stomped angrily at the deck. "I'm tired of all this! I'm tired of shopping, I'm tired of putting up with you two twerps and I'm tired of all these funny-looking people! I want you all to *go away.*"

For just an instant, considering the succession of impossibilities they'd endured the past several days, Kerwin wouldn't have been a bit surprised if everything in the universe except Miranda had suddenly vanished. However, while clearly possessed of a cosmic sense of humor, the universe apparently wasn't ready to collaborate on quite so all-encompassing a joke. Everyone and everything stayed intact.

"Listen sugar," Seeth told her in his usual no-nonsense

tone, "we've all got our butts in the wringer here together, see? Nobody's got time to feel sorry for you. What was that stupid poem you used to torture me with, Kerwin? 'Olympus Decried' or something asinine like that? That's what we got here."

The ship shuddered. Ganun put his drink aside and shouted, "Damage control!"

"All minor, Captain," came a report from across the room. "They're not firing at us."

"I can see that, you incompetent twit! Gracious, if they were firing at us we wouldn't be sitting here discussing the situation. But who *are* they firing at? Not the Prufillians or Oomemians, surely."

"No sir. We have unidentified vessels in four-bee quadrant. They are attacking the Isotat craft and the Isotat are replying."

"And we're stuck in the middle of their formation. Delightful." He took another long swig of his drink.

At about the same time, navigation reported that they were moving. This was of more than casual interest, since the ship's drive had been shut down when they'd been englobed by the Isotat. Ganun remarked on the phenomenon without anticipating anything like a reply. He received one anyway.

They all heard: "You are moving. You are traveling within our transportation field and thus are moving on the same course and at the same speed as we are."

Kerwin stared at the globe with its pale pink lines lacing the creamy surface. The voice had sounded, as before, inside their heads. It was the first time the Isotat had responded to them.

"Look, my friends and I," and he indicated Seeth and Miranda, "we don't belong here. We're just primitive types.

We got sucked up in this conflict accidentally, understand? We don't even have space travel yet. We've only been to our moon a couple of times and our little chemical rockets still blow up all the time and we don't really understand what this is all about. We don't want any part of it. We don't want any trouble. We just want to go *home*."

"Understandable honest primitive reaction," the Isotat responded. "Tough. You are in possession of that." The tentacle not holding the fried Isotat gestured in Izmir's direction. The Astarach had transformed himself into a perfectly serviceable couch, which no one rushed to sit upon.

"A forced relationship between unequals will obtain until we can find a way to transfer *that* from your vessel to one of ours. Only then can we leave you in peace."

The ship shook again. This time the lights went out until the backups could be brought on line.

"Who's shooting at us?" Kerwin asked unsteadily. "What's going on?"

"The Sikan," said the Isotat. "Apparently they too have discovered the existence of that. You call it by name. Izmir. Interesting. They have come to take him. This must be prevented at all costs. You will find the Sikan are not nearly as compassionate as the Isotat. We wish only to take your Izmir with us for study. The Sikan will take him and destroy everything else: us, our ships, you, your ship, those of the other small organic lifeforms who unwisely remain in the vicinity trying to decide what to do next— everything. They can do this because they know that in any battle Izmir will survive for them to examine, even if everything including this ship is obliterated."

"They—they're not going to succeed, are they?" Rail stammered.

The Isotat's reply betrayed no emotion. "For the moment the battle proceeds on equal terms. They have come with more ships. Ours are slightly more powerful."

"I don't want to seem impertinent," Rail continued, "but while we know of the Isotat, I don't think I've ever heard of these Sikan before."

"The Sikan are alien. Truly alien. They are as alien to us as we are to you. You have not heard of them because they come from," and here Kerwin had the feeling the Isotat was looking at him, "the region your people refer to as the Magellanic Clouds.

"They must have been traveling for some time. Even at the considerable velocity their vessels can attain, it takes a while to cross an intergalactic gulf. We have been searching for your Izmir for hundreds of years only. They must have been tracking him for thousands. It is clear they have not come this great distance only to return without the object of their search."

A glance at the battle sphere revealed that both the Oomemian and Prufillian fleets had had the great good sense to depart from the field of combat. It had been bad enough when the ships of those two competing powers had appeared, Kerwin mused exhaustedly. Then the legendary, omnipotent Isotat had come, not with one great vessel but with half a dozen. Now came the Sikan, whose ships were nearly as impressive as those of the Isotat, and who had accomplished the seemingly impossible feat of crossing from one galaxy to another.

Hardly surprising that the Oomemian and Prufillian commanders had chosen rapid retreat. As the Isotat and Sikan warred across open space, they were discharging enough destructive energy to destroy entire worlds. Any mere Oomemian or Prufillian craft unlucky enough to encounter a burst from the unimaginable weapons being employed would vanish like an ice cube dumped in a cauldron of molten iron. Obviously only the Isotat's extended defensive field had prevented Captain Ganun's ship from suffering such a fate.

"We're sorry about your companion." Kerwin nodded toward the extinguished Isotat.

"Someone had to probe. Only so much can be inferred from instruments." The Isotat rocked gently in the air. "We first attempted to transfer Izmir from your vessel to ours when we arrived. This failed. Such a transfer has never failed before. We then came across ourselves to try transfer with physical contact. This also failed."

"He moves freely in a dropshoot field," Rail told it. "He can even slip in and out of the ship at will."

"We have some inkling of what he represents. I assure you we have already brought to bear forces many times an order of magnitude of anything he has been subjected to while in your company. The order of magnitude does not seem to matter. Nothing affects him. You are aware of the pulse-field he generates erratically?" Rail nodded. "Unfortunately, so are the Sikan."

Just his luck, Kerwin thought. They couldn't have waited another hundred years? Or come a hundred years before he'd been born? No, they had to be here now. He glared at his younger brother.

"It's all your fault, dammit."

Seeth growled back at him. "My fault? What do you mean it's my fault?"

"If you'd left me alone in that stupid bowling alley, none of this would be happening. We'd be safe back in Albuquerque. I'd be taking my mid-terms. You'd be happily wasting your life away. We wouldn't be involved in this. We'd be ignorant of everything that's going on.''

"You're ignorant of everything anyway, pinhead."

Insults were swapped between siblings until they attracted even the Isotat's attention.

"We have been monitoring the development of other sentient races throughout the galaxy ever since we gained the ability to travel through space. We have seen whole civilizations destroy themselves before they were able to leave their home world, and watched while others created great empires only to have them fall of their own degenerate weight after thousands of years of sloth and immorality. We have observed new species struggling to rise above physical or mental limitations in order to reach the stars, seen others mature until they were almost worth talking to as equals.

"Some we have helped. Some we have hindered. Most we have ignored. But in the millions of years we Isotat have been monitoring such development, never before have we encountered a race that in such a brief span of time has managed to do so much fighting among themselves without obliterating themselves entirely from the frame of existence as a consequence.''

"I know," agreed Rail readily. "It's their sole claim to uniqueness. It's not much to boast about. I don't think they're very proud of it themselves. All that wasted energy. If only they could learn how to control it, channel it.''

"Perhaps some day they will," said the Isotat. "If there is to be another day. You must realize that the fate of many worlds hinges on the success of our study.''

"Is there anything we can do to help?" Ganun asked it.

"All the weapons you and your people could bring to

bear would scarcely tickle the Sikan's detectors. You can do nothing.''

''Not true.'' Ganun waved his queer flask. ''I can get roaring drunk, goodness knows.''

''Oblivion is a poor refuge,'' the Isotat observed absently. It continued talking, almost as if it was enjoying the companionship of manifestly inferior creatures.

It occurred to Kerwin, when he and Seeth finally stopped arguing, that because of the energy requirements of defensive screens and offensive weaponry, the Isotat might not be able to transfer back to its ship. It might be marooned here. It might even be lonely.

He took a couple of steps toward the hovering globe. ''I'm really sorry the way things have turned out. I guess we're kinda in this together, huh? We, you, everybody. Us against the Sikan, right?''

There was a flash of light. Kerwin felt heat on his face and stumbled backward.

''Wrong. Do not presume too much, you disgusting little carbon composite.''

Seeth caught Kerwin before he fell, smirked down at him. ''So much for interspecies camaraderie, kid.''

''I just thought. . . .'' Kerwin was dazed, stunned, and more than a little hurt emotionally. ''I thought that since we're all fighting these invaders for the same reason. . . .''

''Who says it's for the same reason?'' Seeth helped him stand straight. ''You thought you could talk to the big bulb as an equal? You oughta know better than that, man. Don't take it so hard. I get the same kind of reaction when Iggy and Slop and me go walking through the West Valley shopping mall.''

The Isotat did not apologize and Kerwin certainly didn't think of demanding one. Next time he might find himself on the receiving end of more than a temporary sunburn. The alien continued talking as though nothing had happened which, to its way of thinking, was probably true.

"What might make a difference would be the ability to make use of Izmir."

"Use him?" Kerwin couldn't keep the sarcasm out of his voice. He was mad, however unreasonably so. "Use him for what?"

"The question follows itself. A circular problem. I will contemplate its circumference."

It was hell doing nothing. Ganun continued drinking and was joined by several equally fatalistic senior officers. The ship's guests sat off in a corner by themselves. The Isotat contemplated silently. And every so often the ship shuddered as one of the Sikan's world-annihilating blasts sifted through the Isotat defensive screen sufficiently to remind them of the awesome battle that was searing this tiny corner of existence.

Izmir floated close to the ceiling, blissfully indifferent to the concerns of mere thinking beings.

"I wonder." Seeth glanced over at the unhappy Rail, who looked thinner than ever. "Izmir listens to you."

"I don't know that he listens to me," the Prufillian replied, "so much as it simply suits him to follow my directions lead."

"Well, what if you told him to turn himself into a gun? He's seen guns. He can turn himself into anything. Maybe he could frighten away this Isotat character."

Rail shook his head. "The Isotat are all that stands between us and these Sikan. They are fighting them on our behalf too, remember."

"Says they. All we know about the Sikan is what this Isotat's told us. I don't know about you guys, but me, I don't believe anything anybody tells me straight off. That's a good way to get shafted.''

"It could have killed me when I tried to walk over to it. I mean, I felt enough to know that.'' Kerwin played with the laces of his sneakers. "You could sense the power.''

Miranda ran her fingers down his cheek. The skin tingled. "Got a neat tan.''

"Better than a coffin. You guys heard how it talked. You, me, all of us, we're nothing to it. It's only interested in Izmir. In spite of that, it took care not to kill me. For that matter, it could already have killed everybody on the ship. It hasn't. So I think maybe the Isotat really are the good guys, even if they're not exactly friendly.''

"Maybe.'' Seeth still sounded reluctant. "But only because it serves their own ends to be friendly. I still don't trust 'em.''

The ship shuddered again, only this time it was much worse. There was a sharp, wrenching sensation. Just before he lost consciousness, Kerwin thought he saw the Isotat explode like a giant, floating jellyfish, but he couldn't be certain. It might only have been another protective burst of light.

This is it, he thought, feeling oddly calm. The Sikan have shattered the Isotat defenses. It's all over, finished. He discovered he was not afraid of the darkness, and this made him inordinately proud.

⚡ XII ⚡

When he came to, he found himself lying with his head on Rail's leg. The bony limb wasn't much of a pillow and he sat up fast, shaking. He felt as if a tremendous electric current had been passed through his body. Blinking, he saw Seeth sitting up nearby, rubbing his head. Miranda was in front of him.

Six feet away hovered a series of infinitely intersecting metal strips, with a single blue eye drifting in the center.

Kerwin rose, studied their new surroundings. They were isolated in the middle of a large, unadorned, brightly lit room. The ceiling was many stories overhead. Still shaky, he started off to his left and was almost knocked down again by an invisible field. He and Seeth quickly ascertained that the caging field was fifteen feet in diameter and extended well above their heads.

"Where are we?" Rail looked numbed.

"Not in Kansas, Jack, I can tell you that. Hey, check it out. Company."

A door opened, or rather a hole appeared, in the far wall. Four things that most closely resembled giant levitating squids drifted into the room. Their bodies were short and stubby. Unlike the Isotat, they had eyes. These were large, fiery red-orange in hue, and set with tiny, deep-red pupils. The bodies were striped blue and yellow. Instead of tentacles they had four clawlike grippers located near their heads, two below and two above the angry eyes. The largest was some forty feet long and might have weighed twenty tons.

So it was natural that the prisoners moved to the back of their cage as these impressive creatures approached, staring in at them.

"Sikan?" Kerwin whispered fearfully. He didn't like the looks of any part of their captors.

"Has to be," Seeth murmured back. "Nothin' else could be this ugly."

"For God's sake, watch your mouth! Maybe they can read our thoughts."

"So what? If they wanted to kill us they wouldn't have mailed us over in one piece." He glared defiantly at the nearest monster. "Ain't that right, Jack?"

"Correct." The Sikan who had replied spoke to its companions. "You see? Despite its small size and primitive structure it is capable of rudimentary reason."

"So why didn't you kill us? Why ain't you killing us right now?"

"Sshhh!" Kerwin looked frantic. "Don't give it any ideas."

"We have not disposed of you because of the aura that surrounds you."

"Aura? What aura?" Seeth looked down at himself. "I ain't got any aura on me."

"It links you together somehow," the Sikan continued. "We cannot analyze it entirely, therefore we chose not to tamper with it for now."

Rail straightened a little. "Let me guess. Izmir."

"The object of our long journey, yes. You are linked with it somehow. Therefore there is the possibility you might have some influence over it. We do not destroy what we do not understand. That can come later."

"Then you have defeated beaten the Isotat?" Rail said hesitantly.

"No. The battle continues. The Isotat will not disengage, but we were able by means of a single deft maneuver to slip in briefly enough to transfer you here. They have struck back furiously upon discovering our achievement. We have lost two ships of the Grand Crossing."

"Don't expect us to cry for you," said Seeth.

"The Isotat have also lost one. This is a conflict that will rage on until one group or the other has been utterly defeated. If you have any hopes of preserving your useless lives, and you have any kind of influence over what you call Izmir, you should consider showing us how to utilize this. While you are not worth exterminating, we are aware that to some small organics their lives have value, if only to themselves. If you can show us how to influence this Izmir in any useful manner we would consider placing you intact on a world where you would be capable of survival."

"Is that a promise, ugliness?" Seeth inquired.

"Consider it a formal offer."

"I want to go home!" Miranda had finished crying but was still upset.

"We don't have anything to do with any of this," Kerwin told it, trying one more time. "I told that to the Isotat and now I'm telling you. We—"

Seeth clapped a palm over his brother's mouth. "Don't pay any attention to him, guys. He just makes a lot of silly mouth-noises but he doesn't really say anything. Just likes to hear himself."

"You will be granted time to consider our offer." A slight tremble ran through the floor and the Sikan seemed to draw a little closer together. "The Isotat press their attack forcibly. You will have time, but not much."

With that, they pivoted in midair as neatly as four fighter planes flying in formation and vanished back through the hole in the far wall. The hole closed up behind them as cleanly as if someone had painted it shut.

Kerwin scanned the ceiling, walls. There was no sign of window or camera, but he didn't doubt for an instant they were under constant observation. Not that they could get away with anything in private. They had nothing to get away with. They were so much flotsam, tossed haphazardly onto one beach only to find themselves sucked out by the tide to be unwillingly deposited somewhere else. They'd long since lost control over their fate.

"So they're keeping us alive on the off chance that we might have some kind of control over Izmir." He sat down tiredly. "Like fleas on a dog."

"Come on, brother." Seeth tried to sound encouraging. "We ain't dead yet, man. At least, I don't think we are." He frowned, as if unexpectedly confronted with an uncomfortable possibility.

"No, we still live," Rail assured him. "While we live we may hope. Despair does no one any good."

"Speak for yourself," Kerwin mumbled. "If I want to sink into despair I'm going to."

"The Isotat may yet steal us back."

"Maybe, though they couldn't move Izmir off Ganun's ship. The Sikan have done that."

"I wonder," Rail muttered aloud. "Could it be that the Isotat failed to transfer Izmir to their vessel because they tried to move only him and did not try to take us with him? Perhaps there is some sort of connection after all."

"Be realistic." Kerwin nodded toward Izmir, who had assumed the shape of a cluster of coppery crystals. "We don't have any influence on him. Nobody does. He does whatever he wants. We can't do anything. How could we influence him?"

"Maybe," Miranda said, wiping away the residue of a last tear, "maybe he likes us."

Seeth let out a derisive hoot. "Yeah, sure, right. The thing likes us. If it wasn't for that weird blue eye you wouldn't even be thinking of it as a he. There's no emotion in there. Hell, there's nothing in there. Just stuff."

"How do you know?" she snapped. "I had a gerbil once. His name was Snuffles. People didn't think Snuffles had any emotions either, but he did. Snuffles loved me and I loved him and it didn't matter what *anybody* said."

Kerwin just stared at her, which left it to Seeth to respond. He did so, patiently.

"Honeyhips, Izmir can change his shape and move through walls. He can play ring-around-the-rosy with a spaceship. An Isotat just oh-deed on him. Two gangs to whom the Earth is less than a cigar butt in an ashtray want him bad enough to fight to the death over him, and even they don't know if he's any good for anything. A gerbil he ain't."

"Well I think you're all just, you know, mean." She walked toward Izmir and stood staring up at him. "I think you've all been very mean through all of this by not considering his feelings, if he has any. Not just the Isotat and the Sikan, but the Prufillians and Oomemians and Neanderthals and you guys too. Like, nobody's given any thought to what he might want.''

"Izmir doesn't want anything," Rail tried to explain slowly. "He doesn't respond except when he complies with a direction or two. He just—is.''

"You're such an expert, Mr. Greenface smarty-pants.'' She turned on them. "You all think you're so smart. How do you know he doesn't have any feelings?''

Izmir became a twisting curve, one side mirror-bright, the other jet black. Like the fender of a '57 Eldorado, Seeth thought, except for the everpresent blue eye.

Before anyone could move to stop her, Miranda reached up and ran her hand along the mirrored surface. Nothing happened as she stroked it slowly.

"What's he feel like?'' Kerwin asked breathlessly, waiting for the air to burst into flame around her. "Metal, plastic?''

"I don't know. Kinda tingly like.''

"Cripes.'' Seeth made it into a moan of disappointment. "Here I've been trying to get her to feel like that for days and she gets turned on by a flying bowling ball.''

"Your mind,'' she told him in disgust, "is always in the gutter.''

"Along with the rest of me.'' Seeth didn't sound offended. "That's where me and my friends like to hang out. The rent is low, the cops don't hassle you too much, and nobody bothers about when you filed your last tax return.''

Miranda now wrapped both arms tightly around the glowing, sparkling fender shape. "I think he's cute. Maybe he's just lonely, or unsure of himself. Even unique types can be insecure. Here we've been dragging him all over the galaxy and nobody's ever thought to ask him what he wants."

"He won't communicate, or can't," Rail assured her. "I've tried."

"Yeah? Well what about all that radiation he puts out, huh, what about that?"

"I don't know for certain what it is, but I doubt it's a form variety of communication. That's why I've been so anxious to get him back to Prufillia, where such related phenomena can be properly correctly studied." He looked gloomy. "Now it appears I will never see my beloved home again."

"Doesn't look real promising for any of us," Kerwin agreed. "At least we know now that the Isotat were telling the truth when they said they were the good guys. They sure treated us better than these Sikan."

"There are two ways of looking at that," Rail argued. "You could say that the Isotat just ignored us. The Sikan are not ignoring us."

Kerwin looked at the blank wall that had opened earlier to disgorge their captors. "I don't know, but from what I've seen of the Sikan so far I think I'd much rather be ignored."

"Of course none of you believed that crap about them letting us go if we help them with Izmir."

Kerwin turned to his brother. "Why shouldn't they?"

"Come on, man! These guys are so powerful we must look like germs to them. You don't go out of your way to make germs happy. When you're through studying them you get rid of 'em."

"At least Izmir appears content," Rail observed, "if it is indeed a sign of contentment."

Within Miranda's grasp the Astarach had become a chain of small, swirling, connected loops. They wrapped themselves loosely around her body. Each loop was a different fluorescent hue: red, orange, green, gold, silver. She wore him like a dress.

"You all right?" Kerwin asked her, worried that the chain of glowing loops might unexpectedly contract.

Miranda didn't appear in the least concerned. "I'm fine. Isn't he pretty like this?" She did a slow pirouette, modeling the Izmir dress as if for a gaggle of lunching businesswomen. "He doesn't weigh anything at all. In fact, I don't think he's touching me anywhere, though I can still feel that tingling sensation."

Seeth groaned again.

"I guess he must like me," she added.

"Oh sure," grumbled Kerwin's younger brother. "After all, you don't project anything toward him. No hostility, no concern, no curiosity, nuthin'. Maybe he's curious about the one creature nearby with nothing upstairs but air. Unexplored territory, sort of."

"Give her a break, musician," Kerwin warned him. "You're not doing so hot here yourself."

"None of us is doin' good here."

Kerwin turned back to Rail, indicated the far wall. "How long do you think they'll give us?"

"No way to know. Much depends I should think on how the battle progresses. For now they must be fully occupied in trying to defeat the Isotat. I wish we knew how the conflict was turning."

"Yeah." Seeth was pacing nervously. "You can't see nuthin' in this dump."

"Our prospects are certainly less than sanguine," the

Prufillian declared. "If the Sikan win, we are doomed. If they begin to lose they will try to destroy everything, lest it fall back into Isotat tentacles." A faint smile appeared on his manicured face. "I would like to be present to see them try to destroy Izmir. I am not sure he can be harmed by ordinary means."

"Don't be too sure," said Seeth. "These snails pack more than Saturday night specials and zipguns."

Izmir had spread himself thinner, molding himself more tightly to Miranda's shape while still avoiding actual contact. "He makes a neat dress," she observed, looking down at herself. "I mean, like, you just can't find colors like this even in the best material. It's like you're not wearing anything because you aren't."

"Matter of fact," Seeth commented thoughtfully, "you aren't wearing Izmir. He's wearing you."

"Well, whatever. He's certainly cool and comfortable."

"You humans." Rail was shaking his head. "One of the wonders of the universe and she sees it only in terms of a piece of clothing."

"That's consistent," Kerwin pointed out. "She sees everything in terms of clothing. So you think that no matter what happens we've bought the farm?"

"Agriculture does not enter into it, friend Kerwin. Oh, I suppose the Isotat might find a way to take us back, though their transport system does not seem to be as efficient as that of the Sikan. But the chance exists, if not the likelihood. At least they are from our own galaxy. The Sikan are true outsiders, in the most extreme sense of the term. I can hardly credit that any race would find Izmir of such interest that they would take the time and effort required to make a transgalactic crossing simply in hopes of studying him."

Kerwin was watching as Izmir shifted lazily around Miranda, changing color and form as he did so. "Maybe the Sikan know something we don't. Maybe Izmir has talents and abilities he hasn't revealed yet."

"You don't know the half of it," said a new voice quite unexpectedly.

As unexpected as the presence of a short humanoid figure, which had materialized in the far corner of their cage. He was flanked by two companions, none standing more than three feet high. They were stocky but not squat. One wore a light green three-piece suit, the second shorts and a long-sleeved blue and puce shirt, and the third an outrageously loud, plaid business suit, complete with a wide tie featuring a painted portrait of a nude woman on a shocking purple background.

A contented grin spread across Kerwin's face. "That's fine. It doesn't matter what the Sikan do now because I've finally gone out of my mind."

"Then we all have," Rail told him, "because I see them too."

The three little men walked over and the one in the middle stuck out his hand. "Allow me to make an introduction of myself. I am Brittle."

Not knowing what else to do, Kerwin shook the small hand. The grip was firm without being quite normal. As he drew back his palm, a gentle tingling tickled the skin.

"Aren't they cute?" Miranda commented as Izmir continued to twist and wind around her like a barber pole on vacation.

"Cute, hell," Seeth sniffed. "Catch those threads. Where'd you get the clown suit, Jack?"

The man in the plaid, whose name was Odenaw, replied, "We wished our appearance to be as harmless and familiar as possible so we would not shock you. You have suffered too many shocks already."

Kerwin's gaze narrowed. "How do you know how many shocks we've been through?"

"Oh, we've been monitoring your situation from the beginning. We'd been hoping things would calm down so we could approach you differently."

The third little man said nothing. He kept staring at Miranda. No, not at Miranda, Kerwin realized, but at the manner in which Izmir had draped himself around her.

"Everything's gotten a bit out of hand," Odenaw concluded.

"You could say that," Kerwin agreed. "It started with two Oomemians trying to arrest a bowling ball, and now we've got two galaxies competing for possession."

"Oh, there's more than that involved," said Brittle. "You've no idea how much more."

"I didn't think there was anything more." He could say whatever he wanted to now, Kerwin realized, because he was obviously completely mad. "You know all about the Sikan, right?"

"Oh, we've been around," Odenaw told him. He was tugging on the lapels of his plaid jacket. "It's no big deal. You've seen one galaxy, you've seen 'em all. Massive quasars—now those are worth detouring to visit, but ordinary galaxies are common as hydrogen. Even the food's pretty much the same."

"How did you get here? I mean, in here, with us?" Rail demanded. "I have just about decided that you are real and I am not imagining you, though you could be a trick of the Sikan to unnerve us. Mass delusions are not unknown."

"They're not us, either," Brittle assured him. "Your minds appear to be holding quite well, considering what you've been through."

Off to one side, Miranda was conversing with the third little man.

"Yes, he's kind of becoming when he wants to be."

"As much of him as you can see." The third little man's name was Riztivethariamalian, but he responded to Rizz.

"You mean there's more of him that we can't see?"

Rizz nodded somberly.

"We're Halets," said Brittle. "Like Odenaw says, we know how to get around."

Kerwin stared at him, looked over at Rail who shook his head.

"Never heard of them," the Prufillian confessed.

"Well, that's the idea," said Brittle. "You're not supposed to hear of us. We're very big on anonymity."

"You guys must be pretty big on some other stuff." Seeth gestured at the invisible walls of their prison. "I mean, you got aboard this ship which has got to be really well screened and defended and nobody's showed up to check you out."

"Oh, I don't think the Sikan know we're here yet, though eventually their internal sensors are likely to detect our auras no matter how hard we try to damp ourselves." Brittle looked down at himself. "These aren't our natural forms, of course. Just something we whipped up so we wouldn't alarm you." He glanced at Rail. "No offense, Prufillian."

"What's a Halet?" Kerwin asked.

"Us. Me. We."

"I bet," said Odenaw suddenly, "you folks would like to leave this place."

Kerwin gaped at him. "You're not here. You're just figments of my imagination. Oomemians, Prufillians, Isotat, Sikan, now you guys—it's too much. I can't take anymore. I could handle God showing up, but not Sneezy, Dopey, and Doc."

"No, no." Brittle frowned at him. "I am Brittle, that is Odenaw, and the other is—"

"Never mind, forget it, skip it," Kerwin moaned, sitting down on the deck and holding his head in his hands.

"Oh, I see." Odenaw grinned. "I have referenced the allusion, and a very amusing one it is, too. But inaccurate. I remind you these are not our normal forms."

"What are your normal forms?" Kerwin peeked out between his hands.

"I'm afraid we can't show you that," said Odenaw solemnly. "You wouldn't be capable of relating to them anyhow."

"I don't know why not. We've related to everything else, and some of it's been pretty wild. About the only thing I can't relate to is my brother."

"Same here," growled Seeth.

"This is different." Brittle leaned over and said casually to Seeth, "Like your music."

"Yeah? No bullshit?" He brightened considerably.

"No bullshit. Like I said, we have been observing you for some time hoping events would quiet around you, when in fact quite the opposite seems to have occurred. We could wait until the battle is concluded and simply remove Izmir from the victors."

"You can do such a thing?" Rail murmured in awe.

"Oh yes, but that would mean waiting on death and destruction, and we don't like to see anyone perish unnecessarily, not even members of species as insignificant and immature as your own. That's why we decided to intervene now, before things became worse."

"There's worse than this?" Kerwin said.

"Besides," Odenaw put in, "avoiding Sikan fields is kind of fun, in a primitive, simple sort of way."

Rizz returned to whisper to his companions. Eventually the conference broke up and they turned to face the prisoners.

"We're ready now," Brittle informed them. "You aren't dressed for where we're going, but then neither are we." He laughed at some private amusement.

"Won't the Sikan resist?" Kerwin asked him. "I mean, you can't just. . . ."

His voice trailed away. " . . .Move us like—that."

The Sikan warship was gone. So was their invisible prison. They were standing on a firm, solid surface and a rather warm one at that. Sand shifted beneath his feet. Sandstone monoliths rose into a clear blue sky to north and east, holding back an ocean of dunes. The sand underfoot was white as sugar. A stab of homesickness ran through him. It was just like White Sands National Monument, not far south of Albuquerque. The double star hovering overhead belied that possibility.

Still wearing Izmir, Miranda flung out her arms and turned a small circle. "Imagine! And me without any suntan lotion."

Seeth was already starting to sweat. He began unzipping his leather jacket.

"Yeah, imagine. Inside an hour you'd probably have had alien gumbo picking at your guts. I wouldn't worry about sunburn, sweetskin."

"Oh, I have to. I mean, being, like, so fair-skinned and all. I can't even go down to Galveston for the day without *some* kind of protection." She looked over at Brittle. "You guys wouldn't happen to have any lotion with you, would you?"

"I am sorry," Brittle told her. "We aren't prepared to cope with every little discomfort."

"We're all here," Rail observed in amazement. "Even Izmir. You moved him too."

"It wasn't easy, Quite a strain, in fact. I'd hate to think what might have happened had he been more resistant, but he appears to have taken quite a liking to your single female. That in itself is most interesting. We hadn't thought him capable of that kind of radiation on an emotional plane. But there is so much energy involved here that all things may be possible. Emotion is a form of radiation, of energy. When superstrings begin to twist, who knows what the perceivable results may be?"

"There, you see?" Miranda said. "I told you so. If he has all these, like, fields rotating around him, why not emotional ones as well? Just because you can't detect feelings doesn't mean they aren't there."

"Where are we?" Kerwin was breathing rapidly. The air was thinner than they were used to, but other than having to breathe fast and being a little warm, he felt pretty good.

"Not far from the scene of conflict, actually." Brittle looked skyward without shielding his eyes. "By now the Sikan will note that you are missing, not because of your absence but because of Izmir's. They'll be going frantic trying to relocate him." He chuckled. "They're going to be very confused if they do manage to find him again.

263

That's not impossible. For a primitive lot, the Sikan are quite resourceful and even we cannot completely shield Izmir's erratic pulses from outside detection.''

"I'm not sure I like this." Seeth was looking sharply from one little man to the other. "I mean, you guys show up looking like refugees from the circus and just like *that*," he snapped two fingers, "you move us out of an energy cage and off an alien ship down here to a place that looks almost like back home. No magic words, no buttons, not even a long-distance phone call. How'd you do that?''

"Well," said Brittle softly, "it's not difficult if you know what you're doing. On your world you have developed an artform called origami. It involves folding pieces of paper into interesting shapes. We Halet practice a kind of origami, only we use the fabric of space instead of paper. We just sort of folded things until the point where you were coincided with the point where we wanted to be, and here we are.''

"No kidding? Far out.''

"In a manner of speaking, yes.''

Kerwin chose his words carefully. "You called the Sikan primitive." He luxuriated in the feel of a real breeze as it caressed his face. "Do you have a ship like that around here?''

"We don't bother with awkward mechanical constructions," Odenaw informed him. "We gave up on such devices eons ago. They're messy and you're always tripping over stuff. More trouble than they're worth.''

"Actually, for a bunch of runts I think you've done okay. I guess I ought to thank you for sneaking us away from those Sikan instead of being so suspicious. I can't help it. It's my nature.''

"If you are so all-powerful," said Rail, "why haven't you been noticed before?"

"Think on your own store of knowledge," Brittle advised him. "Until recently, none of you had seen an Isotat. Of the Sikan you knew nothing at all. But the Halet have been around for quite a while. It's just that there aren't many of us and we assume different forms and cover a lot of territory." He smiled at Kerwin.

"By the way, the universe is finite. It's just awful damn big."

"You mean, you travel like Izmir?" Miranda asked him.

"Not quite like Izmir. Similar in a different fashion. We like to observe, keep an eye on things sort of the way the Isotat keep an eye on this galaxy and its inhabitants. So we figure it's kind of up to us to keep an eye on races like the Isotat and the Sikan to make sure they don't get too big for their hypothetical britches."

"Like God?" Kerwin managed to choke out.

"No, no!" Brittle frowned. "We're just folks, just like you. We've just been to school a little longer, that's all."

"When you've been around as long as we have, there's only one thing left to fight against." Odenaw looked up at Kerwin. "That's boredom. But once in a while, say, every five or ten million years, something happens that's of genuine interest. It draws us."

"Like Izmir?"

Brittle nodded, turned contemplative. "We travel incognito. Even visited your Earth once. I spent some time as a tree. Very admirable lifeform. You have plenty of time to sit around and think. If I had to be organic, I think I'd like to be a tree."

"It was Izmir who brought us here," Odenaw went on.

"Just as he attracted the attention of the Prufillians and the Oomemians and all the others. He drew us to him because he was Not Boring."

"I'm still not following all this. Are you guys trying to say that you're millions of years old?"

"Isn't it obvious?" said Brittle.

"Funny, you don't look a day over two mil," quipped Seeth.

Brittle smiled again. "That's what makes you humans stand out among all the other primitive organic races in this bit of space."

"I thought it was our constant combativeness," said Kerwin.

"Oh no, that's not all that uncommon, unfortunately. But you are different. You have the ability to face possible extinction without sacrificing your firm grasp of the absurd. In this one small but important area you have actually vaulted ahead of technologically more advanced peoples like the Oomemians. You have instinctively stumbled upon what might be called the Great Cosmic Silliness, which is the first step on the path to Universal Truth. If you can hang around for a million years or so without snuffing yourselves out of existence, you might really amount to something." He looked past Kerwin and his voice grew somber.

"As for poor, confused Izmir, we've been trying to track him down for, oh, three million or so of your years, give or take a few hundred thousand. He's been very elusive."

Kerwin turned to watch the Izmir-dress flow around Miranda's supple form. "You're telling me that Izmir's more than three million years old too?"

"Oh, a great deal more," said Odenaw enthusiastically. "A great deal more than any of us. He goes back to the Beginnings, but not in this form. There's been a lot of recent development, alteration, changes in field strength and posture. If he wasn't what he is now, he wouldn't be recognizable as such."

"Listen, couldn't you just take us home? I'd like a Coke and a hamburger and I want to find out if I can still make up the exam I missed. I want all of this to disappear. I want all of you to disappear." Kerwin shut his eyes tight. "I'm going to count to ten and you'll all be gone. One, two, three. . . ."

When he reached ten, he opened his eyes slowly. The sun was still hot, the air still thin. Odenaw and Brittle were regarding him with interest.

"You see," said Brittle, "a real grasp of the Cosmic Silliness."

"No question of it," said Odenaw. "Real potential."

"He ain't cosmic, but he's been silly since he was ten," added Seeth.

"Get hold of yourself," Brittle advised the older brother. "There's nothing wrong with you. You've coped this long, you can cope a while longer. Shortly we hope to resolve all that's taken place to everyone's satisfaction." He looked sharply skyward. Kerwin did likewise, but there was nothing to be seen. Not so much as a cloud. Then the Halet looked back at him.

"Wouldn't you like to know what Izmir really is?"

"No, I wouldn't." Kerwin hesitated. "You mean, you know? You really know?"

"Really and truly."

"It took a while to figure it out," said Odenaw. "There wasn't much to go on, even though inference has been an exact science among the Halet for quite a while. That's one of the things that made Izmir so interesting. Interesting enough to bring three of us out to study him. Three is the maximum number of Halet who can be in one place on a solid surface, you see. Otherwise we tend to upset orbital equilibria.''

Brittle was staring at the single blue eye peeping out from among the swirls that now enclosed Miranda in a radiant, rotating gown.

''Izmir is the physical manifestation, the only concrete example, of something your own scientists are just beginning to contemplate. You are familiar with the universal theory of matter?''

''I was just reading about it last week,'' said Seeth. ''Wasn't that in *Rolling Stone,* the one with Dylan on the cover?''

''What kind of matter are we talking about?'' Kerwin inquired hesitantly.

''The missing kind.''

''Oh, you mean the thirty or forty percent that can't be accounted for by current measurements?'' Brittle smiled at him.

''What's he talking about?'' Seeth wanted to know.

''If you add up all the stars and planets and interstellar hydrogen and everything else estimatable, the universe is still missing thirty to forty percent of the matter that all the accepted theories say ought to be hanging around.''

''Very good.'' Odenaw sounded approving. ''Your percentages are a bit high, but that's because your people do not yet possess instruments of sufficient sensitivity to detect much of what remains. Actually, only about twelve percent is missing. We've pretty well accounted for all the rest." He looked again at Izmir. Kerwin turned to look with him.

"You saying that somehow Izmir is the key to all the missing matter in the universe?"

"No, not the key, in the sense you use it," Brittle told him. "We know where the missing twelve percent is now."

"That's right," said Rizz, who'd spent most of his time just staring at Miranda and her unique if temporary outer garment. Twelve percent. Izmir.

"He's it."

⚡ XIII ⚡

Kerwin considered this bit of news very, very carefully. When he did reply, it was with great caution. "I've accepted a lot in the last few days. Prufillians and Oomemians, the Isotat and the Sikan, hundreds of other sentient races, a galaxywide civilization, intergalactic travel and maybe even you Halet, despite your clothes.

"Now, I agree Izmir's weird and can do a lot of amazing things, but to say that he's twelve percent of all the matter in the universe is asking too much. I couldn't buy that even if I was insane."

"You know what they say, bro," Seeth commented. " 'There are more things in Heaven and Earth, Ollie, than ever you dreamed of in your philosophy.' "

"Fine, except it was Horatio."

Seeth shrugged. "Must've seen a different version."

"Yeah. The cartoon one."

"Sorry guys," Seeth told the three Halet, "but I gotta go with my brother on this one. I mean, I'm not the brightest guy in the world, and maybe my interests are more in the arts than the physical sciences, but," and he looked at Miranda, who was lying down on the sand while Izmir shielded her. In fact, he looked so long that he almost forgot what it was he wanted to say.

"Izmir? He ain't any bigger than the rest of us. Again, I ain't no physicist, but it seems to me that if you took twelve or ten or even one percent of all the mass in the universe and rolled it up together, taking out all the space between electrons and nuclei and subatomic particles, you'd still have a pretty good sized something left over. Like a giant black hole, right?"

"Oh, much more massive than that," Odenaw assured him. "More than an entire galaxy, provided natural law was followed. Izmir, however, does not act according to natural law. Which is why he can do things like change shape and position at will and defy all kinds of small forcefields. The only reason he exists in this form at all is that awareness is a form of energy, and energy is only altered matter, and somehow that portion of the missing twelve percent that has been intruded into the universe from where it is presently located has acquired a sort of consciousness."

"Intruded into the universe?" The sense of what the Halet were saying was like a gull, rapidly vanishing into the distance.

"Your scientists may be primitive, but they are not stupid," said Odenaw. "Their percentages may have been off, but the basics of their observations are sound. The reason a substantial portion of the matter that should make up the universe cannot be found is it doesn't exist in this universe anymore. Sometimes the great problems have simple answers."

"What happened to it?" Seeth asked. "Somebody swipe the stuff?"

Brittle did not smile. "Sometime very close to the actual creation of the universe, the force of initial expansion was great enough to shove our missing twelve percent clear over into the seventh dimension."

"Whoa, wait," said Kerwin dazedly. "Are we talking about multiple universes?"

"No. One universe with multiple dimensions. It's very poetic, really. Now, we Halet get around pretty good, but travel between dimensions is one bit of commuting we haven't managed to achieve yet." Brittle was reminiscing. "As I recall, we were goofing around over in what you call NGC 286 when somebody smelled this peculiar shift in spacetime. We've been trying to track it down for several million years. Our task was complicated considerably by the fact that the shift doesn't always announce its presence and keeps moving around."

Kerwin looked to his left. "Izmir?"

"Izmir," Brittle said, nodding. "When we finally located it, we naturally settled in for some long-range studying. We had no idea of the potential with which we were dealing and didn't want to make any hasty moves."

"Sound policy, man," said Seeth knowledgeably.

"What we're dealing with is an intrusion from the seventh dimension, a crack in the fabric of spacetime which has allowed a minuscule portion of that missing matter back into its universe of origin. That it should acquire a rudimentary kind of consciousness and awareness is really no surprise, considering the sheer amount of energy involved.

"Which is what makes our handling of him so touchy. You see, if he were to suddenly snap back into his normal dimension, the resultant reaction in this dimension would manifest itself as the release of a pretty fair amount of energy. Enough to destroy an area, oh, the size of what your people refer to as the local cluster of galaxies.''

"Galactic whiplash," Kerwin muttered.

"More or less. You can't concentrate matter equal to the mass of several million stars in one small place and expect it not to affect its surroundings.''

Kerwin looked back at Izmir, who looked harmless as ever, and Miranda. "Isn't there anything we can do? I've kind of grown accustomed to this galaxy. Can't you just kind of push him back where he belongs?''

"You don't just 'push' twelve percent of all the mass in existence," Odenaw told him. "For one thing, we don't have anything to push with."

"What I can't figure out is why he keeps following us around."

Brittle shrugged. Entirely for their benefit, Kerwin suspected. He doubted Halets normally shrugged, didn't even know if they had anything to shrug with.

"Perhaps he's fond of you. There must be something about your presence he finds appealing. It likes you, it likes your Prufillian friend Rail, and it certainly likes the one you call Miranda.''

The lady in question rolled over and peered across at aliens and humans alike. "I just wanna say, like, I've been listening and I don't buy any of this at all. 'Twelve percent of all the mass in the universe' indeed! Why, he's as light as a feather. He doesn't weigh anything at all.'' As she ran her fingers along Izmir tiny flashes of light trailed behind her fingertips.

"We really shouldn't be here, talking to you like this," said Brittle tiredly. "We've just been tagging along, making our measurements and taking our readings. But the Isotat have been clumsy. We weren't going to interfere because we had hopes this Izmir phenomenon would eventually retract itself and reseal the crack in spacetime. Maybe push over into another dimension. Let them worry about him. Everything would slip back to normal.''

"How many are there? Dimensions, I mean,'' Kerwin asked the Halet.

"We think eleven. Even your scientists have figured out that much. Most of them seem to be pretty empty, but it may be that we simply don't have the means for sensing what's there.

"Anyway, we decided things were starting to get out of hand and that it was time we put in an appearance before clumsy types like the Isotat did some real damage.''

"Now listen,'' said Seeth evenly, "I'll grant you pulled a slick trick getting us out of that Sikan ship and bringing us down here, but how do we know all this stuff about missing matter and multiple dimensions isn't just a line? I mean, look at you guys. You really are just ordinary type runts. Back home nobody on the street would look twice at you.''

"When you're very big and very powerful it's easy to appear big and powerful,'' Brittle told him. "Making yourself look small and insignificant, now *that's* tricky. Takes a lot of thought and energy.''

"So you're really big and powerful.'' Kerwin shot his brother a warning look which, as usual, Seeth ignored. "So if I was to come over there and sock you I'd really be hitting a big powerful thing in the mouth?''

"You wouldn't be able to do that, not that it would affect our actual physicalities anyway,'' Brittle told him. "We could simply stop your hand before contact was achieved. Or dissolve it. Or dissolve you. That would be simple. What would be difficult would be to mimic the actual response of a simple creature such as yourself, complete to broken bones, blood, and bruises.''

"I get it. You'd probably even try to writhe on the ground in pain, right?''

"Exactly,'' said Brittle delightedly. "That would be a real challenge.''

"Then how can we be sure it's all still not part of a line you're trying to feed us?''

Brittle looked thoughtful. "You could come over here and try it. Or I could save time by dissolving your right arm now.''

Seeth took a half-step forward, hesitated. "Man, and I thought I'd met some guys on the street who had good lines.''

"If you didn't want to get involved, why did you? Certainly not for our sakes,'' Kerwin said.

"You'd be surprised. We hold intelligent life sacred. It's pretty lonely out there, especially when you're commuting between galaxies. While we Halet enjoy one another's company, there aren't a great many of us left. So we're always pleased when we run across another new sentient race. There's always the chance of a future relationship, though we can't be friends on an equal basis, of course.''

"I don't know.'' Some of the green fringe covering the back of Rail's head was beginning to turn brown, and Kerwin wondered if the sun was too hot for him. Maybe he needed to be watered. "We seem to be getting along pretty good well okay.''

"Maintaining these humanoid forms is quite a strain for us. We do it because we enjoy the challenge and we don't have many challenges left. You would find our real selves more difficult to relate to." Brittle pointed past the Prufillian. "Izmir is another challenge. A dangerous one."

"Why?" asked Kerwin, alarmed. "You think more of him's getting ready to shift back into our universe?"

"Oh, that wouldn't bother us," Odenaw explained. "We'd simply scoot to a farther place. It would be aesthetically displeasing to watch while several thousand galaxies with their billions of suns and attendant solar systems all, so to speak, went up in smoke, but it wouldn't harm us. No, the danger arises from the possibility that someone might figure out a way to control Izmir by appealing to his rudimentary consciousness."

"You mean, if he could be used selectively, like a weapon."

"Right. If that happened even we wouldn't have a safe place to hide. If you could channel that much matter back and forth between the seventh dimension and ours, you could do just about anything. The ultimate weapon. Absolute power. Call it what you will, but call it Izmir. The situation is unstable and complex."

"Look," Kerwin told him tiredly, "I have an exam to take. That's all I want to do. I'm not interested in absolute powers and ultimate weapons and characters who can flip back and forth between galaxies and. . . ." He sat down abruptly and rested his head in his hands. "And I think my ability to comprehend has just about been overloaded."

Rizz leaned toward Odenaw. "I feared as much. Events have grown beyond their small minds' ability to cope. They are beginning to shut down."

"You must try to help us," Brittle told him.

Kerwin looked up and frowned. "Us? Help *you*?"

"Yes. You see, Izmir responds to you. To the four of you. He will not respond to us. Oh, we've tried, believe me. We produced no reaction whatsoever. Why this odd consciousness should prefer the association of lower forms we don't know, but it's a fact we have to deal with.''

"Maybe we ain't as low a form as you think,'' Seeth said combatively.

"Yeah,'' said Kerwin sarcastically. "I mean, look at you.''

"If you possess unique abilities, we have been unable to discover them.'' Brittle shrugged. "Even so, in a cosmos of multiple dimensions and missing matter, anything is possible.''

"What can we do?'' Kerwin looked back at Izmir and Miranda. "If *you* can't push him back where he belongs, how can we do anything?''

"By persuasion, so that he will retract voluntarily. That means making contact with him. A mind-boggling concept.''

"No way,'' said Kerwin fervently. "My mind's boggled out.''

"Do not give up so easily.'' The three Halet conferred. "Why not come inside our habitat while you are pondering the matter? You might find it more comfortable and we certainly would.''

Kerwin looked at the sand dunes and empty sky. "Habitat? Where?''

"You're standing on it,'' said Odenaw. "We could simply shift you inside the way we shifted you off the Sikan craft, but we worked hard to get this exterior decor just right, and it would be nice to retain the artistic consistency. If you'd follow us?''

He turned and led them toward a cave cut in the base of one of the towering sandstone monoliths. Kerwin and the others followed.

Rail studied the dark opening as they entered. "I do not understand. Do you mean all of this is not real?"

"It's very real." Odenaw sounded slightly put out. "We don't go in for artificialities. Too easy."

"Let's do oceans next week," Brittle said thoughtfully. "I'm tired of desert."

"Sure, why not? We'll have a cluster vote."

Kerwin eyed the tunnel walls warily. It looked like a normal cave. Dry, cool, dark.

Then the cave wasn't there anymore. Neither was the darkness, though it was still cool and dry.

They were drifting, floating as if weightless, though Kerwin still had the normal sensation of weight. He doubted it had anything to do with gravity. They were in an endless open space without visible boundaries. He discovered he could move by walking, though there was nothing to walk upon.

Rail and Seeth hovered nearby. So did Miranda. Izmir had left her to assume the smooth shape of a large silver ovoid. It might have been only Kerwin's unease, but he thought the single blue eye was more active than usual.

Brittle confirmed his supposition. The Halets were drifting close by. "See, we finally got it to react to something." He was whispering animatedly with Rizz and Odenaw.

Off in the distance, Kerwin thought he could make out vast, cloudlike forms. Light twisted and ran through them. They conveyed a feeling of immense size and substance.

Odenaw noticed his stare. "A few of our relations, toned down so as not to cause you mental trauma. Everyone's extremely curious about you and Izmir. They're restraining themselves with difficulty, as are we."

"They're not gods," Kerwin muttered to himself. "They're just people."

"You got it." Brittle sounded approving. "We Halet are just folks. A little bigger maybe, a little more powerful, but with thoughts and feelings just like everybody else. Some things don't change no matter how far you evolve."

There were so many questions to ask. How were all of them existing in what appeared to be a formless, endless void filled with faintly pearlescent air? How was he still able to walk and talk and reason? Better just to accept what he couldn't understand and deal with it as best as he was able.

"Right," said Odenaw, as though Kerwin had spoken aloud.

"You read minds too?"

"Not difficult." The Halet scratched at his hair. "Just a collection of artfully aligned electric charges. If only we could do the same with him." He pointed toward Izmir. "Don't think we haven't tried. If there's anything rational going on in there, we can't tune in to it."

Seeth was turning a slow somersault. "This is your ship, huh? You guys aren't real big on interior decor."

"It changes from time to time. This is mostly for your benefit," Rizz informed him. "We didn't want to overawe you too much."

"I like the colors," Miranda declared. "Really subdued. Neat."

"Thank you," said Brittle solemnly. "I am surprised to find you have the control to admire your surroundings."

"She's different from the rest of us," Seeth told him. "See, her mind, what there is of it, don't run along the same lines as normal folks."

"That's like, funny, coming from, you know, a freak," she replied coolly.

"Your propensity for personal argument is known to us," said Brittle. "Not now, please. There are more important issues at stake that require your attention."

"Hey, maybe we'd all, like, you know, be better off if you guys would just mind your own business."

Kerwin froze, but the Halets didn't respond to the suggestion or the implied criticism.

"That is precisely what we plan to do, Miranda," Brittle informed her, "just as soon as we can assure ourselves that Izmir will not become a threat to us or you or anyone else."

"Well, I think you're all just horrible, picking on him and blaming him for things that haven't happened and like that."

"Miranda, haven't you been listening?" Kerwin asked her. "Izmir's not a person, he's a thing. A portion of an inconceivable amount of mass."

"Person, portion—poo! They're just saying that because they can't push him around like everybody else."

Odenaw looked at Seeth. "You may be right, human. I believe her mind does operate differently than yours. Perhaps that's why Izmir is attracted to her."

"Yeah, sure," said Seeth. "Don't mass abhor a vaccuum?" He executed another slow tumble. "So this is your ship, huh? How big is this cave, anyway?"

"There is no cave," Odenaw told him. "You set down on the sculpted skin of our habitat. We did not wish to shock you too much."

"You mean your ship's inside this planet?"

Odenaw and Rizz exchanged a glance. "We will try one

more time," Rizz said patiently. "There is no ship. There is only the habitat, in which we all presently reside."

"Oh, okay, I get it, Jack. You mean this whole world is your ship, right?"

"Habitat," Rizz corrected him. "Ship is an outmoded term. It implies the utilization of physical instrumentalities. We've not used such clumsy, smelly things for millions of years. We travel by thought, which is a very effective method of propulsion once you learn how to think properly."

"You think we could do that someday, maybe?" Kerwin asked eagerly.

"The idea is premature. Your people haven't reached the point yet where they could make a toy habitat move across a room."

Suddenly all three aliens—he'd almost ceased to think of Arthwit Rail as an alien—went silent and still.

"What is it, what's going on?"

Brittle blinked, looked back at him. "The Sikan. They are preparing to attack. They cannot harm us, but they could do severe injury to themselves. Even the Sikan are entitled to protection from themselves. We are debating how best to cope with this new problem."

"Hey, check out Izmir!" Seeth yelped.

The Astarach was growing, swelling until the ovoid had become several times larger than usual. Energy was running across the smooth surface at high speed. Most disconcerting of all, the single blue eye was racing wildly in all directions.

"Something's wrong." Brittle was concentrating hard on something unseen.

"Is he coming through?" Seeth started backing away from Izmir. "Maybe we'd better get out of here."

"There is nowhere to get out to," said Odenaw quietly. "If anything is going to happen, we would have to be ten billion light years away from this spot to ensure our safety. That is beyond even our capabilities."

"What's he doing?" Kerwin wondered.

"We are not sure." Since Brittle hadn't moved, Kerwin didn't see any point in trying to retreat, either. "We have no idea what is happening."

"Well I do." Everyone, including the Halet, stared at Miranda. She stared back as though they were all deaf, dumb and blind. "I mean, what's the matter with everybody? Can't you see he's scared? *He* doesn't have any place to hide, either. Like, with all this moving around, he's *got* to be unhappy."

"Are you certain of this?" Odenaw asked her.

"Certain schmertain. It's just, you know, a feeling."

"What is it going to do?" Brittle was fascinated that a creature not much more advanced than an amoeba appeared to be serving as a conduit for something as complex and incomprehensible as Izmir.

"Well, like, I don't really know." She smiled hesitantly. "I just have, like, this funny feeling he's going to sneeze or something."

Something happened. Kerwin underwent an instant of complete disorientation that was more total than the Halet's transfer from the Sikan vessel. When it had passed, everything was as it had been.

Except that Miranda was wearing Izmir again.

A cloak, a dress, call it what you would, it was brilliant beyond description. A flowing rush of color and energy that was almost too intense to look upon directly. Kerwin had to squint, and even the drifting Halets were shading their eyes.

It didn't trouble Miranda in the least. "Hey, like, this could catch on. I mean, this is totally rad! Except there's only one of him."

"Not precisely," murmured Odenaw. "There is enough of Izmir to make rather more than one."

"Some threads!" Seeth was squinting through his fingers at her. "Would that light up the Club or what, man?"

"What's happened?" Kerwin asked aloud.

"He's changed his shape again, dimbulb," his younger brother told him.

"No jerkwit. I mean before that. When everything went whacko for a second."

"He moved." Odenaw had drifted closer. "I wouldn't label it a sneeze. There was nothing biological about the reaction."

"More like a burp," said Rizz. "A momentary intrusion, since rectified, of a bit more of Izmir's self into our dimension, with the result that the sun in whose neighborhood we chose to take up temporary residence has gone nova. Fortunately, it was a star without inhabitable worlds circling it."

"It would have been most disconcerting," Brittle pointed out unnecessarily, "had this occurred when he was located on your planet."

"Disconcerting, yeah," Kerwin whispered.

"I hope this is not the beginning of an unstable cycle. There would be cataclysms beyond counting. Unpleasantness. That this has not begun already may in fact be due to your mollifying presence, particularly that of the female to whom Izmir seems drawn."

"If that was a sneeze, Jack, I don't wanna be in the area when he catches a bad cold."

"There is little we can do," Brittle announced sorrowfully. "Our powers are extensive, but we still are subject to limitations. As one of your own philosphers said, we can move worlds around like cookie crumbs. But this is bigger, much bigger. We are out of our depth here."

Kerwin looked thoughtful. "You know, when Arthwit here introduced himself properly, we thought he and his Prufillians were super-powerful. Then we started wondering if maybe it wasn't the Oomemians. Next the Isotat showed up, and then the Sikan. Now you guys talk about moving worlds around like cookie crumbs, commuting between galaxies and studying eleven dimensions.

"I was just wondering what's next up on the scale? I mean, the Prufillians were watching the Oomemians and the Oomemians were watching everybody in their neighborhood and the Isotat were watching everybody and the Sikan came over to check out them. Who's watching you? Are their others above the Halet, or are you the ones on the top rung of the ladder of intelligence?"

"We don't know," said Brittle, spreading his hands. "We suspect, but we can't prove anything. If there's anything or anybody else out there watching us and keeping a jaundiced eye on what we do, it's superior enough to move around incognito. But we do suspect there's something more."

"You mean, like a deity?"

"Hey, I know a wild deity." Seeth reached for his instrument.

"Not ditty, deity." Kerwin shook his head sadly. "The fate of whole races, whole galaxies is at stake here and you make jokes?"

"About the best thing to do, actually," Odenaw declared, "according to the evidence we've been able to put together.'' Symbols began to appear in the pearlescent atmosphere.

"You have your $E = MC?^2$. The Prufillians and Oomemians have their pure catastrophe theory. The Isotat and Sikan know dimensional causation. We've gone a bit beyond all that. Our most brilliant and innovative minds working together down through the eons have succeeded in producing this.''

Kerwin stared at the ranked, indecipherable symbols that glowed in front of him. "What's it mean?"

Brittle sounded proud. "That is conclusive mathematical proof that whatever exists on the next level of intelligence above us possesses a terrific sense of humor. You might call it the amusement equation. Or ontology for airheads. The proof is in the laughter. See, this part here . . .,'' he started to single out a portion of the equation, but Kerwin cut him off.

"Never mind. I'm sorry I asked. Next you'll be telling me that situation comedy is the highest expression of civilized art.''

"Depends on the situation," said Rizz, deadly earnest, "and the comedy.''

"All I want to know is when we can go home, and if there'll be one to get home to.''

"Everything depends on whether or not we can do anything with Izmir and what he represents by extension,'' Brittle told him. He was watching the Astarach as he swirled around Miranda. "He's not likely to be content to serve as a garment forever. The next cosmic burp could be more extensive and much more deadly.'' He raised his voice as he spoke to Miranda. "Can you feel anything, female?"

"Uncertainty," Miranda replied immediately. "Confusion, puzzlement, disorientation."

Odenaw was nodding. "Understandable. Doubtless it has no idea what it is nor how it comes to be in this dimension. Something must be done quickly, before these feelings again manifest themselves physically."

Rizz drifted toward Miranda, taking care not to drift too close, Kerwin noted. "It appears content in your presence. Perhaps you could convince it to pull itself back into the seventh dimension? It may simply be that no one has tried because no one knew what to try. Possibly, if you moved with it, we could reseal the damage to the fabric of spacetime."

"Me? Go with Izmir?" She hesitated, eyed Rizz warily. "I'll bet there's no shopping in the seventh dimension, is there?"

"No one really knows," said Odenaw evasively.

"Sorry. I mean, like, Izmir's cute and all that, but he's not what I'd call a lively date. He doesn't say anything, just sort of gives off vague vibrations. I don't think I'd like, you know, like it in the seventh dimension. Sometimes I'm not real comfortable in this one, but I'm not ready for any radical changes, either."

"You might be saving the entire known universe," said Rizz.

"Hey, that's not my job. I mean, the seventh dimension might be nice to visit and all that but I don't think I'd want to live there." As she spoke, the radiant cloak that was Izmir glowed brighter than ever.

"It's crazy," Kerwin muttered as he stared, "but there is some kind of connection there."

"Why's that crazy?" Seeth wanted to know. "You're

attracted to her, I'm attracted to her, why not everything else?''

''Besides,'' she was saying, ''my date book for the next six months is, like, filled. I couldn't run out on all those boys. My daddy always taught me when you give your word on something, you keep it no matter what. That's just Texan.''

''Miranda,'' Kerwin told her, ''your family might not exist in a little while. Texas might not exist. The whole universe might be scrunched down and sucked into Izmir.''

''Oh poo! Izmir wouldn't do anything like that. He doesn't want to hurt anybody. He's just confused, poor thing.'' She added as an afterthought, ''And Texas will *always* exist.''

''Do you think maybe you could talk to him? About returning to his own dimension? Tell him this is a crummy one anyway, real sloppy, full of black holes and quasars and all sorts of unpleasant stuff.''

''Yeah,'' said Seeth. ''Tell him if he wants to come back and rock some time, maybe we could figure something out, but right now he's kind of taking up everybody else's space.''

Miranda looked dubious. ''I'll try, but I can't promise anything.'' She looked down at herself. ''You sure I couldn't keep just a little bit for one blouse?''

''NO!'' said Kerwin, Seeth, Arthwit Rail and the three Halet simultaneously.

''Honestly, you men! You're always so *serious*.''

There was silence. The distant storm clouds began to close in around the drifting figures, dwarfing the humans. The vast, omniscient shapes pressed close. Kerwin would've been intimidated if he hadn't been so tired. The proximity to so much pure intellect was like a physical presence, a weight pressing heavily on him. Seeth didn't seem as troubled, perhaps because there wasn't as much to weigh upon.

Suddenly Miranda's skin began to glow as a blinding radiance flowed through her. Kerwin thought he shouted her name, but he wasn't sure. It all happened so quickly, much faster than anyone imagined possible.

Izmir broke away from her serene self, tossing off isolated, indifferent bursts of energy, each of which was powerful enough to boost a starship through slipspace. The Halet thoughtfully put up defensive screens to keep their guests from being incinerated. Miranda was not affected.

The light continued to flow from the now-spherical Izmir. It flooded the immense interior of the Halet habitat, forcing the storm cloud shapes to back off. A deep hum filled Kerwin's skull, coming not through his ears but directly inside his head. Far away, Miranda said, "Oh dear, I think he's getting ready to sneeze again, you know?"

Like.

Total disorientation, burst of heat and light. It faded as rapidly as it occurred.

Then they were drifting soundlessly once more. The clouds retreated into the distance, soft musical sounds filling the empty air between them.

"Well," Brittle announced into the silence, "that was really something!"

"Truly," Odenaw agreed. "We moved just in time."

Kerwin turned a slow somersault. Miranda no longer wore the glowing cloak. No hovering pyramid or twisted trapezoid clung to her, no waterfall of color or cold flame. Izmir was gone. The Halet confirmed it.

Miranda was trying to stifle a sniffle. "He did it for us,

you know. For all of us. Not just for me. That was the last feeling I got from him. It was hard for him, too, but he found a way to do it—go back to where he came from. You know why he poked through in the first place? Because he was lonely. He just wanted some company because he didn't know what to do with all of himself. I mean, like, if you were twelve percent of all the matter in the universe and you were stuck over in some foreign dimension, wouldn't you wonder what it was like where you came from?''

"Heavy," Seeth murmured, nodding agreement.

"He finally decided, when I talked to him about it, that maybe he's not on, like, the same wavelength as this dimension anymore. Like people preferring Nikes to Converse, you know?''

"What is she talking about?" Brittle asked.

"Footgear," Kerwin told him.

It was the Halets' turn to look confused.

Miranda went on. "I tried to convince him that if he stuck around and kept sneezing or burping or whatever it was he was doing that he was going to do a lot of damage and hurt a lot of innocent thinking beings. So he managed to squeeze himself back through the crack and seal it up behind him.''

"You did well," Rizz told her solemnly. "The whole universe owes you an unpayable debt.''

She shrugged. "Hey, like, no big deal, you know?''

"Where are we?" Kerwin asked. "It felt like we moved again.''

"We skipped across a considerable distance just as Izmir returned to his proper dimension, because we feared possible side effects," Brittle told him. "We're in a section of space your people call—actually I don't believe they have a name for it. We left behind a few new quasars that are going to puzzle your astronomers no end when they locate them. They won't display a normal red shift. You can tell them they're the result of Izmir's homeward journey. There's also a unique supermass whose driving mechanism they won't be able to explain. That's what you get when you seal spacetime.''

"Yeah, right, we'll tell 'em all about it,'' said Seeth impatiently. "Does this mean we go home?''

"Poor Izmir,'' Miranda was saying. "He was so alone. But I think he understood.''

"He must have,'' said Odenaw, "or he wouldn't have gone. Maybe he can project his consciousness through without intruding mass. Sort of make some mental visits.''

"Oh no,'' she told the Halet. "He can't do that because he doesn't exist anymore.''

Everyone stared at her. "I mean, like, the consequences must be obvious to everybody. When he snapped back into the seventh dimension he, like, folded into himself. All that mass just overloaded. There was, you know, a big explosion. A big bang, I think they call it. Anyway, the seventh dimension isn't empty anymore. It's all full of Izmir.'' She looked thoughtful. "You think, like, maybe *this* dimension was empty at one time, except for something like Izmir that got bored with being all alone and decided to fold in on itself and blew up to form everything else?''

"No telling,'' said Rizz quietly. "I don't believe anyone's ever seriously proposed a theory that the universe was born out of suicidal loneliness.''

"Why not, Jack?'' said Seeth. "Why shouldn't mass need a psychiatrist like everybody else? I mean, existence is nuts anyway.''

"Much to ponder," said Brittle. "For now there remains the much smaller question of how best to get you home. We cannot do it ourselves. Even our screened presence would register a little too strongly on your people's detection devices. However, we can return you to the vessel you last traveled."

"Ganun won't understand, but he'll go along," said Rail. He smiled at his human friends, all three eyes blinking simultaneously. "I'm sure he'll be able to slip you home quietly."

"What about the Isotat and the Sikan?" Kerwin wondered.

"Both will continue to search the region we left in haste. Finding nothing but undisciplined, raw energy, the Isotat will return to their travels. Their chance of securing an ultimate weapon gone, the Sikan will start on the long journey back to their home galaxy. There is no reason to pursue conflict when the cause has absented itself. Only you humans do that."

✂ XIV ✂

Ganun and the rest of his people were too shocked by the sudden appearance of their missing guests in their midst to object to the fantastic tale they had to tell. There was a lot of whispering and sideways glances before the crew returned to their duties.

As a guest himself, Yirunta was able to spend more time with his distant cousins than any member of the regular crew. The Neanderthal leaned back in the lounge in the common room and regarded them thoughtfully.

"So the universe exists as the result of suicidal loneliness?"

"Maybe," Kerwin replied. "That's a theory of Miranda's. It may all be just a big joke."

Seeth burst into the common room. He was cradling his petal instrument. Several off-duty crew members crowded close behind him. Kerwin glimpsed other alien shapes in their huge, hairy hands.

"Hey, give Mom a hug for me, big brother, and Dad too, if he'll take it. I'm not going home."

Kerwin gaped at him. "What are you talking about?"

The off-duty crew members pushed into the room. "I've

been rappin' with some of the guys, see? They're all amateurs like myself. We've been jamming and talking and they like my stuff. Say it's just primitive enough to catch on big back on House. Bimuri here says he thinks he can line us up some good gigs in a city called Asaria."

The tallest of the new arrivals nodded. "Big money for sure."

"You can't do that!" Kerwin yelped. "What are your friends going to say?"

"Hey, I'm independent, man. If I drop out of sight and show up again in ten years, the most anybody's gonna say to me is 'Hi, Seeth, what's happenin', man?' I'll just tell 'em me and my band's been touring, which'll be the truth. The boys assure me there are ways to work a little Earthside visit now and then without upsetting the cops." He was grinning hugely. "Told you I was due for a real break. I'm not gonna blow it."

"A star is born," Kerwin muttered. "Swell. Go on, if you want to. Me, I've got a test to make up."

"Hey, no sweat. Just tell the profs what you've been doing."

"Sure."

"Goodness knows you must have stories to tell," said Yirunta. "All this talk of Sikan and Isotat and crossing intergalactic gulfs and these mysterious Halet is a bit much to believe. Yet the danger is past. Our instruments find no trace of the field Izmir put out. Even Ganun has accepted the gist of your tale, if not the details."

"It doesn't matter," said Rail. "As for myself, I am resigning my post as espial and going into interior decorating. I've had enough."

Kerwin looked across the room. "What about you,

Miranda? You just saved the entire universe. You must be worn out. I don't guess you're free Saturday night?''

"Sorry."

"Sunday?"

"Can't make it, like."

"Next Saturday?" It occurred to Kerwin that he was begging, but he didn't care.

"Well—I'll have to check my book, you know? Maybe."

Maybe. Kerwin felt better than he had at any time since he and Seeth had been watching Rail bowling back in Albuquerque. That was a long, long time ago.

Miranda stretched out her perfect legs and smiled up at the ceiling. "I feel, like, bad for Izmir. It's probably better for him this way, though. And it's not like I had any choice, really. I mean, I do have a date for this weekend, and if Izmir had kept hanging around and sneezing it might have frightened him away.

"Besides which, it would have, like, you know, ruined my hair."

BESTSELLING
Science Fiction
and
Fantasy